A Candlelight
Regency Special

BT. pretty good

CANDLELIGHT REGENCIES

A Suitable Marriage

Marlaine Kyle

A CANDLELIGHT REGENCY SPECIAL

Published by
Dell Publishing Co., Inc.
1 Dag Hammarskjold Plaza
New York, New York 10017

Dell ® TM 681510, Dell Publishing Co., Inc.

ISBN: 0-440-18406-1

Printed in the United States of America
First printing—December 1981

For my daughter and son-in-law,
Elaine and Jeff Clark,
with such love.

1

Upon the departure of Mr. Havner, the estate manager, a portentous silence fell over Lord Dahlmere's house in Grosvenor Square on this rainy March morning in London. For all the house's inhabitants, from the old lord's granddaughter, Lady Cynthia Chattington, down to the lowliest kitchen maid, knew that Mr. Havner would not have traveled up from Hampshire, the weather and the roads being what they were, except under the most direful circumstances. Felicitous news could wait upon the weather or the mails; redoubtable tidings more often could not.

The essence of those tidings was generally perceived as having to do with finances—or rather the lack of them. How the large staff of servants, from Tom the stableboy to Hobson the butler, had come by their surprisingly comprehensive knowledge of the master's affairs, it would be difficult to trace exactly. Certainly neither Lady Cynthia, her grandfather, nor her late father's cousin, Lady Sedgegood, ever forgot themselves to the extent of decrying a shortage of funds in the presence of the servants.

Lady Cynthia's brother, Viscount Bramford Chattington, was, it must be admitted, another kettle of fish. Lord Bramford had a streak of wildness in his character, typical of a certain class of young peers, that led him into a variety of peccadilloes, both financial and otherwise, which it was hoped would be moderated by that gentleman's increasing maturity. Since Lord Bramford had been known to lay a sizable wager on how many times a particularly dithering young lady of the ton would giggle in the course of a half hour, it was not surprising that he frequently found himself in dun territory. This was not generally felt to be a reflection upon Lord Dahlmere, who was often understandably in a choleric mood as the result of his grandson's latest tangle.

On the other hand, Lady Cynthia's bill at the dressmaker's was known to be shockingly overdue. And Lady Jersey, while attended by a considerable number of ambitious mamas at Almack's one evening recently, had been overheard to remark that Lady Cynthia had worn the same gown to two ton parties during the past month. Lady Jersey *had* been considerate enough to add that such a black-haired, gray-eyed beauty as Cynthia Chattington had less need of an extensive wardrobe than many of the season's marriageable misses. Unhappily that daunting patronness of Almack's had then somewhat mitigated the effect of her compliment by saying what a pity it was that the girl had no fortune.

The entire incident had been reported to Lord Dahlmere's housekeeper, Mrs. Hench, by the dresser of Lady Bloomhedge, who had been one of the mothers attending Lady Jersey at the time. In similar manner did the latest

10

on-dits pass through all the London houses of the quality in a matter of days. Therefore, it was not perhaps surprising that the baron's staff had half guessed at impending disaster even before the appearance of Mr. Havner.

Now that he was gone, the servants, sensing the desolate mood that was emanating from behind the closed door of Lord Dahlmere's study, managed to find numerous pressing tasks in other parts of the house. All except Hobson, whose reputation as fearing neither man nor beast made it incumbent upon him to take his stand in the hallway outside the study where he waited upon events. His courage had not long to maintain itself. Scarcely a quarter of an hour after Mr. Havner had been shown out of the house, the study door was abruptly opened and Lord Dahlmere, wearing a maroon morning coat and a thunderous scowl, directed that Lord Bramford, Lady Cynthia, and Lady Sedgegood attend him in the study immediately.

"I believe, sir," said the butler in commendably cool and steady tones, "that Lord Chattington has gone out. I heard him not this half hour past instruct his groom to bring his curricle around."

"Gone out!" Lord Dahlmere's beetling white brows drew down as the dark eyes beneath looked accusingly at Hobson. "The devil confound it! Where has that young pup gone at this hour?"

Hobson's countenance remained admirably composed. "I regret that I cannot say, sir."

"Cannot or will not?" bridled Lord Dahlmere.

Hobson, who had known the young lord since he was an extremely mischievous toddler and who had been caught out, on more than one occasion, covering up for his lordship, received this accusatory question calmly.

11

"The viscount did not see fit to inform me of his destination," responded Hobson equably.

"Poppycock!" Lord Dahlmere said crossly. "He is attending a prizefight or a horse race or something of that sort."

Hobson repeated that he could not say, but admitted that he was hard put to imagine anything else that could have gotten his lordship out of bed before noon.

"I want him sent to me immediately upon his return," the old lord ordered darkly.

Hobson said that his lordship could depend upon it; he would see to the matter, and in the meantime, he would inform the ladies' abigails of the master's instruction.

The summons found Lady Cynthia and Lady Sedgegood at breakfast. "You may send word to Lord Dahlmere," Lady Sedgegood instructed her maid, "that Lady Cynthia and I will join him on the instant we have finished our meal." That plump, mettlesome lady never liked being "sent for like a schoolroom miss," and even though she was a guest in Lord Dahlmere's house, she was there less as a poor relation than as a necessary personage whose services were required to chaperon Lady Cynthia in her second London season.

When her maid continued to hesitate timidly in the doorway, understandably reluctant to deliver what must seem a set-down to the old lord, Lady Sedgegood said sharply, "Stop *hovering*, Eunice, and do as you are told!" For a lady whose household staff in the country numbered three, she could sound surprisingly as if she were accustomed to directing an army of servants.

When the maid was gone, Cynthia said, "I expect we had better go without much delay, Cousin Alice. Grandfather's mood these past few days is nothing to cavil at."

Lady Sedgegood gave her a speaking glance while applying butter to a hot muffin. "I hardly need remind you, Cynthia, that I do not find the necessary exigencies of London social life particularly soothing to *my* mood either. I cannot think how anyone can prefer it to country living." Lady Sedgegood had married twenty years earlier and had been widowed for nineteen of those years, most of which time she had remained in residence at her small country estate in Sussex, quite content with the sparsity of village society. She worked in her gardens, carried soup and clothing collected from more fortunate acquaintances to the neighborhood poor, and took tea with the village vicar's wife twice a week. She lived, in short, so much the life of a spinster of moderate means that people often forgot she had ever been married. To own the truth, there were times when Lady Sedgegood herself wondered if her marriage were anything more than a barely remembered dream.

"Nor can I conceive," that lady continued with asperity, "what can be gained by putting Cook into a great taking because we have not eaten her meal."

"Well, I suppose you may be right," Cynthia said doubtfully. "And, of course, it is generous above all things of you to come up to London again when I know how you could not wait to get back home after last season." Cynthia dimpled prettily. "It was most disappointing, I expect, not to get me married off during my come-out year."

"Fiddle!" remarked Lady Sedgegood, helping herself to pear marmalade. "You are just coming on twenty, still young to marry in my opinion. Although I am sure not many women of the ton would agree with me. One imagines they feel that since a woman must marry in any case,

13

the sooner the better. I daresay you will have to marry soon enough. Few of us are fortunate enough to be allowed to go our own way alone if we so choose."

"Why, Cousin Alice," said Cynthia, "you sound almost as if you regret your own marriage, as if it was not happy."

Lady Sedgegood fixed her with a green-eyed stare. "What is that to the purpose? A marriage must be *suitable,* but whether it is happy or not is of little consequence in the majority of unions with which I am acquainted. To say the truth, my lord and I were together for such a short time and that so long ago that I cannot remember if I felt happy. I was well enough satisfied, I expect, and since then the life of a country widow has come to suit me admirably. Of course, being a widow is more acceptable in the eyes of society than being one of those poor, piteous creatures who was never able to catch a husband."

"So you own I am not *quite* at my last prayers," Cynthia remarked lightly. "Though what gentleman will have me without a fortune, I cannot well imagine." Both ladies knew this was said half in jest, for Cynthia had turned down two perfectly respectable offers of marriage during her first London season.

"One who is not in need of any fortune other than his own, my dear," Lady Sedgegood replied with candor. Although many of the gentlemen of the haut ton were on the lookout for an heiress to repair their fortunes, she had enough confidence in her young cousin's beauty and spritely personality to believe that she would, in time, make a good marriage. She *could* wish that Cynthia's penchant for impulsive action was not quite so pronounced and that the comely miss could behave in a slightly less shatter-brained manner at such times. Nevertheless, she had taken careful note of the coterie of young

14

admirers who paid court to Cynthia at every social gathering and felt that the girl could walk away with a most eligible husband if her crochety old grandfather didn't press her to make a hasty match.

Recalling the baron's peremptory summons, Lady Sedgegood experienced a slight stirring of concern and decided she had delayed long enough to make her point and it would be the better part of wisdom not to keep that gentleman waiting any longer. She pressed a snowy napkin to her lips and said, "Shall we join your grandfather now?"

When they had been admitted to the study, the baron went immediately on the attack. "Are you ladies quite sure you can spare me this little time?" he inquired in a tone of ominous gruffness. His eyes took in his granddaughter's pertly elegant nose, arching black brows, and dark-lashed gray eyes, all of which were enchantingly set off by a gold-colored morning dress of French merino, and he was in danger of forgetting his frustration over the sizable dressmaker's bill that lay in his desk drawer unpaid and, it now appeared, would continue to do so. Lord Dahlmere increased the fierceness of his frown, determined not to weaken in the face of his granddaughter's charm.

That young lady ignored the frown and went around the desk to kiss his lined cheek. "Of course, we can spare you as much time as you wish, Grandfather. Had we known your business was urgent, we would not have stayed to finish our breakfast."

"Though what can be so urgent as to have to be discussed *before* breakfast, I cannot think," said Lady Sedgegood with a sniff as she sat down in a convenient chair and settled her skirts about her ample body.

Lord Dahlmere shot her a darkling look and, motioning Cynthia to another chair, began to pace back and forth across the Persian rug behind his desk. "I suppose it is too much to expect that either of *you* knows where Bramford is?"

"Do you mean he has risen from his bed and gone out already?" asked Cynthia, feeling a sense of indefinable alarm at her grandfather's grim demeanor. "What has he done to put you in such a fret?"

"I am not in a fret, miss!" fretted Lord Dahlmere, coming from behind the desk to circle a Sheraton side table and pace in front of the fireplace. "But I would like to know where I might locate that rattle-pate when a family crisis arises. I cannot conceive how such a cork-brained pup can be my grandson." He stopped pacing momentarily to glare at Lady Sedgegood. "Takes after his father's side of the family, I daresay."

"Unless I mistake the matter," retorted that indignant lady, "his mother's side of the family boasts a few crackskulls, too!"

"Family crisis, Grandfather?" intervened Cynthia, perceiving that, for once, the baron was not in a pucker over something her brother had done. Indeed, it occurred to her that it might be much more serious than that. "It is what Mr. Havner told you, isn't it? Oh, I knew it had to be something very grave to bring him up from the country."

Lord Dahlmere stopped pacing again, glanced absently at the French ormolu clock on the mantel, and returned to the desk to draw the dressmaker's bill from the drawer. Turning to Lady Sedgegood, he inquired, "By all that's wonderful, madam, what are you preparing the girl for—the Prince Regent's court? I know the royal dukes are in

16

search of wives, but I hardly think Cynthia is under consideration."

"I certainly hope I am not!" exclaimed Cynthia. "They are all so very *old*." She got to her feet to peer over the desk at the bill. "Gracious! That does seem an exorbitant amount."

Lady Sedgegood pulled herself up stiffly in her chair. "Surely, sir, you cannot expect the girl to go into society in such unadorned gowns as she was used to wear in the country. A dottier notion I never heard! Such a blot on one's escutcheon could never be overcome."

"I daresay she is right," said Cynthia in a conciliatory tone.

"*Furthermore,*" Lady Sedgegood continued in high dudgeon, "Cynthia's wardrobe is quite sparse compared to most of the young ladies with whom she must constantly be compared. A girl with no fortune must needs present a respectable appearance or there is no hope at all of her being offered for. Not that *I* care a fig for that, but I collect *you* do, Lord Dahlmere, else why have we come up for the season at all?" Having delivered what she considered an unarguable case, Lady Sedgegood fell silent, prepared to wait as long as necessary for Lord Dahlmere's acquiescence in the matter.

To both the ladies' surprise, the baron did not take the opportunity to sail into the fray. Instead, he seated himself behind the desk and, laying aside the dressmaker's bill, assumed an expression that in anyone less proud-spirited might have been described as crestfallen.

"Well, that is neither here nor there. I must insist that there will be no more dressmaker or milliner bills. It may even be necessary to dispose of this house and return to

17

Hampshire before the season is over."

"Oh, that is coming it a little too strong, sir," protested Lady Sedgegood, put considerably off the mark by this speech.

Lord Dahlmere turned a glowering look upon her. "I assure you, madam, I do not refine too much upon the matter. Mr. Havner has informed me that the failure of our last two corn crops has left me in possession of hardly a farthing to bless myself with. I see no other solution than to sell this house, since it is not entailed while the Hampshire estate is."

"Then that is just what we shall do," said Cynthia readily. "I care little for society, Grandfather, and would as leave pass the remainder of my days in Hampshire."

This announcement caused the other two to look with some amazement at the girl, for until that moment she had given every appearance of enjoying herself immensely in London.

"Very prettily said," remarked Lady Sedgegood disparagingly. "Where, I daresay, you intend marrying the stableboy or one of the innkeeper's want-witted sons! But it will not do. Surely you, sir, can see that. If I may put it bluntly—"

At this point Lord Dahlmere interrupted rudely and begged to be informed when she had ever put an opinion any other way.

To which Lady Sedgegood responded, "I shall let that pass since I intend making no apologies for speaking my mind."

"I expect not!" mumbled the baron. "Should have had a man to take you in hand years ago."

Lady Sedgegood pretended not to hear this and continued, "It is as plain as a pikestaff that your granddaughter is your most valuable asset in the present circumstances—provided she remains in London."

The baron's eyes narrowed ponderingly at this remark and he fell into abstracted silence for a moment. Then he stirred and said, "Dashed if you aren't right for once, madam!"

Not expecting such ready acceptance of her opinion, Lady Sedgegood cast a troubled look at her young cousin and took another tack. "Not that these things can be rushed, Lord Dahlmere. No, no—that would not do at all. And if it should fall out that Cynthia does not make a suitable match this season, why I collect there will be another corn crop before next year. She is, after all, not yet twenty."

Cynthia, quickly grasping her importance in the matter at hand, fell in with her grandfather in her usual impulsive manner, for she could see that the notion had eased some of the worry lines in his forehead.

"Well, there is an end to our worries. I shall marry a rich husband before the season is out."

"Famous!" Lord Dahlmere beamed on his granddaughter. "Sensible girl! Takes after my side of the family."

"The two of you are running ahead a great deal too fast," exclaimed Lady Sedgegood, who was beginning to wish that she had not been so quick to point out a solution. "I only meant to suggest that Cynthia has a right to a life in society—not that she should be sold forthwith to the highest bidder!"

"But, of course, I shall be," remarked Cynthia, dampened not at all by her cousin's cynical rejoinder. "Isn't that the purpose of a girl's come-out? She is put on display so that the gentlemen of the ton may look her over and decide if she is worth an offer—very like the cattle at Tattersall's."

Lord Dahlmere gave a disconcerted little cough at this, but Lady Sedgegood noticed that he did not have the grace to disagree.

"You see, Grandfather," Cynthia continued, hardly faltering, "you need not cudgel your brain over the matter of money any longer. Only explain to the dressmaker and our other creditors that payment will be forthcoming within a short time. Now, if I may be excused, I must go and decide which of my gowns would be best to wear to the Bloomhedges' ball tomorrow night. It seems I must start my campaign without delay."

As his granddaughter hurried from the room, Lord Dahlmere settled back in his chair, a faint expression of worry overshadowed by the bloom of hope on his face. Lady Sedgegood, on the other hand, was in a state of agitation. "Indeed, sir!" She fixed the baron with a baleful stare. "This is the outside of enough! Only conceive what you are doing, encouraging that child to throw herself at the head of the first wealthy gentleman who shows an interest in her, regardless of how well they shall go on together."

"How came you to be so missish, madam!" the baron responded, stung by her criticism. "What else is the season for? Oh, I will own that we generally put it more delicately. But Cynthia is right, you know. It is little more than an auction, only of young ladies rather than horseflesh." He cleared his throat rather more loudly than was necessary. "If you will excuse me now, I have correspondence to see to."

Thus dismissed, Lady Sedgegood had little choice except to withdraw, but not before she pronounced her opinion that Cynthia would have them all in a hum over the morning's business and that the baron's judgment had been quite overdone.

2

Cynthia was abovestairs with her maid, Mary, looking over her ball gowns, when voices below told her that her brother had returned. She flung a puce sarcenet gown across her bed, saying, "This one will be just the thing, Mary. I seem to remember that one of the flounces needs mending, but you are so very good with the needle that poses no problem. I haven't worn it since early last season, so perhaps no one will remember it."

Mary, a rawboned red-haired woman of thirty, with a prodigious sprinkling of freckles on her pale skin, surveyed the puce gown with an expert eye. "An added bit of lace here and there would make it look different."

"Wonderful idea," said Cynthia, glancing toward the door. "I will leave it in your capable hands, Mary. But now I must hurry down and speak to Bramford before he goes in to Grandfather." She left the bedchamber in a whirl of gold-colored skirts.

Descending the stairs, she saw her brother handing his

caped driving coat and beaver to Hobson. Lord Bramford Chattington was a slender, dashingly handsome young man with curly hair of the same inky color as his sister's and eyes tending more toward blue than hers. Although he was a year older than she, Cynthia's bosom harbored a strong maternal feeling toward him. This was, no doubt, the result of Lord Bramford's being sickly as a young child while she had always been the image of robust health. She had used to sit beside his sickbed, telling stories and playing games to keep him pacified so that he would not overexert himself, which was his wont, and bring on more symptoms.

"Bram," she said in a low but urgent voice as she reached the front hall. "I must speak to you before you see Grandfather. Does he know of your arrival as yet?"

Hobson turned from the ebony wardrobe where he had placed the viscount's coat and beaver. "I was about to announce him, Lady Cynthia."

"No, wait—" Cynthia glanced worriedly toward the closed study door.

"I do not think that Lord Dahlmere will wish to be kept waiting any longer," said Hobson. "I myself do not care for a rake-down, either, if I may say so without being impertinent."

Cynthia looked somewhat amused and wondered when Hobson had started to concern himself with the fact that a statement of his might be considered impertinent, since many of his utterances could easily be described in such a manner. "You will forgive me, Hobson, if I cannot credit this new retiring pose of yours. If anyone receives a rake-down, I daresay it will not be you."

"Well, look here, Cyn," Bramford interpolated, looking very grim for such a usually carefree gentleman. "Might

23

as well brave the old lion in his den. Get it over with, whatever it is."

"Not until I speak with you," Cynthia insisted and, laying hold of the sleeve of her brother's excellently tailored kerseymere coat, pulled him toward the green saloon. "Hobson," she added, casting the butler a limpid, imploring look, "I am sure you will know what to say to Grandfather if he emerges before Bram and I have finished our talk."

Hobson looked as if he might disagree, but then he straightened his shoulders and replied, "Very good, my lady."

"I say, Cyn," remarked Bramford petulantly, "let go of my coat. I'm here, ain't I? Have to tell you, old girl, you're getting to be an out-and-out virago." He walked across the saloon and turned to face his sister, who was closing the door. "No help for it, you know. Have to ask the old boy for some blunt. Might as well do it and let him tell me what a rapscallion I am. Get it over with."

"That is just what you cannot do!" exclaimed Cynthia, following her brother into the room and taking her stand in front of him, hands on hips.

"Course I can," returned Bramford imperturbably. "Where else am I to get it?"

"I don't know, Bram. The payment of your debts will have to be postponed, I expect," said Cynthia firmly. "Mr. Havner has been here and thrown Grandfather into a taking. There is no money for tailors—or anything else."

"No money?" inquired Bramford incredulously. "But that ain't possible, Cyn. Has to be some money somewhere."

"No, there is not," reiterated Cynthia with emphasis. "I have decided to get a rich husband as soon as ever I can.

In the meantime, you will have to lie low and wait. If it is too embarrassing for you, you can return early to Hampshire."

Bramford's handsome face fell, and walking to a green satin chair, he flung himself into it. "Can't wait for you to leg-shackle a rich 'un, Cyn. Could take months, even if you are a pretty chit. Got no fortune and—don't mean to insult you, old girl—but you're too much of a hoyden for most men."

Bridling, Cynthia returned, "Oh, you're a fine one to cast aspersions, Bram."

The worried frown creasing her brother's face gave way momentarily to a grin. "Didn't say *I'm* the catch of the ton either."

"Well," she went on, "in future I shall be more decorous and—biddable."

The viscount laughed aloud. "Don't try bamming me, Cyn. Know you too well by half."

Undaunted, Cynthia said, "If you know of another way to rescue us from disgrace, pray tell me. If not, go to Hampshire and rusticate for a while."

He fingered the intricate folds of his snowy cravat and, frowning, did not reply immediately. After a moment he muttered, "Hampshire ain't far enough. Not even certain the Continent would do, but I don't want to go there, anyway."

"You cannot offer a better plan than mine," concluded Cynthia. "Nor did I think you could. I am resigned to the necessity of a hasty marriage. When I have fixed the interest of the right man, I expect we can get a special license . . ." Her voice trailed away as she turned to peer musingly out one of the saloon's long, beautiful Georgian windows.

"Devilish plucky of you, Sister, but it won't do. Unless you can manage it within the sennight."

She turned to survey her brother's despondent face. "No woman of quality could get herself married that quickly. But stop fretting yourself with all this talk about the Continent. The tailor will wait."

"Ain't my tailor, Cyn. Wish it was. Far worse imbroglio than that."

Indeed he did look much abashed. "Is it gaming debts?"

"Should have asked me that last week," Bramford told her gloomily. "Could have said yes then. But a gentleman has to pay his gambling debts, you know, or he'd be shunned at his club."

"Don't tell me," broke in Cynthia, "that you borrowed money from Lord Caverset! Though *that* would be a wondrous thing, since Cavey's pockets are as often to let as yours."

He lifted his face to give her an affronted look. "Borrow from Cavey? What do you take me for, Cyn? May not be a nonpareil, but I ain't so ungentlemanly as to borrow from my friends."

"Well, what *has* made you look so Gothic?" demanded Cynthia, losing patience.

"Found myself in such a coil I had to go to a moneylender. Eight days ago."

"I don't believe it!" gasped Cynthia.

"Well, could have been nine days. I don't recollect exactly. In no mood to quibble about it, either."

Cynthia gritted her teeth. "I am not referring to the number of days. I can't believe you went to a moneylender! Bram, I cannot think of anything so—so *dissolute*. Why, I have heard tales of what such men *do* to people who can't pay them! Dumped in the Thames—or worse. Oh, Bram, you must have been foxed."

"Won't say I hadn't had a few drinks," owned the viscount. "But I wasn't foxed. Remember it all quite clearly. Promised to pay within the week. Gave my word as a gentleman on it. Signed the vowels, too."

"Of all the bird-witted, buffleheaded . . ." sputtered Cynthia.

"Can't call me anything I haven't called myself," interrupted her brother. "Should have known by looking at him that nag couldn't win. Swaybacked, you know."

"A horse race! So that is what put you into debt again. I might have known."

"Thought I'd been given a sign. Horse's name was Chestnut. Just the night before the race I'd met a—young lady—"

"A light-skirt, you mean?" inquired Cynthia baldly.

"Well, ahem—guess you could call her that. Pretty girl, though. Smashing chestnut brown hair. Told me to call her Chessey."

"Ah ha," said his sister dryly. "When you realized the horse's name was Chestnut, you thought Fate had smiled on you? Truly, Bram, I despair of your good sense."

The viscount pulled himself from his slouched position on the chair and straightened his cravat. "Needn't be so prickly about it. Cavey thought the nag was a sure thing, too."

"I might have managed to give Cavey's opinion *some* credit," said Cynthia, reining her temper with great difficulty, "if I did not know that he is as often in dun territory as you are." She began to pace restlessly about the saloon.

Watching her, the viscount said, "Went to call on Higgins this morning to ask for an extension. The shabster wouldn't hear of it."

Cynthia ceased her pacing, her gray eyes narrowing reflectively. "You say the moneylender's name is Higgins?"

"That's the man. Deuced uncivil fellow, too, if anyone should ask my opinion. Lives on Clarges Street across from that old house where Cavey's great-aunt used to reside. Threatened to call on Grandfather, so it really don't signify whether I tell him now or Higgins tells him in the next day or two, does it?"

Cynthia resumed her pacing. "I have to think about this."

"Won't do any good," the viscount informed her reasonably. "Already cudgeled my brains till I'm exhausted. Nothing more of a dead bore than having to think about money. Nothing for it but to tell Grandfather."

"No!" Cynthia was adamant. "Promise me, Bram, that you won't tell Grandfather. He has too many worries as it is, and he isn't in the pink of health this past twelve-month. You must go in to him and convince him that you've seen the error of your ways. Tell him you've sworn off gaming—"

"Won't tell him about Higgins if it means so much to you, Cyn. But I shouldn't imagine he'll believe the other. He's old, but he ain't all about in his head, you know."

Cynthia might have taken further issue with her brother, but at that moment Hobson opened the saloon door and coughed discreetly. Cynthia turned to the butler with an impatient little gesture of one hand. "What is it, Hobson?"

"Lord Dahlmere, my lady. Demanding to know when the viscount is coming in to him. He heard our voices in the hall. I shouldn't think he'll be kept waiting much longer."

Bramford got to his feet, giving Cynthia a sideways glance. "Here I go, Sister. Wouldn't care to come in with me, I don't expect?"

Cynthia shook her head emphatically. "Remember, Bram, no mention of Higgins—and promise me you won't do anything about him yourself until we talk again."

"Can't imagine what I could *do* without the blunt." He straightened his shoulders and left the saloon.

Hobson closed the door, and Cynthia, left alone, went to stand again at the window, gazing out at the rain that continued to fall in a fine drizzle, soaking the garden that lay between the house and the low rock wall bordering the property. She recalled once more the tales she had heard concerning the unpleasant end of certain unfortunate people who had failed to repay their moneylenders. She had no way of knowing whether the tales were factual, but even the possibility that they might be made her shiver.

She *must* do something to help Bramford and prevent her grandfather's learning of this latest indiscretion of her brother's. Several minutes passed, during which she continued to stare unseeing out the window, before the idea occurred to her of calling on Higgins herself. It had been her experience that an attractive, helpless-appearing female could sometimes accomplish what a gentleman could not. Doubtless Bram had lost his temper and insulted the man, whereas she was determined to be calm and reasonable in presenting her brother's case.

With the idea barely formed in her mind, she acted. Finding Hobson still in the entry hall, she said airily, "Oh, Hobson, please fetch a post chaise at once. I have a few visits to make."

29

"But it is raining, my lady," Hobson pointed out quite unnecessarily, a look of suspicion slowly dawning on his face.

"I am well aware of that," Cynthia said, not at all daunted, "and you needn't mention my leave-taking to Grandfather—unless he asks for me, of course."

"Naturally, I shall have to tell his lordship if he asks, my lady," said Hobson, looking affronted, "since it is not my place to tell Banbury tales to my betters."

"I'm going up for my wrap, Hobson," Cynthia said, ignoring the censure in his tone. She hurried toward the stairs.

"If I may be so bold, my lady," Hobson persisted, his suspicion growing, "would you not prefer me to send for Lord Dahlmere's carriage and the groom?"

Having already reached the bottom step, Cynthia turned back to say, "No, I would not. Grandfather may wish to—to go to his club, and I shouldn't like him to be in any way discommoded after the morning he has had."

"I do not think he will be going anywhere in this weather," remarked Hobson dryly.

"I cannot stand here brangling with you, Hobson," returned Cynthia, losing patience. And then she added imperiously, "Fetch the post chaise at once." Without waiting for his reply, she hurried on up the stairs.

In her bedchamber Mary was seated on a low stool mending the flounce on the puce ball gown.

"Mary," said Cynthia, putting on a pelisse of light gray wool and Limerick gloves, "I have decided to make a few visits."

The maid put aside the ball gown, saying, "I'll fetch my coat, ma'am."

"Pray continue with your mending," Cynthia said

quickly. "I'm only going to the Larchmonts'—and perhaps the Bagbees'. I shan't need you with me, Mary."

"But you can't be thinking of going alone!" said Mary, so astounded by her mistress's statement that she failed to realize for the moment that she was questioning the wishes of a member of the quality.

"It is only for a short distance," said Cynthia firmly and added, inventing hurriedly, "Bramford may decide to accompany me. Now where is my cap—oh, here it is," she concluded as she donned the head covering and tied the lappets under her chin in a black bow.

She departed the bedchamber before her abigail could think of further objections.

Set down on Clarges Street, Cynthia found her courage deserting her. The thought had occurred to her that it might be a good deal wiser to employ a go-between. But whom could she trust, other than herself, to act promptly on Bram's behalf? Gazing for a moment at the tall, somewhat ramshackle-looking house that was across the way from the residence where Lord Caverset's great-aunt had used to live, she decided to walk the length of the block first to bolster her flagging determination. By the time she had returned to stand in front of the Higgins house, she was wishing herself back in her snug bedchamber at Grosvenor Square.

From a window in the house—which was, in fact, a lodging place for several gentlemen—the Earl of Graybroughton, Lord Kenyon Marlbridge, caught sight of the young woman who was pacing back and forth in the rain. Much intrigued, he raised his quizzing glass to study her. His piercing blue gaze took in an exceptionally pretty girl wearing a gray pelisse of a fine woolen material with black curls escaping around the edges of her cap in charming, if damp, disarray.

The earl, who had traveled down to London only three days earlier from the largest of his country estates in Northumberland, had come to the house to pay a call on an old soldier—one of the four gentlemen lodging there—with whom he had served in the Peninsula and whom he had not seen for almost three years. Having been informed by his old friend's valet that his master had gone out, Lord Marlbridge had been about to return to his Bedford Square mansion when he caught sight of the girl outside.

When the girl, who was obviously well-bred and just as obviously alone, took a few slow steps toward the house, the earl let his glass fall on the end of its ribbon and muttered to himself: "Good God! What can the chit be about?" Silently he cursed the men in the girl's family for allowing her to pay a call on a gentleman unaccompanied. But then it came to him that it was more than probable that the gentlemen he was silently maligning knew nothing of this visit, which was likely a secret assignation with some totally unsuitable rake. Never having clapped eyes on any of the lodgers, other than his old friend, he could not guess who the scoundrel might be for whom the featherbrained chit had fallen head over ears. Nor could he imagine why he should feel in any way obliged to intercept the girl and send her on her way.

Nevertheless, as he saw her step up to the front door, he hurried across the room and entered the small kitchen where the valet was enjoying a cup of tea with the housekeeper. At sight of the earl, both of the servants blushed furiously and came to attention.

"I'm sorry, sir," croaked the valet, "we—we thought you had gone."

"Never mind that," said the earl. "There is a young woman outside who appears to be in a somewhat indelicate situation. I may find it necessary to bring her in here, and if I do I would like the two of you to stay out of sight. If I need you, I will call."

"But, of course, my lord," said the valet, obviously relieved at not being given a rake-down. "We will do just as you say."

The earl hastily picked up his hat and gloves and crossed the apartment in long strides. Entering the main foyer of the house, he reached the front door just as the young woman, evidently despairing of her repeated tapping at the door being heard, stepped hesitantly inside.

Cynthia came to an abrupt halt, startled into momentary speechlessness by the sudden appearance in front of her of a tall man with dark auburn hair, deep blue eyes, and features that were striking although too rugged for conventional handsomeness. He was impressively turned out in an exquisitely cut forest-green coat with brass buttons, tan inexpressibles, and top boots.

Cynthia found herself in the extremely unusual circumstance of groping for words, for the man could not have been farther removed from her mental image of a moneylender. Indeed, if she had not seen him in this house, she would have taken him for a peer of the realm with the most impeccable family connections. The man clearly found his business a lucrative one. This hateful thought brought her chin up and gave her the impetus to meet his arrogant stare levelly.

After a moment he bowed slightly. "Your servant, ma'am."

"I," she informed him, "am Lady Cynthia Chattington." She waited to see what effect the name would have on him. But if there was any effect at all, it was not apparent.

He merely inclined his head and said, "I'm Kenyon." The earl had decided to give away as little as possible until he knew more of why such a clearly high-born young woman had brought herself to this highly unlikely house.

"Oh—" Her mouth formed a pretty O, showing straight white teeth. "You must be Higgins's associate."

"May I ask your business here, Lady Chattington?" the earl inquired.

"My business," she informed him haughtily, "is with Higgins, but if you are his associate—"

"Perhaps if you would come into my—er, study," said the earl, "we might discuss the matter." Without waiting for her acquiescence, he opened a door to the left and gestured for her to precede him into the room.

"So you *are* Higgins's associate," concluded Cynthia, brushing past the man with her head held high. "Why didn't you say as much?"

She found herself in a square room the furnishings of which, although shabby, were cozily arranged before a fireplace where the embers of burned logs gave off a pleasant warmth. Shelves on one wall were filled with books. It was not the sort of room she would have imagined belonging to this man who called himself Kenyon. Undoubtedly, she thought scornfully, he spends most of his money on tailors. She moved to the fireplace and sat down in one of the chairs drawn up before it.

Kenyon laid his hat and gloves on a side table and remained standing, his back to the fireplace, his hands clasped behind him, and his long, muscular legs spread slightly. "Well, now, Lady Chattington. How may I be of service to you?"

"Pray do not play the innocent with me, sir! You know very well why I am here."

The man did not move. "Perhaps," he responded finally, running long fingers through his thick auburn hair, "I would like to hear the reason from you before I commit myself to—anything."

"Well, of course, I will tell you what you already know," said Cynthia with an air of asperity. "Would it amuse you to hear me plead for my brother? Well, I will tell you, but I *shan't* plead, no matter what you do to me, sir!"

The earl suppressed a smile and looked critically at her fashionable pelisse, which clung damply to her body, and the little mud-splattered half boots peeping out from beneath it. "This brother of yours is a fortunate fellow. Not every sister would expose herself to the elements and—"

"Men who are in the odious business of living off other people's misfortunes?" finished Cynthia with virtuous disapproval.

"Quite," said the earl, more intrigued than ever.

"I can't allow you to go to my grandfather, you see. He is old and not entirely well—and, besides, you may as well know that he hasn't a feather to fly with." Cynthia fixed him with a gray-eyed stare. "So, sir, it would be quite useless for you to go to him in any case. He can't pay you what Bramford borrowed." The black-lashed eyes narrowed suddenly. "I warn you that if my brother should come to any harm, *I* will know who is behind it and I will make certain he is apprehended."

"Ah," said the earl, beginning to get a glimmer of what the chit was babbling about. "I collect that Higgins has loaned your brother money which he cannot repay." He shook his head, a slightly incredulous look on his rugged face. "Lord Chattington must be a rattle-pate, going to a man like Higgins!"

"Lud, you are a strange sort of moneylender!" said Cynthia, raising her black brows at him. "I wonder that Higgins keeps you on as his associate since you seem to care so little for the abominable business in which you are engaged together. Or are you merely trying to fob me off by pretending to mislike it?"

The earl did not reply to this, but strolled across the small room to glance out the window to where the dreary drizzle continued to fall unabated. "What," he inquired after several moments, "does your brother intend doing about his debt?"

"Doing?" repeated Cynthia impatiently. "But that is just what I have been telling you! There is nothing he *can* do. One cannot extract blood from a turnip."

He turned to look at her in a disdainful sort of way. "So he has sent *you* here to speak for him."

Cynthia stiffened. "Neither Bramford nor my grandfather knows I am here. I didn't even bring my abigail, for I do not wish word to get back to them. I daresay that Bram lost his temper with Higgins—he has what my grandfather calls a short wick—and I wanted to explain to the man that it is really *quite* useless for him to hound Bram or Grandfather about the matter."

"And you actually expect Higgins to be satisfied with that?"

Cynthia's brows went up. "Well, I am not such a featherbrain as that, sir! No, *I* shall make all right but, of course, I must have some time to accomplish it."

"*You!*" The earl's dark expression changed from disdain to amusement, and one hand came up to smooth the intricate folds of his cravat, an unnecessary gesture since he looked quite as if he had just left his valet after two hours' ministrations. "How shall you accomplish this feat? I suspect you have visions going round in that precipitous brain of yours of becoming an actress or something of that sort, but I think I can tell you with confidence that your grandfather will not hear of it."

"Fustian! Naturally he will not. Nor do I have any desire to go on the stage. My plan has more assurance of success than that! I have decided to marry a rich husband before the season is out."

The earl, composing his countenance, said, "I beg leave to tell you, Lady Chattington, that you will have to put a damper on such harebrained impulses as calling on moneylenders alone if you expect to leg-shackle a wealthy gentleman of the ton. And," he added, his features breaking into a grin, "something tells me it is rather ingrained in your character to act first and think about the wisdom of it later. In truth, I expect you are asking yourself at this very moment how you came to be here."

Cynthia got to her feet abruptly, smoothing the wrinkles in her pelisse and staring with distaste at the tall auburn-haired man before her. "You are without any notion of how to carry on a proper conversation with a lady of quality, you know," she said with a haughty little sniff, "but one can hardly expect better of a *moneylender.*"

The earl bowed slightly and tried to keep from breaking into a laugh. "Just so, ma'am."

In spite of her words, Cynthia found herself admiring his wardrobe and refined accent. He must be a gentleman who has come down in the world, she told herself, and has taken to this nefarious means of repairing his fortunes. "And now I wish you may tell me how soon you expect

Higgins, for I can't think whether I ought to wait for him or come back at a later time."

"I fancy I can assist you there. Higgins won't return for hours, I expect. But you needn't come to see him again, either, for I shall explain the situation to him. I think I may say that you will be given the time to carry out your—ah, maneuvering."

"Well, I must say this is most commendable of you, sir. And, of course, you and your associate *will* have your money—let us say within a sennight after my marriage."

The earl muttered something under his breath about buffleheaded females, which fortunately Cynthia could not make out, and then he insisted upon seeing her outside, hailing a post chaise, handing her inside, and instructing the driver, in admirably authoritative tones, to see that the passenger reached her door safely. Perhaps, thought Cynthia as she settled back against the squabs, there was hope for improvement in his manner yet, for she fancied that he had taken to heart her criticism of his behavior. Undoubtedly she would have thought otherwise if she had seen the scowl on the earl's face as he reentered the house and heard the words that issued from his lips.

"Hell's teeth! Wretched chit needs a husband, I daresay, since neither her grandfather nor her brother seems able to keep a rein on her. But he had better be strong-willed or she will cause the poor fellow to run mad!"

In spite of his chagrin, he discovered in himself a most uncharacteristic protective feeling for the little termagant. He decided it must be because, with those damp black curls, she reminded him of the bedraggled puppy he had rescued from starvation when he was still in short coats. Consequently, he inspected the doors leading into the various lodgings and, spying one that displayed a card marked Higgins, tapped it impatiently with his knuckles.

After some moments the door was opened by a small, swarthy-skinned man with more mud-colored hair on his upper lip than on his head. Before the earl's haughty blue eyes, the fellow's manner changed from one of scurrilous incivility to what could only be described as groveling.

"Higgins?" barked the earl, not bothering with civilities.

The fellow started at the peremptory tone and smiled ingratiatingly, exposing sharp yellow teeth. "At your service, sir. May I be so bold as to hope you may honor me by entering my humble lodgings?"

The nostrils of the earl's aristocratic nose flared with distaste. The place smelled of onions and cabbage and an unwashed human. Baldly ignoring the invitation, the earl restrained a desire to pinch his nose between his long fingers and said, "Understand you hold the vowels of young Lord Chattington."

"Why, yes sir." Higgins's bony hand tried vainly to smooth his dingy cravat. "Fine young lord, if I may say so, sir. Relative of yours? Overextended himself a bit at the horse races, I fear. Tut, tut—"

Cutting through the man's blathering, the earl inquired, "How much?"

"Why, er—ahem, sir. Please grace my poor quarters with your noble presence while I consult my books."

"Devil take it, man!" roared the earl, losing the remnants of his patience. "Stop quibbling and tell me how much!"

Blinking, the moneylender named an amount that was less than the earl had feared—but more than he could have imagined tossing away in aid of a total stranger a half hour earlier. From what that harebrained chit had said, there was little hope of a reimbursement from her brother or her grandfather. Silently maligning himself for his soft-headedness, he brought forth the notes from his coat pocket and, counting out the correct amount, thrust them into Higgins's eager hand. "I'll have the paper, if you please."

"Er—yes, sir! Tut—" Higgins scurried into the smelly murkiness of the room, returning shortly with a scrap of rough paper bearing the signature of Bramford Chattington.

The earl poked the scrap into his coat and fixed Higgins with a quelling stare. "If you ever again lend so much as a farthing to Lord Chattington, I'll see you in Newgate." With that direful threat, he strode from the house.

3

Upon entering the Bloomhedges' ballroom the following evening flanked by her Cousin Alice and Bramford, Cynthia was immediately spotted by two gentlemen who made their way toward her from opposites directions, reaching her side at nearly the same moment.

"Good evening, Lady Sedgegood," said Lord Pendleton, the younger of the two, bowing over Cousin Alice's hand. Only two or three years older than Cynthia, he was stick-slim with pale blond hair and rather pinched features. "The color of that gown, my lady, becomes you exceedingly." Lord Pendleton's compliment might have been taken more seriously had he not been gazing past the recipient to her young cousin.

"Fustian, Pendleton!" Lady Sedgegood gasped, still out of breath from climbing the stairs to the ballroom. "Yellow always makes me look sallow." She glanced down at her ample bosom, frowning. "I never can resist it when I see it on the bolt, all the same." The gown in question was one she had had for a good many years; it had been refurbished for the season with a few rows of brown lace.

Lord Pendleton, who was peering deep into Cynthia's gray eyes, was only vaguely aware of what Lady Sedgegood was saying, but he managed another enthusiastic compliment concerning the yellow gown, well aware of the wisdom of a gentleman's being in the good graces of the chaperon of any young woman upon whom he has fixed an interest.

Unfortunately, while he had been flattering the chaperon, a rival for Lady Cynthia's attention, Lord Ainsley Silverstone, a short pudgy gentleman with a smooth cherubic face that seemed at odds with the fact that he had recently passed his thirtieth birthday, had engaged her in conversation.

"May I hope to have the pleasure of the first dance with you, Lady Cynthia?" Lord Silverstone was saying.

"I have been yearning for that honor myself," Lord Pendleton put in testily, piqued at being outflanked by the pink-faced Lord Silverstone.

"Cousin Alice," Cynthia said with what seemed dutiful concern for her cousin's comfort but was, in truth, a maneuver for time. "You must find a chair at once. You look tired already. There, I see one beside Lady Sommers. I shall come back to you before we go in for supper."

Lady Sedgegood made good her claim on the empty chair as Cynthia turned a dazzling smile on the two gentlemen before her. "How very considerate of you both to concern yourself with rescuing me from conversation with the chaperons, which is certain to run to their latest aches and ailments. I cannot think why you should be so kind to me."

Bramford, who stood just behind her, snickered in her

42

ear. "Coming it much too strong, Cyn," he mumbled under his breath.

Cynthia continued to smile at her attendants. "I very much regret, however, that I have promised the first to my brother." She shared a conspiratorial look with the two gentlemen, whose faces had fallen at her announcement. "Bramford is still in need of practice, I fear, so I must perform my sisterly duty. But I know how we shall go on. I shall have the first boulanger with you, Lord Pendleton. And Lord Silverstone, nothing would please me more than to stand up with you for the set of country dances, sir." Clutching firmly at her brother's coat sleeve, she continued, "Come, Bram. The orchestra is about to begin."

"Dash it, Cyn," complained Bramford as soon as they were out of earshot of the two gentlemen. "You know I don't care a rush for dancing."

"Now don't go all Friday-faced," she said cajolingly. "If you are ever to make the proper impression on the lady of your choice, you must learn, at least, to pretend otherwise."

"There ain't no lady of my choice," argued Bramford, still trying to pull his coat from his sister's grasp. "Don't mean to marry until I'm past thirty, so there ain't a need to dance *now*. Besides, I promised to meet Cavey in the game room."

Cynthia halted in her progress toward the dance floor and stared up into her brother's blue eyes. "No more gambling, Bram! You promised."

"Did no such thing," retorted that gentleman with a grimace. "Strangest coincidence. While searching through a drawer for a missing neckcloth this morning, I came across some notes I'd tucked away for a rainy day. A sign, you might say."

"I've had too much of your signs by half!"

He shrugged. "Mean to begin to repair my fortune this very night. Of course, the stakes are never high at these balls, but it's a start."

"Rattlecap!" Cynthia uttered. "How you can even go *near* a gaming table when that is the very thing that has put you in the briars to begin with, I cannot think! Higgins's associate—that brassy Kenyon fellow who fancies himself a pink of the ton if one is to judge by his dress— but, let that pass, for he *was* willing to speak to Higgins about waiting for payment until my marriage. But if you think for one moment that another groat will be forthcoming from *those* odious creatures, you are indeed short of a sheet!"

"Don't fly up into the boughs." Bramford's sculptured mouth thinned with impatience, and he smoothed his curly locks with a finely manicured hand. "I've learned my lesson when it comes to moneylenders." He glanced over his shoulder, seeking an escape route. "Now let me out of here. They're starting to dance."

"I'll not be made an out-and-out fibster by my own flesh and blood," Cynthia told him severely, forgetting for the moment her lecture on gambling, "and you heard me tell those gentlemen that this dance was promised to you."

A bark of laughter escaped Bramford. "*That* was your first Banbury tale of the evening, Sister, but I'll go bail it won't be the last."

"I do not wish to come to cuffs with you in the middle of a ballroom, Bram," Cynthia said in exasperation. "But you must stand up with me. I wish to consult you on a most serious matter. And do stop making those horrid faces!"

Bramford gazed toward the chandeliered ceiling briefly, calling upon heaven for patience, and then, knowing well it was easier to humor his sister than to win an argument with her, he led her onto the dance floor, muttering, "If your toes land under my feet, you'll have no one to blame but yourself."

In a better humor after a moment, he inquired, "Pray inform me, what freakish set of circumstances has prompted you to petition *me* for advice, since you are so fond of telling me I have windmills in my head? Besides, you must own, Sister, that when it comes to advice you are far better at giving it than taking it." There was good-humored teasing in the accusation. He was not one to stay out of sorts for long, and although Cynthia could be the most vexing of women, he was extremely fond of her.

She smiled at a couple near them and, lowering her voice, said, "I want you to acquaint me with the two or three wealthiest gentlemen in attendance tonight."

Bramford's dark brows shot up. "Lord, Cyn!" At her warning frown, he modulated his tone so that his next words could not be heard by other dancers. "Still bent on that crackbrain scheme to leg-shackle a rich husband, eh?" He glanced about the ballroom, then grinned suddenly. "Fancy I can take some of the wind out of your billows. Clap your eyes on that tottering old gentleman dancing—or at least shuffling about—with Anne Bloomhedge. I will lay a wager that the poor girl is holding him up, for he'll not see seventy again. Take a good look, Cyn. He's the richest man here tonight and recently widowed. On the catch for a young wife, I hear."

Cynthia's gaze raked the gentleman in question, who

45

was smiling rather foolishly and very bemusedly into poor little Anne Bloomhedge's fresh young face. He was slight and bent-shouldered with thin white hair. He wasn't as decrepit as Bram was making out, but he was much too far past his prime for Cynthia to envision facing him at meals every day—much less sharing with him the more intimate aspects of marriage.

Seeing her regretful look, Bramford chortled, "See, you don't fancy that un. Well, there's Lord Dexcord. He's much younger, but then you will have to listen to an unending stream of pointless, repetitious conversation punctuated by those barks of his every word or two. Puts one in mind of a hunting hound."

"Don't be unkind, Bram." Cynthia's sisterly reprimand was automatic. "Lord Dexcord suffers from a mild lung condition and he never barks. He merely clears his throat. Although I will own I must surely go distracted if I had to listen to him do it day in and day out."

"Don't forget the nights!" interposed Bramford. "I shouldn't wonder if he does it in his sleep," he added with evident relish. "Perhaps you could live apart. He has several country estates, and if you organized things cleverly, I collect you could always be in residence where he was not."

"You needn't imagine you can flummery me into abandoning my plan," Cynthia returned, "for I can think of no other way out of our present predicament. Oh—look toward the door." A sandy-haired gentleman dressed in impeccable fashion had entered the hall accompanied by a buxom matron wearing an atrocious purple gown and a gold turban slightly askew on a tangle of reddish hair.

"Isn't that Lord Percy Farthing?"

"With his redoubtable mama," Bramford said. "Wherever poor Percy goes, Lady Farthing is not far behind. Heard at my club that Lord Farthing wanted to offer for a lady two years ago, but his mama gave it as her judgment that the chit had too many opinions of her own. Settled the matter, I can tell you."

"I seem to recall," Cynthia mused, "that Lord Farthing's uncle left him a sizable fortune."

"Indeed he did," confirmed Bramford, "and even before that he was well set up. His father left a large estate."

Cynthia watched the tall figure of Lord Farthing and his lumbering mama as they halted to engage in conversation with Lady Bloomhedge. "How old is he?"

"Thirty-five, I daresay."

"He's very pleasant looking," Cynthia noted.

"Cyn," said the viscount critically, watching the speculative expression on her pretty face, "he ain't bad to look at, but it won't do. He ain't the man for you!"

"I beg leave to take issue with you," she said, a stubborn note coming into the voice. "He's wealthy and presentable and not too old—"

"I collect he's a very worthy man," Bramford said, laughing, "but he's a mama's boy. I'm devilish fond of you, Cyn, but it won't do at all. You'll never get past that old dragon! She'll choose the wife for Percy, and it won't be a self-willed hoyden with a tongue as sharp as a needle."

"What a dog in the manger you are, Bram!" she exclaimed, both indignant and amused. "You say you are fond of me, and then you heap insults upon my head."

"Only saying the truth, old girl," replied Bramford equably. "When Lord Farthing marries, it will be to some retiring, biddable, blushing miss who will permit Lady Farthing to run her life as well as Percy's. Believe me, you

47

wouldn't thank me if I encouraged you to join yourself to Lady Farthing's household. You will have to live with her, you know. She'll never allow Percy to set up an establishment of his own."

"I daresay," Cynthia said, "that I am a better judge of what will suit me than you are. And I am sure there is no need to remind you that our straitened finances force us to make the best of what is at hand."

"No need at all," he interrupted with a rueful smile. "Dashed embarrassing when a gentleman can't even stand good for drinks for his friends."

"Well then, you will introduce me to Lord Farthing."

The dance came to an end and Cynthia laid claim to her brother's arm before he could escape to the game room. "Come, we'll make our way to where the Farthings are standing and you can strike up a conversation with him."

"Hardly know the man, Cyn," muttered Bramford. "Feel like a deuced fool." In the event, however, Bramford managed the meeting adroitly, pretending to recognize Lord Farthing only at the last moment.

"Farthing!" he exclaimed, all pleasant surprise. "Haven't seen you since we were at Tattersall's last month. Are you satisfied with the grays you bought?"

"Quite," replied Lord Farthing. His tone was low, as if he were unaccustomed to speaking up for himself. As things progressed, it appeared that this was indeed the case, for Lady Farthing interrupted in a loud, strident voice, elaborating on her son's reply.

"Sixteen mile an hour tits, those two!" she boomed. "Chattington, ain't it? Lord Dahlmere's grandson, ain't you, boy?"

Bramford made his bow and displayed his most disarming smile. "Your servant, ma'am. My grandfather's health

48

prevents his attending many social evenings, but when I tell him that you were here, I am certain he will regret having missed this one."

"Nothing of the kind," said her ladyship crudely. "That crotchety old rumstick will own himself fortunate to have avoided me. Nearly come to cuffs every time we meet."

"Know what you mean, madam," said Bramford gallantly. "Grandfather can be as cross as crabs. Pleasure to meet someone who ain't intimidated by his gruff ways."

"Eh, what?" inquired Lady Farthing with a cackle. "It takes more than a leaky rattle like old Dahlmere to intimidate *me!* Stroke of good fortune that you seem to take after the other side of the family in looks. The Dahlmeres were all knocker-faced."

"May I present my sister, Lady Cynthia Chattington?" Bramford interposed. "Cynthia, Lady Farthing and her son, Lord Farthing."

With a hesitant smile and half-lowered lashes, the perfect image of a shy, retiring miss, Cynthia turned to Lord Farthing.

That gentleman bowed over her small hand. "Ahem— Chattington didn't tell me he had such a lovely sister." He smiled down at her, an expression of bemusement lurking in his hazel eyes.

"Oh, la, sir!" Cynthia chirped. "You make me blush with such pretty compliments."

From the corner of her eye she caught the astonished look on Bramford's face. Even Lady Farthing did not appear to believe that Cynthia could be brought to the blush so easily. "Humph!" she announced. "Lovely is as lovely does, eh, Percy?"

"Very true, mama," Lord Farthing agreed, "and if I

may venture an opinion, I am certain Lady Chattington's ways are as lovely as her face."

Lady Farthing's eyes narrowed suspiciously. "Ain't you the gel that fell into the Hallums' fishpond at the breakfast last season? Disgraceful behavior!"

Cynthia batted her eyes innocently. "I fear you have me confused with some other girl, Lady Farthing. Perhaps it was someone who looked like me."

"Eh, what? You ain't got a twin, do you?"

"No, my lady," replied Cynthia, "but, of course, there were a number of dark-haired girls out last season."

When Lady Farthing's piercing gaze was attracted elsewhere, Cynthia shot a warning look at Bramford, who appeared to be choking behind his hand.

"Come with me, Percy," Lady Farthing bellowed. "I see Lady Swinson has arrived. Must talk to her about the rout I am planning next month."

Lord Farthing's attention was still on Cynthia. "May I have the honor of the first waltz, Lady Chattington? That is, if you are permitted to waltz."

"Oh, yes, sir," Cynthia assured him. "I was approved by the patronesses of Almack's last season. And I should like above all things to stand up with you for the waltz."

As soon as Lord Farthing was gone, a laugh, too long held back, exploded from Bramford. "Quite a Cheltenham tragedy you enacted, Sister, but if you will take my advice —which you confessed yourself in dire need of earlier— you'll set your sights on some other gentleman. You'll never steer Percy Farthing into parson's mousetrap! Not with Lady Farthing watching every move he makes! Did you ever see such a horrid rudesby as that female? Had all I could do to keep from choking when she brought up that incident at the Hallums' last season."

"I hope I convinced her that she had mistaken me for someone else," Cynthia said. "It wasn't my fault, you know."

"Never is, to hear you tell it."

"It's true! Hetta Larchmont *pushed* me—because Lord Pendleton was paying too much attention to me, and after she had told everyone that he was about to offer for her."

"You must own," Bramford said with a grin, "you *did* provoke her, calling her a mutton-face."

"That was only after she said *I* was behaving like a dasher and didn't have a presentable party gown to my name because of Grandfather's nipcheese ways. She insulted our entire family, calling us shabby-genteel."

"So *that* was what made you fall into such a twitter," Bramford remarked. "Better not let Lady Farthing see you in a similar state. Oh, oh, here comes Pendleton to claim his dance. Understand he has two left feet. Well, you've gotten yourself into the suds this time, Cyn."

"Lord Pendleton," Cynthia said with a sweet, if spurious, pleasure as that gentleman approached. "I feared you had forgotten me."

Lord Pendleton assured her that such an eventuality was not even within the realm of possibility as he led her onto the dance floor, where he continued to layer his conversation with flowery compliments pertaining to the color of her eyes and her cheeks and the Grecian cut that framed her face with charming curls, a style that gentleman proclaimed to be slap up to the mark. Lord Pendleton was too prosy by half for Cynthia's tastes, but she managed to parry his poetic fancies prettily.

During her first London season Cynthia had polished the habit of easy intercourse with gentlemen, first learned at small gatherings in the country. She had a fund of social chitchat available for such occasions as the Bloomhedges' ball, and after she had perfected the ability to stay out of the way of his "two left feet" and persuaded his lordship to stop poeticizing, she talked easily with him—and with the other gentlemen who sought her company that evening, laughing a great deal and engaging in lighthearted flirtation.

It is true that when Lord Farthing came to claim his waltz, she underwent something of a metamorphosis, becoming ever so much more demure and shy. She managed, instead, to draw him out without his being aware that she was doing it and listened with a rapt expression upon her face as he talked of his high-toned racers and Farthingate, his ancestral home, where he and his mama would retire at the end of the season.

As the waltz ended, that gentleman owned himself astonished to have talked so much more than was his general habit. Cynthia refrained from suggesting that *anyone* so much in Lady Farthing's company would find the occasions when he was able to speak at any length rare indeed.

"It must be that you are such a good listener, Lady Cynthia," he told her warmly. Noting his use of her Christian name for the first time, from which Cynthia took heart that she was making good progress with the gentleman, and perceiving that he did not usually find it easy to talk to females, she said, "Oh, sir, you held me spellbound, I assure you. Your country home sounds so idyllic. I confess I prefer the country to the city. Something tells me that you share that opinion."

"Why, yes," admitted the gentleman, much struck. "How did you guess?"

She lowered her lashes. "I hope I will not sound bold if I say I sensed we were kindred spirits."

"Dashed if I don't believe you're right! I say, would you care to have the supper dance with me? We could continue our conversation over the collation. I will tell you about my new dairy cows and a new pasture grass I am experimenting with."

"You honor me, sir! La, we shall have all the other girls turning quite green with envy! Indeed, I am all aquiver to hear about your cows." She saw Lady Farthing bearing down on them. "I believe your dear mama is looking for you. And there is my cousin beckoning. Good-bye until the supper dance, my lord."

Lady Sedgegood gestured for Cynthia to be seated in the chair next to her own. "I've just spoken with Bramford and have learned that you are going on with that hey-go-mad scheme. I confess, I had hoped it was nothing but a distempered freak that you would have forgotten by now."

"Whatever are you talking about, Cousin Alice?"

"Don't bat those big gray eyes at me, my girl. Before you carry this ridiculous notion of yours too far, I must warn you that your grandfather despises Lord Farthing's mother. Lord Dahlmere and I often find ourselves at opposite opinions, but in that I must own I am inclined to agree with him."

"Grandfather may have taken Lord Farthing's mother in dislike—indeed, I cannot blame him—but I daresay he will like Lord Farthing's money well enough," retorted Cynthia impertinently.

"I watched you waltzing with him," Lady Sedgegood informed her young cousin, "toadying and looking as demure as a nun's hen!"

"Did I?" Cynthia asked earnestly. "Well, to say the truth, dear cousin, I felt like an utter pea-goose. Being shy and retiring is a dead bore. But never mind. I shall go on well enough, I expect. Lord Farthing is a pleasant enough companion when he can be separated from his mama."

"I promise you," Lady Sedgegood said forthrightly, "that such occasions will be rare indeed."

Her cousin's prophecy proved all too true. Lady Farthing's eyes never left her son and the pretty black-haired girl during the supper dance, and as the couple went in to supper, she attached herself firmly to Lord Farthing's side. Further, she dominated the table conversation, pausing only now and then to fix Cynthia with a baleful stare and announce, "You still look to me like that gel who fell into the Hallums' fishpond. Eh, what?" And when Lord Farthing departed the table to refill their punch cups, his mother leaned toward Cynthia and said stentoriously, "Percy ain't a man who takes ballroom flirtations seriously, you know. And, of course, the dear boy will never marry without my approval. Someone older and settled, that's the sort of gel who will suit my Percy."

"Indeed, ma'am," Cynthia responded, keeping her temper with difficulty, "it is not every mother who takes such a marked interest in her son's welfare."

"Eh, what?" bellowed Lady Farthing, somewhat taken aback, for she was at a loss to know whether she was being complimented or insulted. Fortunately, Lord Farthing returned at that moment and forestalled a direct attack.

Unable to engage Lord Farthing in conversation while his mother continued talking, stopping only long enough to draw breath, Cynthia had to content herself with casting shy smiles in that gentleman's direction. These were clearly not lost on their recipient, for several times his pale cheeks flushed pink and his gaze lingered on Cynthia's lowered lashes and pert nose.

When, as they returned to the ballroom after supper,

Lady Farthing announced that she very much feared she could feel one of her prostrating headaches coming on and thought it imperative that Percy escort her to their house at once, Cynthia lost all hope of advancing her campaign further that night. Just before leaving the ballroom, Lord Farthing surprised her by whispering into her ear when his mother's back was turned and begging permission to call on her the following afternoon.

Cynthia said that she would look forward with the utmost eagerness to seeing him then, and as she watched the Farthings taking their leave of their host and hostess, she congratulated herself on getting her campaign off to a propitious start.

She then sighed with relief because, with the Farthings gone, she could be more herself and enjoy the remainder of the ball. It was at this juncture that she received the greatest shock of the evening. Lord Silverstone, come to claim her for the country dances, stopped to speak to Lady Sedgegood, probably intending to position himself as high in her good graces as Lord Pendleton.

"Have you heard, madam, that the Earl of Graybroughton has put in an appearance here tonight?"

"The earl?" inquired Lady Sedgegood with intense interest. "You don't mean Lord Marlbridge!"

"Exactly so!" Lord Pendleton said. "I believe he arrived just before we went in for supper. Causing quite a flurry among the ladies."

"Why, I haven't heard anything about *him* for ages! I was acquainted with his father years ago, but the old earl has been gone these five years and more. I am told that the on-dits three years ago had it that the present earl was something of a recluse—and, indeed, to my knowledge he hasn't come down for the season in years."

"That is very true, my lady," confirmed Lord Silverstone. "Until three years ago he was with the troops fighting Boney in the Peninsula. Upon his return he retired to one of his country estates—in Northumberland —and the London hostesses had despaired of ever uprooting him from there and getting him to London. My own mother has shed tears over his numerous failures to accept invitations to her parties."

Cynthia, who had been listening to this exchange with growing curiosity, asked, "Where is he? I must see this man of mystery."

Lord Silverstone craned his short neck for several moments and then said, "I believe he's the center of that group of pinks over there by the door. He's the tallest of the lot. You can see the back of his head just through there."

Cynthia stood on tiptoe so that she could peer over another young woman's shoulder. The back of the earl's head was covered with thick auburn hair. Its color and the broad shoulders, clad in a finely tailored ivory-colored evening coat, looked faintly familiar to her. What she could see of the earl put her in mind of someone—although she could not think who.

She was cudgeling her brain for the answer when the earl turned to glance idly about the dance floor. Momentarily, his faintly arrogant blue-eyed gaze made contact with Cynthia's gray-eyed stare. It was then that Cynthia's heart very nearly jumped into her throat.

Kenyon, the moneylender, was standing in the Bloomhedges' ballroom, masquerading as the Earl of Graybroughton and behaving for all the world as if he were to the manor born!

4

The man Cynthia knew merely as Kenyon did not appear in the least discommoded at espying her across the ballroom. Holding her gaze, he inclined his head and smiled crookedly in a way that could only be described as insolent.

Cynthia tore her eyes from his face, and laying a hand across the bodice of her puce gown where her heart thudded at a far too rapid pace, she said in a breathless little rush, "Lord Silverstone, the heat is excessively oppressive in here. Do you suppose we could forgo the country dances in favor of the punch bowl?"

Lord Silverstone pronounced himself in favor of this change in the programme and begged permission of Lady Sedgegood to escort Lady Cynthia for a stroll on the terrace after they had refreshed themselves. Lady Sedgegood gave them leave with the added instruction that they were to return to the ballroom when the country dances ended. Then, waving them away, she turned to the elderly matron at her side and exclaimed, "Well, Lottie, the Earl of Graybroughton is here. Quite a feather for Druscilla Bloomhedge. I was acquainted with his late father, you know. A regular rake-shame in his younger days, the old earl was, but after his marriage they do say he became all that is proper."

"Not an uncommon tale, you must own, Alice," replied Lady Sommers.

"Just so," concurred Lady Sedgegood, shaking her head over the peculiarities of men.

A while later, strolling on the terrace, Cynthia was intent on learning more about the earl from her escort. "It seems strange that he would suddenly put in an appearance after refusing all invitations for so long."

"Not so strange," commented Lord Silverstone. "It's as plain as a pikestaff that he's come to London on the lookout for a wife. Why else would a man who shuns society in favor of country pursuits and reading—for they do say he is inclined to the bookish—put himself through an ordeal that must needs be a dead bore for a gentleman of that ilk?"

Cynthia, who knew of the man's secret life, could think of a number of far less innocent reasons for Kenyon's appearance in London at the height of the season. What better time or place for preying on ramshackle young blades such as her brother? As for his appearance at the Bloomhedges' ball, Cynthia was very much afraid that she knew the reason for that, too, and the thought made a shiver go up her spine.

"Are you cold?" inquired Lord Silverstone with the greatest solicitousness. "Shall I fetch your wrap?"

"No, no," Cynthia declined. "We must be getting back to the ballroom in a very few minutes at any rate. W-what makes you think the—er, earl has come to London in search of a wife?"

"My dear Lady Cynthia, even the greatest rogue unhung among the quality must enter the matrimonial state eventually. Oh, I don't mean to imply that the earl is a rogue, although they do say he has had some adventures in the petticoat line. He is now two or three years past thirty, and it is time he married and set up his nursery."

"Well, of course, you are undoubtedly right," Cynthia murmured, but she was thinking that she pitied the poor unsuspecting lady who fell under the spell of the gentleman in question. But surely he could not carry out his masquerade right up to the marriage altar! It was one thing to pretend to be the earl in a London ballroom, but quite another to marry under false pretenses and wearing an assumed name into the bargain. Unless—Was it even remotely possible that he actually *was* the Earl of Graybroughton?

On the sudden thought she asked her escort, "Have you ever seen the earl before tonight?"

"No," he admitted, "but that is hardly surprising, considering his reclusive manner of life and the fact that Northumberland is so far from London." This information did nothing to clear the fog of questions that was swirling in Cynthia's head. Seeing there was no other news to be gained from that source, she suggested that they return to the ballroom.

As she stepped across the threshold, Bramford hurried to her side. "Been scouring the house for you! Oh, hallo, Lord Silverstone. I wish you will excuse us. I must have a private word with my sister."

Lord Silverstone took his leave, albeit reluctantly, and

not until he had extracted Cynthia's promise to stand up with him for another dance before the evening ended.

"By Jupiter, Cyn! Thought I'd never find you."

"You might have asked Cousin Alice," Cynthia told him, "and saved yourself running about until your collar points were wilted."

"Well, I couldn't find *her,* either. I think she must have gone in for some punch, although I missed her *there* as well. But never mind. I've met the most bang-up fellow, not by half as top-lofty as he might be, considering that he's as rich as royalty, or so everyone is saying. Wouldn't even venture to guess how many girls are on the catch for him, but I do think you ought to give it a go, anyway, for I'll put you up against the best of 'em—only try to remember to keep your tongue in your head."

"What are you running on about?" she interrupted. "I only went for a stroll on the terrace with Lord Silverstone. It couldn't have been for more than ten minutes. And what has drawn you away from the gaming table? Lost your nest egg, I daresay."

"No, I didn't! And what the dickens do you mean strolling on the terrace with that pie-faced Silverstone when I'm trying to find you so that I can introduce you to a gentleman?"

"Well, I had no idea that you were searching for me. How could I?" She sighed impatiently. "So that is what this is all about? Well, I find this passing strange, Bram. A while earlier you were doing your best to discourage me from trying to fix the interest of a gentleman—and now you wish to introduce me to one!"

"Dash it, Cyn, I didn't fancy any of those other fellows as a brother-in-law. But it's Charlton House to a Charley's shelter the earl could get a rein on you, and he ain't got a freakish, cow-mouthed mama, either. In fact, he ain't got a mama *or* a papa, for they've both stuck their spoons in the wall—"

"Bram!" Cynthia uttered wrathfully. "You *can't* be speaking of the Earl of Graybroughton!"

"But of course I am! I told him all your good points—for which you might spare a word of thanks instead of ripping up at me like this—and he said he would be pleased to be introduced to such a paragon of maidenly virtue!"

"Oh, how abominable of you! And I don't care a straw what he said. Not that I believe for one moment that he meant it. I should think you would know when someone was bamming you, but if that horrible creature is rag-mannered enough to face me—"

"Cyn!" Bramford was looking incredulous. "How can you speak so of the earl? Dashed shabby thing to say, old girl. I wouldn't have believed it of you. If you're turning shrewish at such an early age, I fear you will make a horrid old lady—"

"Oh, be quiet!" she said crossly.

It did seem that she had been right in her suspicion as to why Kenyon had shown his face at the Bloomhedges' ball. She had no doubt now that he had somehow learned that *she* would be there and had come to demand payment of Bram's IOU. Since that was the case, she did not hold out the frailest hope that she would be able to avoid him for the remainder of the evening. She wondered distractedly if she ought to take a swooning fit and allow Bramford to escort her home. But since she had never fainted in her life and had little patience with those who did, she supposed her brother would merely stare at her prone body through his quizzing glass and tell her to get up and stop making a cake of herself. No, she would have to think of something else.

But before she could, her worst fears were realized. Suddenly a tall figure loomed at Bram's elbow. "Ah, there you are, Chattington. I understood you to say that you wished to introduce me to someone."

"Oh, hallo, Lord Marlbridge!" Bramford turned to look up into the rugged face that was half a head above his own. "May I present my sister, Lady Cynthia Chattington?"

"Your servant, ma'am," said Kenyon with a twinkle in his eye. "I must say you are a small package to contain all the sterling qualities which your brother assures me are yours." The man was mocking her!

"My brother is a shocking fibster, sir!"

"Indeed? I beg leave to form my own judgment in the matter. May I have the honor of the next dance—if you haven't already promised it."

"Oh, no," Bram said baldly. "She ain't promised this one."

Maneuvered into a corner, Cynthia could not but accompany Kenyon onto the floor. She was so furious that she couldn't even speak for a moment, though whether she was more angry at her brother or at the odious Kenyon, she could not have said.

To her chagrin the orchestra struck up the strains of a waltz and Kenyon encircled her with one arm, an action that in any other gentleman of Cynthia's acquaintance would have seemed perfectly proper, for it *was* the accepted stance for the waltz, but in the present instance struck her as most audaciously familiar.

"You are shaking like a blancmange, Lady Cynthia," he observed. "Since we both know you are no bashful, gooseish miss, something tells me that you are angry."

After assuring herself they could not be overhead, she sputtered, "Well, of course I'm angry! I s-should just like to know how you have the brass to walk in here masquerading as a member of the nobility!"

"Are you concerned for me—in case I should be caught out?" Kenyon's mouth curved in a sardonic grin that further provoked her.

"I assure you, sir, that nothing would give me greater pleasure than to see you exposed in your true colors!"

A deep chuckle escaped him. "Lord, but you *are* hot in the spur! Well, I am persuaded, Lady Cynthia, that your brother failed to mention *all* of your qualities. A quick temper and a sharp tongue, for two. You wouldn't be Irish, would you?"

"Well, I *did* have an Irish grandmother, though I can't conceive why that should be of the least interest to you. If you will heed my advice, sir, you will take your leave of London as fast as ever you can—before all these people discover that you have been bamming them."

"Draw bridle, my girl!" said Kenyon dampingly. "I assure you that, even if I were not the Earl of Graybroughton, my being caught out in a Banbury tale is very much in question. The earl is known to be a stranger in London, and I very much doubt that anyone present would readily recognize the earl if they saw him."

"You said *if* you were not the earl," Cynthia exclaimed. "Does that mean that you *are* the earl?"

"I am not such a cabbage-head as to believe you will take my word for it. However, you may ask anyone here tonight and have your answer, for I am told I favor my father."

"Oh, I know what *they* will say. You have flummeried them all! Y-you even have the audacity to *look* like an earl!

63

And you will please stop laughing at me in that unfeeling way."

"I can't help but laugh, Cynthia, for here you are raking me down for pretending to be something I am not—when I saw you doing the same thing not an hour past."

"Gammon!" Cynthia blurted. "What *are* you talking about?"

"I watched you at supper with Lord Farthing. Poor fellow was quite taken in by your bag of moonshine, although I fancy his mother was not. Am I to assume that Percy Farthing is the gentleman whom you have settled on to rescue your family from dun territory?"

"Ah ha!" said Cynthia. "The veneer is rubbing off, isn't it, Kenyon? I knew all along why you showed your face here tonight. You mean to put pressure on me to repay my brother's loan! Well, you may be the Earl of Graybroughton—although I still am not convinced of that by half— but the same people who are fawning over you tonight will cut you in an instant if they learn the wicked means by which you made your fortune. I, sir, know the truth of the matter!"

"Oh, you do, do you?" said his lordship with awful sarcasm.

"I expect you were thrown into quite a dither at being seen running tame in that *moneylender's* house by a member of the quality. But see you I did, sir! I know you are Higgins's associate, and that you call yourself by the ridiculous name of Kenyon in your—other life."

"As to the suitability of my Christian name, you shan't put *that* in my dish along with everything else! My father pinned that appellation on me when I was far too young to lodge a protest."

"Well, that is neither here nor there. I told you at

that—that purse-leech's establishment that there is no money for repayment of the note until I marry."

Kenyon's brows rose. "I must tell you that you have an odd notion of how moneylenders operate. Did you imagine that a pretty face would touch the heart of such a personage? If so, you are far wide of the mark, my innocent."

"Oh, for shame!" Shock and indignation had caused Cynthia's voice to reach such a pitch that several couples near them turned to stare. Realizing that she and Kenyon were becoming the center of attention, she felt her cheeks grow hot and lowered her voice to a hoarse whisper. "It is a blessing your poor parents have passed on, for if word ever spreads as to how you can go on so famously with your carriages and your wardrobe and your country estates—well, your family name will be tarnished beyond salvaging!"

"For once, hoyden, I am in complete agreement with you!" returned Kenyon, a warning light in his eyes. "So we shall strike a bargain. You will not breathe a word of what you have just said to me to anyone else—and I shall not demand payment of your brother's note at the present time. You must own, however, that I am to be excused for taking an interest in how your plan is progressing, seeing that my own good fortune—not to put too fine a point on it—is hanging on your success or failure. And I promise you, I shall own myself astonished if you make any headway with that jerry-sneak Percy Farthing!"

"Allow me to inform you, sir, that Lord Farthing has asked permission to call on me tomorrow!" Cynthia retorted in chilly accents.

The earl eyed her in speculative silence for several moments but at last replied, just as the waltz came to an end, "Poor silly corker."

When he had returned her to Bramford and departed, her brother said rudely, "Couldn't believe my eyes, Cyn! You were *arguing* with the earl. It is fortunate that no one else seemed to notice, but I know you too well. What you could find to brangle over with a man you have just met, I can't think. If you don't learn to put a damper on that temper of yours, you are going to find yourself at your last prayers!"

"What makes you suppose," returned Cynthia, firing up, "that I shouldn't prefer being at my last prayers to spending my time with such a rascal as—"

"He ain't a rascal!" exclaimed Bramford, deeply offended. "And why you should be so top-lofty when we ain't got sixpence to scratch with, I wish you will tell me. It's coming to something when a man tries to steer the nonpareil of the season in his sister's direction and is treated to a tantrum for his pains!"

"Oh, Bram," cried Cynthia, suddenly tiring of the entire affair, "you don't know half of what is transpiring here and—oh, dear, there is Cousin Alice, looking quite wretchedly bored. I am going to tell her we are ready to depart."

Lady Sedgegood proved more than willing to call it an evening, and after they had expressed gratitude to their host and hostess, the butler had their carriage brought to the door. When they were settled back against the squabs and the carriage was headed in the direction of Grosvenor Square, Bramford announced that if anyone should ask for his opinion he would say that, except for the unexpected appearance of Lord Marlbridge, the evening had been one of the dreariest he had ever had the misfortune to experience.

When Cynthia voiced a hearty agreement, adding that she had not found the earl at all remarkable either, Lady Sedgegood inquired in astonishment how she could say such a thing when she had been particularly marked off from the other young ladies by Lord Marlbridge's invitation to waltz with him. Cynthia could depend upon it, Lady Sedgegood continued, that the incident would be the talk of the haut ton for days. That good lady confessed that she would not be at all surprised if what had transpired that evening had turned Cynthia into the brightest belle of the season.

"What nonsense!" said Cynthia contemptuously. "Belle of the season, indeed! I wonder that even you have allowed yourself to be bamboozled by such an odious blackguard as the Earl of Graybroughton!"

If Cynthia had denied God and England in the same breath, Lady Sedgegood could not have been more shocked. When she had recovered enough to speak, she predicted that her young cousin was coming down with the megrims, for she could conceive of no other explanation for her positively freakish utterances.

Cynthia merely heaved a deep sigh that verged on a moan and covered her eyes with one small hand, holding her peace on the remainder of the journey home, a course of action that was difficult indeed. For she would have enjoyed avenging herself by telling the awful truth about the earl. However, she remembered too well the warning light in that gentleman's eyes when he had struck the "bargain" with her. Unless she wished a demand to be lodged with her grandfather for immediate payment of Bram's IOU, she must needs keep her own counsel.

5

Shortly after noon the next day Cynthia and Bramford were enjoying one of Cook's hearty repasts in the breakfast parlor. At least the viscount, who was layering his third hot muffin with butter and orange marmalade, could certainly be said to be enjoying it. Already dressed for the day in a camel-colored coat, leather breeches, and top boots, his cravat arranged in the style known as the Oriental, Bramford—if his appetite were any indicator—did not have a care in the world. Cynthia was well aware of the reason for her brother's good spirits at an hour when he was, more often than not, still abed. It was her revelation that payment of his IOU had been postponed indefinitely.

The knowledge did not cheer her, for *she* knew that the price of Bramford's lightheartedness was her own silence concerning information so damaging to a member of society that, were it spread about, it would rock the ton to its very core. She had spent a good portion of the early morning hours, after retiring, recalling every aspect of the

Bloomhedges' ball, particularly what had transpired after the arrival of Kenyon. She no longer had much doubt that he was the Earl of Graybroughton, for even a scoundrel such as he could not hope to carry off such a blatant masquerade. It was a grudging admission, and the earl's impeccable family connections in no way mitigated, in Cynthia's mind, his calculated choice of money-making schemes, which was far worse than if he had gone into trade. And even *that* course of action virtually assured one of being snubbed by the quality.

Wearing a pale green promenade dress, her black hair in a very becoming mode, caught up behind with tiny ringlets at each temple, Cynthia might have looked in high croak to anyone who did not know her as well as her brother.

"You've hardly touched your breakfast, Cyn," commented Bramford, popping a tasty morsel into his mouth. "Fit of the blue-devils that overset you last evening appears to be hanging on. Daresay it's the thought of promenading in the park with Lord Farthing."

"What makes you think so?" inquired Cynthia disinterestedly.

The viscount's eyes twinkled mischievously. "Unless I mistake the matter, you are wondering how you shall carry on with that Cheltenham tragedy you began last evening for a full two hours or more this afternoon."

"Nonsense!" retorted Cynthia. "The trouble is that I didn't sleep well last night."

"Heigh-ho! Don't tell me your conscience was pricking for pulling the wool over Farthing's eyes."

Cynthia sniffed. "Don't be absurd."

Her brother's look was one of high amusement. "Care

to lay a wager on how long you can play the blushful miss before you start kicking up the dust?"

"No, I do not!" Cynthia flared. "Need I remind you that it is your disgraceful penchant to place a wager on anything and everything that has put us in this mingle-mangle?"

"Crop failures in Hampshire had more to do with it than I did," Bramford told her, much affronted. "And by all that's wonderful, Cyn, how else do you expect me to pass my time in London?"

Cynthia might have given him a few choice suggestions had not Hobson appeared at that moment, looking down his long nose with disapproval. "I've just shown Lord Caverset into the study, my lord. I told him you were at breakfast, but he has taken it upon himself to wait."

Cynthia could well imagine the icy stare that such insistence must have elicited from Hobson. The butler regarded Lord Caverset with dislike and suspicion. The old retainer was convinced the young lord's bosom companion was a disgraceful scattergood whose influence was the chief cause of the viscount's improvident manner of life. For Cynthia's part, she was not at all sure who was leading whom. Nor did she imagine that Bram's and Cavey's ramshackle ways were very different from many other young lords of their age and position. The fact was that Hobson's excessive fondness for her brother caused him to turn a blind eye to that gentleman's faults. It was Lord Caverset's misfortune to be the most convenient scapegoat for the butler's displeasure.

"Well, don't leave him kicking his heels in the study, man," Bramford said. "You know Cavey is like one of the family. Why didn't you show him in here?"

"Since you ask me for my opinion, sir," Hobson said

portentously, "I feel myself bound to say that I consider social calls at this early hour not quite acceptable. Any further opinion I might have of Lord Caverset's conduct is something I wouldn't demean myself by divulging."

"The devil you wouldn't!" Bramford remarked provocatively.

The butler received this charge without a blink, and when further told to escort Lord Caverset to the breakfast parlor, he merely said primly, "If that is your wish, my lord."

"Do you imagine I would waste my breath on something that was not my wish, you old jackanapes?"

"Since it is not my place to pass judgment on my betters, sir, I am sure I cannot take it upon myself to venture an opinion," replied Hobson in frosty accents.

"You need not scruple on *that* head at this late juncture," said Bramford in exasperation, for Hobson was capable of ignoring the most blistering set-down with complete sangfroid. "And bring Cavey here at once."

"As you say, sir," replied Hobson as he went to carry out the viscount's instructions, every line of his stiffly retreating figure communicating his disapprobation.

If Lord Caverset was aware of Hobson's disapproval, however, it did not trouble him in the slightest degree. He bounded flamboyantly into the breakfast parlor, his pale brown hair arranged in the currently popular Brutus style, his hands and cravat glittering with rubies, and made himself comfortable in a chair at the table. Although Bramford was frequently impressed by his friend's dash, Cynthia thought the rubies, particularly at this hour, made him look gaudy and overdressed. They were, she thought, in even worse taste when one considered that the

71

sale of the jewels would have gone a long way toward disposing of Lord Caverset's long-overdue debts.

"What has rousted you out at this hour, Cavey?" asked Bramford, pushing the platter of muffins within easy reach of his friend's long arm.

Lord Caverset examined the offering with obvious relish, then extended a beringed hand to help himself to a muffin. Recollecting his manners rather belatedly, he said, "Good afternoon, Lady Cynthia. I hope I am not committing a social solecism by arriving while you are still at breakfast."

"Fustian, ~~Cavey! Of~~ course you are not," Cynthia assured him.

"Thank you for saying so. I say, Bram, always did say your sister was as sound as a trout! Can't think how the two of you could spring from the same parents, you rascal."

"You ain't one who ought to be casting aspersions, Cavey," replied Bramford good-naturedly.

Lord Caverset grinned. "You can't insult me this morning, Bram. I say, ain't it a bang-up day?"

"Since I haven't been out yet, I shan't venture an agreement," Bramford said, "but it seems to me that Hobson said earlier it was clouding up to rain. Anyway, I would like to know where you disappeared to last night just when I was starting to win."

"Had an important appointment, old boy."

"At eleven o'clock at night?" said Bramford doubtfully. "Well, whatever it was, it's put you in a rattling good humor."

"Indeed it has," Cynthia concurred. "And since I know you so well, Cavey, I suspect that you have somehow improved your fortune since the last time you were here, when you were looking as grave as a judge."

"Not to dress it up in clean linen, I am about to come into possession of more blunt than I ever dreamed of having." Lord Caverset's expression put Cynthia in mind of a cat who had just swallowed whole his mistress's despised tame songbird.

"Why, you rake!" Bramford exclaimed, beaming at his friend. "You've had a sure tip on a race! Can't think of anything else that could plunge you into such raptures. Well, speak up, man! Tell me the news and we'll decide how we shall find the blunt to take advantage of it."

"Afraid I can't do that, Bram."

"What do you mean you *can't?*" Bramford's eager expression had become incredulity. "When have we ever had secrets from each other? Come now, Cavey, stop bamming me and tell me your news."

"Can't," repeated Lord Caverset calmly.

"Then why'd you come calling at all?" inquired Bramford petulantly.

"To see if you'd care to accompany me to Bond Street. I'm having some new coats tailored. After that I collect we might stroll over to Gentleman Jackson's."

"Gentleman Jackson be hanged!" exploded Bramford, his well-known "short wick" flaming up. "I've no intention of being seen in the company of a gentleman who don't think enough of our friendship to tip me off when he's on to a sure thing. Never thought you to be such a shabster!"

"Don't fall into a twitter, Bram," Cynthia intervened. She turned to Lord Caverset. "For my part, you shall have my undying gratitude if you will keep your 'sure things' to yourself, Cavey. Bramford is going to have to curtail his gambling, and I daresay it wouldn't do you any harm to follow the same course."

"Can't expect a lady to understand gentlemanly endeavors," said that gentleman tolerantly. "I recommend that you come with me to Bond Street, Bram. Nothing like the hustle and bustle of the shops to lift a churlish mood—even if it should rain."

"How you can have the effrontery to call me churlish," Bramford ejaculated, "when you have just insulted me at my own breakfast table, I cannot conceive!"

"Confound it, Bram!" Lord Caverset's patience seemed to have spent itself. "Are you coming with me or ain't you?"

"Course I'm coming," announced the viscount, apparently forgetting that he had just expressed outrage at the very idea. "If you imagine you can gull me into believing you ain't got a tip on a horse, you're dotty. Oh, no need for you to look abashed. My blood's up, Cavey, and I mean to ferret out your news if I have to dog your footsteps all day!"

Still brangling like a couple of aged, cross-tempered lapdogs, the two gentlemen left the breakfast parlor, sparing not even a farewell for Cynthia, who merely shook her head sadly and wondered how she could make her brother face the seriousness of their financial affairs.

Pushing aside her still-full plate, she left the table and wandered into the green saloon, where she found her cousin bent over her embroidery hoop.

"I'll have Eunice go fetch your embroidery, if you will join me in my occupation," said Lady Sedgegood, glancing up.

"I'd make a tangle of it," Cynthia replied, wandering over to a window to peer out with a dismal expression on her face. Hobson's prediction of rain, it seemed, was not going to be fulfilled. The clouds were breaking up, and shafts of hazy sunlight dappled the garden.

"What's got you on the fidgets?" asked Lady Sedgegood, thrusting her needle through the linen of her sampler.

"I promised to go for an outing in the park with Lord Farthing, and I confess I don't feel up to social chitchat today."

"Are you taking Mary?" asked her cousin, her tone stiff with disapproval. "Or am I to act as chaperon?"

Cynthia heaved a sigh. "I don't know." She moved away from the window and lowered herself into a green satin armchair. "Since I perceive that you have taken Lord Farthing in dislike, I expect I had better take Mary."

"It's not Lord Farthing I mislike," said Lady Sedgegood. "It's his mother. Have you told your grandfather that a member of *that* family is coming to call on you?"

"No," Cynthia admitted. "Nor do I feel it is necessary at this juncture. If Lord Farthing and I go on well together this afternoon, why I collect there will be time enough to tell Grandfather before a second visit."

"Well, I shall have a few words to say to the baron myself," Lady Sedgegood said, snapping a thread with her teeth. "It's his encouraging you to dangle after a rich gentleman that put this ridiculous idea into your head in the first place. And don't try to tell me that you've developed a *tendre* for him, either."

"I shan't go so far as to make that claim, Cousin Alice," admitted Cynthia, "but you yourself said that love is not a necessary requisite in a marriage—so long as it is suitable."

"I will own I may have said something of that sort,"

Lady Sedgegood admitted, "but I did not mean to provoke you into hurling yourself at the most unsuitable gentleman among the quality."

"Pooh, Cousin Alice, Lord Farthing is surely all that is *suitable.*"

Lady Sedgegood looked up from her hoop to fix her young cousin with a baleful eye. "I mean that he is unsuited to *you,* Cynthia. Your natures could not be more unlike. And before it is too late I hope your good judgment will prevail over this buffleheaded notion of yours that you must play the heroine and save the family's name. If you must marry in a trice, you would do better to attempt to fix the interest of someone like the Earl of Graybroughton, although I will confess *he* may be a bit above your reach, considering his eminent eligibility and the many girls of fortune who are available and—"

"Lud!" interrupted Cynthia. "I would consider it a great favor if you would stop speaking of that *man* as if he were Prinny himself."

Lady Sedgegood frowned her puzzlement. "I can't think why you fly up into the boughs every time the earl's name is mentioned. His manner at the ball last night was all that is proper. Everyone said so. And he deigned to honor you particularly."

"He—he insulted me," Cynthia faltered, frustrated at being unable to voice her real view of the gentleman in question.

"Don't be a silly pippin!" exclaimed the astonished Lady Sedgegood. "I am sure a man of the earl's breeding would do no such thing. What did he say that you mistook as a blot on your escutcheon? No doubt he used a unique turn of phrase or—"

"Oh, never mind," Cynthia said wearily. "I have a

dreadful headache, so if you will excuse me, Cousin, I shall try to rest awhile before Lord Farthing arrives."

Lady Sedgegood gave it as her considered opinion that this was the very thing that Cynthia ought to do, and she watched the girl leave the saloon with an expression of total bewilderment on her plump face.

"What *has* come over that child?" she muttered to herself when Cynthia was gone. "I daresay I was right last night and we are in for a siege of the fever or something of that sort." She sighed distractedly. "Well, perhaps a rest will be what is needed to pluck her up." She smiled fondly, adding, "The foolish pea-goose."

Abovestairs the pea-goose, far from resting, was pacing about her bedchamber, glancing often at her clock, and dreading the outing that was fast approaching.

Eventually she succeeded in reminding herself that Lord Farthing was so much more acceptable to her sensibilities than the other wealthy gentlemen whom Bram had pointed out to her, that she really ought to be willing to endure even the obstreperous Lady Farthing when occasion demanded. Today she would have Lord Farthing safely out of his mama's clutches, so she would make the most of the opportunity. With this in mind, she decided definitely against taking Lady Sedgegood—who would most certainly put a damper on Cynthia's campaign with her quelling glances—in favor of her abigail.

After informing Mary that she would be in need of her services that afternoon, Cynthia gave her reflection in the glass over her vanity a close scrutiny. She dropped her lashes and pressed her soft lips together slightly so that the dimple in one cheek was prominently displayed. A modest sideways glance with the irrepressible dimple suggesting a bit of the flirtatious was just the thing, she decided, as she practiced the look several times while continuing to study herself in the glass.

The green promenade dress with its high military collar and frogs was well chosen, too, she assured herself. By the time Mary entered to tell her that Lord Farthing was waiting downstairs, Cynthia had succeeded in convincing herself that she would actually enjoy the afternoon.

Her studiously engendered mood carried her down the stairs in a swirl of green skirts and into the library, where Lord Farthing's pleasant, if bland, face lighted up at the sight of her.

"How do you do sir?" she inquired brightly.

"Capital, Lady Cynthia," he said as he bowed over her hand. "And if I may be permitted to say so, you look—ahem—charming—yes, charming."

"La, sir, I give you leave to utter such prettily said phrases whenever the impulse strikes you!"

A startled bark of laughter escaped Lord Farthing, and realizing that she might have put too bold a face on it, Cynthia added with a blushful half smile, "Oh, I can't think what came over me to speak so immodestly, Lord Farthing. No doubt it is the excitement over your coming to call. I confess I hardly slept at all last night."

"Well, ahem—Lady Cynthia, if you are too tired for a foray in the park, perhaps we should stay here and . . ."

Envisioning her grandfather's reaction should he come face to face with Lord Farthing in his house without advance warning, Cynthia hastened to assure the gentleman that she was transported by the thought of a stroll with his lordship and, further, she expected the fresh air would be quite bracing to her constitution.

"I shall go and call my abigail to accompany us."

78

"Oh—that will not be necessary, my lady," Lord Farthing said, color flushing up in his pale face in a way that made Cynthia suspect he had hoped to be alone with her.

She laughed trillingly. "Sir! You cannot expect me to accompany you without a chaperon! No, I am convinced you are too proper a gentleman to suggest such a naughty thing, so I collect you are jesting."

"Ahem—my lady, you mistook me. I meant to inform you that your abigail's services will not be required because the—er, headache that made it necessary for Mama to leave the ball early last night has not been dispelled, and she has high hopes that taking the air will be beneficial."

"I am sorry, Lord Farthing," Cynthia said, blinking, "but I am not sure I understand you. Will your mama be taking the air in the park?"

"Exactly so," said his lordship. "She awaits us in the carriage. I expect you have noticed that when a notion lodges in my mother's brain it is quite stuck there. And she was suffering so with the headache that I could not bring myself to behave so ungraciously as to refuse her request to accompany us."

"No," agreed Cynthia, her spirits sagging to the toes of her polished promenade shoes. "One cannot be rude to one's mama, and you are quite the most considerate of men to take such account of Lady Farthing's health."

Lord Farthing exhaled a long breath, clearly relieved at Cynthia's response. "I say, you are quite the most understanding lady of my acquaintance—not missish and willful like certain ones I could name. I assure you, there are some who would fly into a pelter at being accompanied on an outing by a gentleman's mother."

"You don't say so, sir!" exclaimed Cynthia, gathering her forces. "Well, I hope that I shall never be so self-

79

indulgent. And indeed," she added with a blatant disregard for the truth, "no one of my acquaintance has ever named me willful. Please excuse me while I inform my abigail of the change in plans and fetch my pelisse."

In spite of her audacious claim in the library, it would have been difficult to imagine a more willful manner than the one that had overtaken Cynthia by the time she entered her bedchamber. "You shan't be accompanying me and Lord Farthing, after all, Mary," she informed the abigail in strident tones. "I have just learned that the gentleman's mother will chaperon us."

"I collect, my lady," Mary ventured, recognizing the fire in her mistress's eye, "that you are not well pleased by the news."

"Lud!" exclaimed Cynthia, stomping her foot. "Lord Farthing may not perceive what that abominable old termagant is about, but I promise you *I* am not such a gudgeon! The headache, indeed! I am not so addle-pated as to be taken in by *that* Canterbury tale."

"No, miss," agreed Mary, suppressing a smile, her amusement causing her to add with uncommon audacity, "for I have noticed that dissembling females do recognize one another."

"Just so!" agreed Cynthia heatedly, too angry with Lady Farthing to spare a set-down for what might, in other circumstances, have struck her as impertinent. "I fancy that I can carry on a charade as long as *that* woman!"

Mary coughed discreetly. "If I may be so bold, my lady, I wish to remind you that those who know your true self are excessively fond of you in spite of your human failings. And if I should be asked for my opinion, I would say that

80

Lord Farthing may consider himself the most fortunate of men that you have decided to encourage his attention."

"Thank you, Mary," said Cynthia fondly. "As for my true self—all in good time. Now, where is my pelisse. Oh, there it is." She donned the wrap and, straightening her shoulders resolutely, descended the stairs to meet Lord Farthing.

The scene that met Cynthia's eyes when she was handed into the waiting carriage bore eloquent testimony to Lady Farthing's ability to enact a Cheltenham tragedy with consummate skill. Her ladyship sat slumped against the squabs, moaning softly. Cynthia settled herself into the seat facing Lady Farthing and arranged her face in an expression of sympathetic concern.

Ignoring Cynthia, Lady Farthing cried dramatically, "Thank God you have come back at last, Percy! What can have taken you so long?" At this point she spared an accusatory look for Cynthia.

"Dear Lady Farthing," Cynthia said, "please accept my condolences for your indisposition. It is to be hoped that the afternoon air will relieve your symptoms. Indeed, it does seem stuffy in here."

"Oh, Percy!" quavered Lady Farthing, holding out a limp hand and disregarding Cynthia's speech.

"Yes, Mama, I'm here," said Lord Farthing soothingly. He took the limp hand and patted it, seating himself beside his mother. As the driver urged the horses forward, he inquired solicitously, "Where are your asafetida drops? Or perhaps you would prefer a little lavender water sprinkled on a handkerchief."

"Yes, yes, the lavender water, please," said her ladyship, reviving sufficiently to push away the bottle containing the drops. When her son offered a freshly sprinkled handkerchief, she sniffed it deeply. "So refreshing! You always know just what to do to make me better, dearest Percy."

The lady's turban, a ghastly orange this time, had fallen over one eye. She raised a weak hand to settle it more securely. "I hope I shall not look as draggle-tailed as I feel when we reach the park."

"Nonsense, Mama," her son assured her. "You look just the thing, don't she, Lady Cynthia?"

"Oh, indeed," Cynthia agreed. "Why, your skin has quite a healthy glow to it, my lady, which one might think surprising for one expects such a grave indisposition to leave the skin pale. I expect your color may be caused by this overheated carriage." She favored her opponent with a dazzlingly innocent smile.

"Eh, what? I daresay you are right, my gel, or else I am flushed with fever, for I have been feeling hot and cold by turns sitting here alone and waiting for the two of you. Oh, Percy, do keep my smelling salts at hand in case I should feel another spasm coming on. I do believe that Timmons' cordial has disagreed with my stomach. Oh, my nerves are quite shattered!"

"There, there, Mama," soothed Lord Farthing in a pandering tone that made Cynthia wish to scream. "We are just coming into the park now. I shall leave the carriage doors open so that you may receive the benefit of the fresh air while Lady Cynthia and I stroll nearby. The groom can call us if you need me."

"The lavender water seems to have settled my stomach, dearest," announced Lady Farthing, "and I am convinced that a stroll will work further benefits. I shall have to hang on to you, Percy, in case I feel faint." This speech had increased in vigor astonishingly as it progressed. And for one who, upon leaving Lord Dahlmere's house, had given every appearance of being almost beyond human aid, her ladyship's improvement in the few minutes required to reach the park was nothing short of miraculous.

The park pathways were heavily populated with strolling couples who had left their carriages parked on the grassy verges to take advantage of the balmy springlike weather, which might be swept away at any time by a March cold snap.

Lord Farthing stepped down to help his mother alight. Once Lady Farthing had pronounced herself steady enough on her feet to stand alone, he turned to hand Cynthia out of the carriage. They chose a path at random, and with Lady Farthing clutching her son's right arm and Cynthia's small hand resting lightly in the crook of his left, the trio began their promenade.

Within minutes Lady Farthing's addiction to being in on the latest on-dits had taken clear precedence over her ill health. "Ain't that Anne Bloomhedge with Lord Silverstone?" she inquired. "Last night she was dangling after that doddering old fool, Henchside."

Recalling the pained expression she had seen on Anne Bloomhedge's face when she was dancing with the gentleman Lady Farthing had dubbed "that doddering old fool," Cynthia thought that her ladyship was doing it much too brown.

"Oh, I am sure you have misjudged Anne," she said impulsively. "I have always thought her to be very prettily behaved."

"Eh, what?" Lady Farthing scowled at this hint of disagreement with her opinion. "The gel's a flirt! All young gels are flirts these days—flitting about and making eyes—

and falling into fishponds!" She leaned forward so that she could give Cynthia a hard-eyed stare.

"I say, Mama," said Lord Farthing, casting Cynthia an apologetic smile, "I do not think you are being all that is just—painting all young ladies with the same brush."

"Humph!" retorted her ladyship. "I ain't quite so easily bamboozled as you are, Percy!"

"Surely you don't imagine falling into a fishpond could be a flirtatious act, my lady," Cynthia couldn't resist remarking. "I daresay it would leave one looking quite limp with all that water streaming from the ends of one's hair. Not that I actually witnessed the incident you refer to, madam."

Cynthia caught a glimpse of Lady Farthing's jaw working furiously and as soon as the injudicious words were out began berating herself for giving her tongue so much rein. However, she was not to suffer her ladyship's wrath at the moment, for Anne Bloomhedge and Lord Silverstone, with Anne's abigail trailing at a discreet distance, joined themselves to the trio.

When greetings were exchanged all around, the rosy-cheeked Anne, a young lady of an age with Cynthia and one whom Cynthia had come to consider a friend during the previous season, launched into a spirited rehearsal of her parents' ball on the night just past.

"You seemed to be enjoying the party, Cynthia," she remarked, "but I did wonder when I learned you had left before the end."

"Cousin Alice had grown weary," Cynthia explained, "and so we thought it just as well to take our leave. It *was* a fine party, though, Anne."

"Indeed, Lady Cynthia," spoke up Lord Silverstone, "I

confess myself disappointed that you had to leave before I could claim my promised dance."

"Oh, gracious, Lord Silverstone," Cynthia began, intending to confess that she had quite forgotten her promise to that gentleman. She thought better of it in time, however, and continued, "I'm sorry there wasn't time to find you and explain that I had to go. May I be forgiven, sir?"

"Oh—certainly." Lord Silverstone did not have it in his nature to hold a grudge when his indulgence was being entreated by so pretty a young lady. "I must warn you, though, that I shall press my claim at the next ball."

"Well, you did stay long enough to waltz with Lord Marlbridge," Anne said somewhat breathlessly. "I must own myself *quite* envious of the honor bestowed upon you, Cynthia."

"Why? Because the Earl of Graybroughton asked me to waltz?"

"Well, of course!" Anne clasped her plump hands in front of her bosom as she spoke. "Mother was utterly transported because the earl chose *her* ball to make his first appearance in society after so long."

"I say, did you meet him, Farthing?" inquired Lord Silverstone. "A great gun, don't you agree?"

"He did strike me as a right one," admitted Lord Farthing readily. "Must say he had all the ladies in raptures."

"Quite," said Lord Silverstone, his round moon face taking on an expression of wistful regret. "All of them smitten by him, I should judge."

"Humph!" stated Lady Farthing. "Spittin' image of the old earl. *He* had all London on its ear in his bachelor days, you may be sure."

"Oh, did you know Lord Marlbridge's father?" Cynthia asked curiously.

"Know him! Why, I came within ambsace of marrying him. If Percy's father hadn't come along and stolen my heart, I daresay I might have, too!"

Cynthia received this announcement with a great deal of doubt, for she could not conceive of Lady Farthing—even a much younger, slimmer Lady Farthing—capturing the attention of a nonpareil. "And you say the present earl looks like his father?" she asked thoughtfully.

"Two peas from the same pod," pronounced Lady Farthing, laying to rest any lingering doubt that Cynthia might have been harboring that the earl was an imposter.

"I wonder who he will favor with his particular attention?" breathed Anne Bloomhedge, clearly yearning to be the fortunate focus of the earl's regard. "Did you go on well with him during the waltz, Cynthia?" This question was put quite longingly.

"There is hardly time to forge a fast friendship during a single waltz," Cynthia told her. "In truth, I found the man—somewhat overbearing."

Anne's mouth fell open and the two gentlemen turned to stare at Cynthia oddly. "Why, how can you say so?" Anne demanded, going immediately to the earl's aid. Clearly the girl was very nearly head over ears for the man already.

Lady Farthing cackled suddenly. "Gave you a setdown, did he, gel?" She seemed to find this quite hilarious. "Fellow's got more sense than I gave him credit for. Eh, what? Ain't going to be taken in by a pretty face and simpering ways." Her ladyship shoved an elbow into her son's ribs. "Take a lesson, Percy!"

"I beg leave to inform you, my lady," Cynthia exclaimed, flaring up, "that in the event it was quite the other way around. It takes more than a title to make a gentleman, and so I told the earl!"

"Ahem—" Lord Farthing cleared his throat in the shocked silence that followed Cynthia's pronouncement. "I say, Lady Cynthia, what did the fellow say to put you into such a taking?"

"Well, I shouldn't like to repeat it in polite company, I assure you," said Cynthia, sniffing.

Lady Farthing hooted at this and gave her son another dig with her elbow. "He *is* a trump, eh, what?"

Lord Farthing's mouth thinned. "A rigid stickler, he may be, Mama," he announced with uncharacteristic bravado, "but on that head, I must say no gentleman would insult a lady, whatever the provocation, not that I believe Lady Cynthia provoked him."

"Course she did!" chortled Lady Farthing rudely. "Made a cake of herself, I expect."

"I am sure you are rarely mistaken, my lady," Cynthia said, her tone dripping with feigned sweetness, "but I behaved with admirable restraint, considering . . . everything. And I am sure we can find something more interesting to discuss than the earl. *Your* indisposition, for example, your ladyship. I confess I am quite amazed at your remarkable recovery since we left the carriage."

"Indeed, Mama," intervened Lord Farthing, "you do seem much improved. Nothing like a long walk to stir up the humors."

"Just so, dearest Percy," said her ladyship, giving Cynthia a speaking glance. "But I must own I am beginning to feel faint. I am very much afraid we shall have to curtail our promenade and return to the carriage."

Cynthia was certain this was a sudden notion, one intended as punishment for her impudence.

"What an inconsiderate ailment," Cynthia purred. "It *does* seem to come and go so."

"We will go back then," Lord Farthing conceded. "We must take our leave of you," he added for the benefit of Lord Silverstone and Anne Bloomhedge, who murmured their good-byes and continued their stroll. "I wish you will not be too disappointed at such a precipitate departure, Lady Cynthia," he said, near to staggering under his mother's weight, for she had gone limp against him and he was finding it necessary to support her as they turned toward the carriage.

"I have no doubt that you must console your mama," Cynthia returned, managing with an awesome effort to control her temper. "So we shall say no more about it."

"Lady Cynthia," gasped Lord Farthing, struggling under the near dead weight of his obese parent, "you are all that is accommodating and unselfish."

At this, Lady Farthing groaned loudly.

6

At about the same time that Cynthia was following Lord Farthing and his mother back to the carriage, Kenyon, attired in a dove-gray coat and darker gray breeches, the only bit of frippery on his person a solitary modest-sized diamond adorning his cravat, was being served a very hearty tea in his library by his valet, Drabney. A thick tome covering several aspects of the science of agriculture lay open, facedown, on the Aubusson carpet beside his favorite reading chair.

Drabney lifted a snowy linen napkin from the silver tray resting on the side table and, flipping it open smartly, spread it across his lordship's knee.

"What is all this?" inquired Kenyon, his auburn brows rising as his intensely blue eyes took in the varied offerings before him. "Salmon, ham, three kinds of sandwiches, fruit compote, and *four* kinds of cakes. Did Mrs. Drabney perhaps think I was having a rout?"

"No, sir," replied Drabney smoothly. "My wife has set

it as her main goal in life to tempt your palate. If I may say so, my lord, she is a tolerably accomplished cook. I hope you will forgive what you might consider an overindulgence on her part, but we come so seldom to London and—well, sir, she has been fretting herself that her cooking might in some way be to blame. That is, sir, she has it firmly fixed in her head that you may consider her cooking well enough for the country, but not quite up to the mark for town."

"Lord, Drabney!" exclaimed the earl, selecting one of the small sandwiches. "Your good wife has few peers, even in the kitchens of Carlton House, and well she knows it!" His blue eyes laughed into the valet's serious hazel ones. "No, that's all a hum, my man. I perceive that the culinary creations being piled on my plate at every opportunity are a not-very-subtle form of blackmail."

"If I may speak my mind, sir," said Drabney, coming stiffly to attention at the earl's elbow.

"By all means," returned the earl equably.

"I feel it would be beneath me to reply to such an *unjust* charge."

"Doing it too brown, Drabney," Kenyon said, amusement quivering in his voice. "You and your excellent wife mean to make it as difficult as possible for me to quit London any time soon." He glanced into the valet's stoic face. "Can you look me in the eye and swear that my sister has not enlisted your aid to that very end?"

"Lady Witherspoon has only been here once since your arrival, my lord."

"Doesn't answer my question, though, does it?"

Drabney seemed to take this as an affront to the earl's sister, whom he considered so beautiful and genteel as to be above the touch of most mere mortals. "I hope your sainted sister may be forgiven, sir, for wishing you may perform all the duties your exalted station in life has laid upon you."

"Oh, quite," said Kenyon with a crack of laughter. "But Maddy's not up to sainthood *yet,* and she can't resist meddling here and there. I have the oddest dislike, however, of going into wedded shackles before my own time and by any other than my own choice."

"I am certain Lady Witherspoon is only trying to be helpful, knowing as she does that you *will* marry—when you are ready, of course. But it is not my place to remind you of your duty as the only son, my lord."

"Nor of my advanced age, either," said Kenyon helpfully.

"No, though you are of a perfect age for marriage, or so I would say should anyone care for my judgment, but may I be permitted to observe that a gentleman must go into society to find eligible ladies that he may choose a soul mate."

The earl set his teacup down with a rattle and dabbed at his twitching mouth with a corner of his napkin. "Never knew you to wax so poetic, Drabney. Soul mate, is it? I must tell you that I am *excessively* obliged to you and my very helpful sister for having my interests so much at heart! But if the ladies I met last night are prime examples, I fear you both may have a protracted wait."

"I daresay you will like them better on further acquaintance," commented Drabney hopefully.

"Dashed unlikely," returned the earl. "I have the most marked abhorrence for simpering, tittering females and, alas, they all fit that category admirably—except for one—"

"Yes, sir?" Drabney inserted expectantly, grasping at

91

the reed. "You found one who is different from the rest—more to your refined tastes, perhaps?"

"Good God, she *is* decidedly different!" ejaculated the earl. "Far worse than the others!"

The valet cleared his throat. "It may not have occurred to you, sir, but your—ah, noble bearing and—ah, high standing may have been somewhat intimidating to the lady. What I mean, sir, is that she may not have displayed herself to best advantage because of being so—ah, dazzled."

"No, no," contradicted Kenyon. "That old dog won't hunt, Drabney. The chit wasn't the smallest part dazzled. In fact, she had the audacity to tell me, in the middle of a waltz, that I was a disgrace to my family's esteemed name."

"*What, sir?*" said the shocked valet, startled out of his proper demeanor. "She must be dicked in the nob!"

A muscle alongside the earl's wide mouth jerked. "That is as may be, Drabney, but it is my judgment that the girl simply has an extremely vivid imagination and probably reads far too many romances. Never knew such an exquisite face to cover a brain so inclined to soar into the realms of fancy at the drop of a hat. If you can imagine all the wild hoydens you've ever known rolled into one, Drabney, you'll have an idea of the lady's character. I swear she has heaped more insults on my name on the two occasions when we have met than I've received in all of my life before."

The valet frowned and suggested, "She may be a bit high-strung."

"High-strung! Merciful heaven, yes!" agreed the earl, laughing outright. He finished another cake. "Well, I've done my best by Mrs. Drabney, but it would take four of me to finish all of this. Give her my compliments on the spice cake."

"Yes, sir," said the valet, collecting the tray and moving toward the door, a deeply thoughtful expression on his face. "Will you be looking in at Almack's tonight, sir?"

Kenyon heaved a put-upon sigh. "Can't think how I can avoid it. Lord Witherspoon's out of town and Maddy has requested my services as escort. I am resigned to letting her trot me out for inspection now and then."

"Have you decided to stay through the season then?" inquired Drabney in admirably careless tones.

"Well, the roads are still uncertain to the north. And I wouldn't like to bring my sister's wrath down on my head, either, so I intend to stay at least long enough to satisfy her." He reached for his book and, finding his place, began to read.

"Very good, sir," said Drabney, a satisfied smile lurking about his mouth as he left.

Entering the kitchen, Drabney addressed his pink-cheeked, white-aproned wife in portentous tones. "I shouldn't like this to be noised about, Abby, but if you was to ask for my opinion, I should be bound to say that I consider the earl to be on the horns of a dilemma."

"Do you say so, luv?" said Mrs. Drabney, turning from the stove to regard him with curious interest. "And what sort of a dilemma would that be?"

Drabney folded his arms across his liveried chest and observed knowingly, "One with a lady in it, if I am any judge of his lordship's moods." His tone left no doubt whatever that he was not only *any judge,* but the prime authority on that subject.

"Oh, how luverly," exclaimed his wife, clasping her hands in front of her ecstatically. "Sit down, luv, and we'll have our tea and you can tell me everything." She scurried about, bringing a plate of sandwiches and cakes, cups and teapot to the table. At last, she took her seat facing her husband and waited with bated breath.

Drabney lifted a sandwich from the plate and gazed at it reflectively for a moment. Then he took a bite, chewed slowly, and swallowed before he said, "I hope I am above engaging in servants' gossip."

"Oh, *Horace,*" his wife said on a note of supreme exasperation. "How can it be servants' gossip when you are having a comfy coze with your wife?" She frowned suddenly. "I don't know how there can be a dilemma just because his lordship has an interest in a lady. For myself, I'm that happy to be staying in town for a spell, which we must do if—Unless—Coo, luv, you can't mean he's lost his heart to a dasher!"

Drabney's narrow look was censorious. "I would hope the earl is too sensible to become involved in more than a discreet—ah, liaison on *that* front."

"Well, then—"

"I don't name myself among the earl's close confidants, but I can say that the only lady who has brought herself to his lordship's attention since his arrival in London has the peculiar habit of assailing him with the most vile imprecations whenever they meet."

Mrs. Drabney's mouth fell open. "Coo! Sounds as if she's all about in her head."

"So I said to his lordship, madam," agreed Drabney, stirring his tea, "but he disagreed with me as quick as a flea's leap. It appears that we shall have to wait upon further events."

In the house in Grosvenor Square, Lady Sedgegood had

taken it upon herself to inform the baron of his grand-daughter's latest brainstorm, not wishing to be blamed later should Cynthia actually manage to bring about such a farfetched alliance, a not very likely eventuality in Lady Sedgegood's considered opinion, or embroil them in some shocking scandal, which was much more possible, one might even say probable.

She was admitted to the study just as the baron had finished his tea. He was sitting in a leather armchair, his left leg heavily bandaged and propped on a footstool. His lordship was not the most agreeable of companions at the best of times, and when a victim of gout he was never very far from irascibility.

"Hobson says you are bound to have this tête-à-tête," said the baron, glaring at Lady Sedgegood and finding her yellow dress particularly nauseating after just having eaten. "Might as well come in. I collect you have come to pry loose a few more farthings for useless baubles, but you'll be wasting your breath. I'm quite run off my legs already, and I've no more patience for scattergood females."

"Pray, sir, what have I done to earn such a trimming from you?" inquired Lady Sedgegood, coming into the room and settling herself amidst a billow of yellow cambric in a chair facing the baron's.

"What have you done in aid of the situation?" countered his lordship. "And there's no need to remind me that I invited you to chaperon Cynthia for the season, for I am well aware of it. I told you then and I tell you now that there is no one else to see after the girl. But I never intended to hand you a carte blanche to commit every frivolous extravagance that came into your head. That dressmaker's bill is outrageous beyond anything," said the baron inaccurately but with utter sincerity, "and every time I look at it, I want to do violence to *someone*."

Her ladyship flicked a glance at the bandaged foot. "Your present circumstance," she said, refusing to be drawn in, for she had other fish to fry, "would seem to render the gratification of such brutish impulses ineligible. No doubt you have been sitting here with your foot throbbing, working yourself into another dither over that bill. Well, sir, I will be more than content to return to my home the minute you give me leave. While I remain here, however, I shall consider it my duty to try to keep Cynthia on a *relatively* sane course. And that brings me to the reason for this meeting. I feel you should be apprised of her latest tangent."

"Dash it, woman! Stop circling around and around like a deuced vulture and say what's on your mind!" He paused, throwing a fulminating glance at the lady.

"Since our interview with you Monday, your granddaughter has chosen a husband for herself—though the gentleman in question has no inkling of what is in store for him, I assure you—and she has sallied forth this very afternoon in pursuit of her quarry."

"Upon my word, a fine sort of chaperon you are!" said the baron, suddenly detecting another flaw in the lady before him. "I reminded you on the occasion of our last meeting that the reason any girl is introduced into society is so that she might find a husband—the whole world knows that!—and it is surely the fondest wish of any *proper* chaperon to see that mission accomplished." He winced suddenly at a particularly vicious twinge in his foot, then added grimly, "What's more, if Cynthia has gone out with a gentleman, why didn't you accompany them?"

"In fact, I offered to do just that," replied Lady Sedge-good tartly. "But the gentleman's mother insisted on playing the role of chaperon, or so Mary informs me."

"Women!" snapped the baron, sweeping that half of the world's population aside with a contemptuous gesture. "It is the girl's place to provide the chaperon. What sort of mother makes so bold as to do a thing like that?"

"Well you might ask, sir!"

"Who," uttered the baron crossly, "is the gentleman upon whom Cynthia has set her eye?" Then, struck with a sudden explanation for the freakish behavior of the gentleman's mother, he added, "I warn you, I'll not have a Frenchy in the family."

"That is one tangle I collect you need not unravel, for if Cynthia is even acquainted with a Frenchman I am not aware of it," said Lady Sedgegood with unruffled reasonableness. "No, this gentleman is known to you, my lord, or at any rate, his mother is. He is Percy Farthing."

"Oh, God's beard!" croaked the baron, utterly astounded. "I'll not have my family allied with that—that *woman's!* Why, she is the crudest, most brazen, vulgar creature—and she has never ceased to make the most slanderous statements about me ever since I refused to fall in with the scheme hatched by her and her father to marry her to my elder son. Poor Oliver, God rest his soul, actually shuddered every time the woman's name was mentioned in his hearing. Nor could I blame him. No, no—this foolishness must be ended at once."

"I hesitate to contradict you, sir, but I must remind you that Cynthia believes she is saving *you* from disgrace, and you yourself encouraged her to find a rich husband. Percy Farthing, by all accounts, is certainly that. Furthermore, your granddaughter is not the sort to acquiesce in the face of ultimatums." Lady Sedgegood took a deep, bracing breath before continuing. "It pains me to say it, Lord Dahlmere, but *you* are responsible for the mulish streak in Cynthia's nature, for you brought her up."

The baron directed a searching look at Lady Sedgegood from under beetling brows. "Madam," he said in testy tones, "I confess you are right about Cynthia's not taking to ultimatums. Don't suppose that disgusting slattern is afflicted with some ailment of a terminal nature?"

This switch of topics in mid-speech was followed with practiced ease by Lady Sedgegood. "Lady Farthing? Quite the opposite. I should say she will hold for a long while yet."

"Humph! I daresay Cynthia will tire of the woman's Turkish treatment soon enough." He scowled thoughtfully. "Anyway, I can't conceive of any son of *hers* being up to Cynthia's weight."

At that moment the young lady who was displayed to such advantage in that conjecture stalked into the foyer, slamming the door behind her, and marched past Hobson, whose lifted brows spoke volumes.

In the study Lady Sedgegood said, "That must be Cynthia now."

"Bring her in here," ordered the baron, wincing at another pain in his foot. Lady Sedgegood stepped into the foyer just as Cynthia started toward the stairs. "Your grandfather would like to see you for a moment. His gout has him confined to his chair, I'm afraid."

Cynthia made as if to protest, but then thought better of it. She entered the study ahead of her cousin, going directly to her grandfather and brushing a kiss across his cheek. "I am sorry you aren't feeling well, sir."

"Cursed foot!" complained the baron. "Well, it won't

kill me. Nor do I believe that too much port makes it worse, despite what that sapskull of a doctor says. And don't try to fob me off with solicitations about my health. I'm told you've been out with the Farthings."

Cynthia glanced at Lady Sedgegood, who had returned to her chair, but found no support in that lady's face. She tossed her black curls. "Yes, I have been, Grandfather. We went to the park, but we had no more than arrived when Lady Farthing took a weak spell and had to be helped back to the carriage. It was plain as could be that she was shamming, but Lord Farthing is quite blind to her trickery. He seems somewhat taken with me," she announced immodestly, "and it has thrown his mama into the most Gothic pet." It was clear that the thought of being the cause of Lady Farthing's discomfiture was not unpleasing to Cynthia.

"I *did* try to tell you," observed Lady Sedgegood, "that this plan of yours was not at all the thing."

"Why, I collect you are mistaken, Cousin Alice," said Cynthia. "Lord Farthing is a most unexceptionable gentleman. He is well-mannered and pleasant. It is his mother who is the troublemaker. But when Lord Farthing and I are married, I shall see that there are miles separating her from us."

"Hah!" responded Lady Sedgegood. "If you ever manage to remove Lord Farthing from her house, I shall own myself astonished."

Cynthia's small chin jutted stubbornly. "As Lord Farthing's wife, I shall have more influence on him than his mother."

Lord Dahlmere cleared his throat. "Cynthia, the Lord knows when we'll be out of dun territory, but we ain't in such a horrid hell as to require your marriage to someone —unworthy of you."

"Pooh, Grandfather," Cynthia returned lightly, for she had noticed that the worry lines etched in that gentleman's face were, if anything, deeper than on Monday. "I daresay it is your fondness that gives you such a jumped-up opinion of me. And I am excessively fond of you, too—but I should like to be excused now. I must find Mary so that she can arrange my hair and help me choose a proper gown. You haven't forgotten that we are going to Almack's this evening, have you, Cousin Alice?"

"My memory," Lady Sedgegood told her dryly, "is as good as it ever was."

Cynthia merely nodded absently and hurried from the study, her mind already flying ahead to the coming evening.

Lady Sedgegood and Lord Dahlmere exchanged glances. "Dashed if I don't think she's wearing the willow for the fellow!" said the baron, having fallen under the spell of his granddaughter's beautiful eyes, which had glowed with warm sincerity when she confessed to a particular attachment to him. "I suppose," he added with uncommon reasonableness, "we must consider putting personal prejudice aside if Cynthia's heart is engaged."

Lady Sedgegood got to her feet. "Fiddle! Cynthia's heart does not even enter into the matter. It's her *temper* that has been engaged." With that dogmatic statement, she swept from the room.

In her bedchamber Cynthia tugged the bell pull to summon her abigail and began to drag dresses from her wardrobe. "Oh, there you are, Mary," she observed quite unnecessarily a few moments later when the abigail entered the chamber. Frowning, she lifted the gown she held in her hand so that the late afternoon light coming through the window fell upon it. "These last year's muslins look so schoolmissish. I can hardly conceive that I actually thought them the first stare of fashion when they were new!" She tossed the sprigged muslin atop the pile of muslins, cambrics, and gauzes on her bed. "I collect," she said, her tone taking on a wistful note, "that it is one thing to have one's mind full of balls and routs and alfrescos and all that is pleasing to oneself, and quite another when one is contemplating the serious business of entering the matrimonial state."

"I should hope, miss," stated Mary, "that my lady would not be contemplating marriage for any other reason than to please herself."

"Mary, we all, you know, must sooner or later reach the age where we must put duty and family loyalty above our private—sensibilities," said Cynthia gloomily.

Mary did not know whether to be amused at her young mistress's sudden, if not quite believable, mature wisdom or to feel anxious about the grimly rigid set to her ladyship's jaw, as if she might burst into sobs should she allow her feelings full scope. She decided that perhaps the best course was to try to divert Lady Cynthia's attention. "I have always thought, miss, that you look especially lovely in the sea-green Berlin silk."

This ploy seemed to have its desired effect, for Cynthia turned back to the wardrobe and lifted the silk from its place. "I rather like this one myself, Mary. I always thought the floss trimming so very modish. I think this style looks best with my hair in the Grecian mode, don't you?"

"Yes, miss," agreed Mary, relieved that her ladyship

now seemed engrossed in her toilette. "Perhaps I could weave a satin ribbon among the curls."

"Oh, yes, please," Cynthia responded. "We shall have to hurry, too, for I do not think Grandfather's mood will admit of my late arrival at the dinner table, even though I do not feel as if I could swallow a bite."

As things fell out, Lord Dahlmere did not feel up to putting in an appearance at the dinner table himself and was served his meal in his bedchamber. Nor did Bramford return before Cynthia and Lady Sedgegood had dined and set out for Almack's Assembly Rooms, a fact upon which Cynthia commented anxiously. "I do hope Bram has not gotten himself into another hobble."

Shortly after ten o'clock the missing gentleman sauntered through the portals of Almack's with Lord Caverset at his side. Cynthia saw that her brother had returned to Grosvenor Square before arriving at that discerning establishment, for he had changed into knee-breeches, a fawn-colored coat with a matching waistcoat, and a neck-cloth so intricately arranged that it must have taken his valet the better part of an hour to do it. Bramford, although beautiful to behold, was quite overshadowed by his bosom companion, who positively glittered in a hugely padded rose-pink coat with extremely long tails, striped stockings, and satin knee-breeches.

Lord Caverset was immediately surrounded by several admiring pinks of the ton, and Bramford found himself on the fringe of the squeeze and, not caring for any position but the center of attention, deserted his friend, muttering crossly that *he* should certainly not like to be found basking in anyone's reflected glory.

He spotted Cynthia just as her current dancing partner

was returning her to the sidelines and made his way toward her.

"If that don't beat the Dutch!" he observed peevishly, quite as if his sister could read his mind.

She could not, however, and mistook his meaning entirely. "But I always thought you approved of this gown," she said, glancing down to see if a bit of floss had come loose.

"Ain't referring to the gown," asserted Bramford, which brought a smile of relief to her face. Her brother might be a shocking gamester, but he had a near unfailing eye for suitability in fashion. "You look as fine as sixpence. It's Cavey. Been itching to land him a facer all day!"

"Well, yes," concurred Cynthia with a tiny giggle. "I have always thought that Cavey had enough height and slenderness to adopt extravagant styles, but I didn't think he had the brass to enter Almack's—which *is* somewhat staid, you will admit—in such an outlandish rig as that! I noticed Lady Jersey giving him the once-over, but I rather think she was too stunned to speak."

"Bought it today," said Bramford, "and me telling him all the while that it was garish. Set him back three hundred pounds."

"Gracious!" Cynthia was staggered to learn that a single costume could be so dear. "Why, how can he ever find the means to pay for it?"

"Just so," said Bramford darkly. "Not only that, he ordered *five* other coats as well. Pulled out a roll and paid for the whole lot with hard blunt. If he ain't had a run of luck at the races, I'm a Chinaman!"

"Well, depend upon it, if that is the case, he will soon have his pockets to let again," Cynthia said with disapproval.

"Says his future's assured," Bramford told her with an air of imparting the biggest humbug of all time. "As if anyone's future at the Turf was ever assured! Dashed smoky, that's what it is! I know Cavey! If this sudden affluence *is* gaming wins—and I don't know what *else* it could be—willing to lay you a monkey there's something havey-cavey about it."

"You don't mean you think Cavey's gotten involved in a *fixed* race!" Cynthia's gray eyes were as round as platters. "Oh, Bram, how shameless of you to accuse your old friend of something so unsavory!"

"No need to get up on your high ropes. Ain't saying anything about a fixed race. Thing is he won't let *me* in on it. Always before he couldn't wait to pull me in. Been after him all day. Even said I'd refuse to acknowledge him when we meet on the street if he didn't tell me. Just looked at me in the strangest way and said he didn't suppose *that* would hasten his taking off by more than a day or two! Queer start, that's what *I* say."

Cynthia's face had taken on a thoughtful expression. "Bram, do you remember Cavey telling us once about that cousin of his father's who made a king's fortune in the woolen trade? I wonder if he died and left it all to Cavey."

"Shouldn't think so!" stated Bramford. "Cavey and his father were always devilish shamed that anyone in the family would become a *merchant*, even if the fellow did make a ripping good go of it. Felt it put them all under a cloud, wouldn't have the cousin in the house. Cousin said he'd leave his money to a foundling home before Cavey or his father had a groat of it."

"Hmm," mused Cynthia. "Sometimes when people are ill, you know, and feel they are dying, they start to think of their relatives in a kinder light."

"Get windmills in their heads, you mean?" interpreted Bramford. "Don't sound likely to me, for Cavey's cousin called him a dirty dish to his face not twelve months past. Ran into him in Bond Street. Kicked up an awful row. Besides, I shouldn't think Cavey would scruple at telling *me* if he'd been made his cousin's heir. *I* ain't a tattlebox."

"I am sure no one has named you one," Cynthia told him, seeing the indignant scowl deepening. "And I suppose it is Cavey's right to keep his source of funds a secret if he chooses to do so. You shouldn't take umbrage."

"Confound it, Cyn! You can't think I am going to totter all over London playing shabby-genteel while my *closest* friend since nursery days puts Prinny to shame with his extravagances! No, I'll have the truth of it! You ain't the only member of the family that likes a challenge, old girl!"

"If that is a veiled thrust at my expression of interest in Lord Farthing—"

"Ain't veiled at all," said Bramford, smiling for the first time since entering the hall. "Incidentally, where is the fortunate gentleman? Don't tell me he's got your ticket already! Didn't think he had that much in the upper works."

"His mama is ailing," Cynthia admitted, sniffing.

"Oh, well! Has to play nursemaid, does he? I recommend you enjoy yourself while you can then. Expect Lady Farthing won't approve of any frivolous behavior after the betrothal. Expect you'll be spending your time with your embroidery and the pianoforte and helping Percy's mama with her correspondence."

Rather than respond in kind, which was her usual reaction, Cynthia bit her lip and glanced about the hall with an expression that put her brother in mind of a bird who has just discovered it's caught in a snare.

"I say, old girl," he remarked, "didn't mean to get your damper down. Only bamming you, you know."

"What?" She regarded him quizzically. "Sorry, Bram, but I wasn't attending." She further bewildered her brother by refusing the offers of several young gentlemen and going to sit beside Lady Sedgegood, who was in loud conversation with an ancient dowager equipped with an ear trumpet.

7

Cynthia had rather expected to meet Lord Farthing at Almack's, but it did not look as if he were coming at all. As Bram had pointed out, she ought to be flirting and enjoying herself, for one was never able to be quite so carefree after one became a married woman. Of course, there were other pastimes for wives, for Cynthia had noticed that a married woman could go about with a whole gaggle of admiring bachelors in her wake and no one remarked overmuch on it. In fact, if the rumors could be believed, any number of the young matrons of the ton actually took lovers and their husbands looked the other way, as well they might for *they* were frequently involved with actresses and other such fast females.

Cynthia had always thought such behavior unbecoming and had engaged in romantic flights of fancy in which she was married to a dashingly handsome gentleman whom she adored and who loved her above all things, and, of course, in these daydreams there was never any desire for lovers by either party.

Her mind began to drift into one of these fancies, this time with Lord Farthing in the role of her husband. She tried to imagine the house they would have in London and how she would decorate it—after she had paid off Bram's IOU, of course, and taken care of her grandfather's debts. But the daydream simply wouldn't *go*. It seemed flat. She couldn't imagine Lord Farthing taking her in a masterful embrace and covering her face with kisses—or scooping her into his arms and carrying her up the wide, marble staircase of the house she always dreamed she would inhabit one day to her green and gold bedchamber where—well, she wasn't absolutely clear about the intimacies that would follow, but she was convinced they would be quite wonderful. After all, they were always referred to in romantic novels in the most extravagantly poetic terms, with the gentleman vowing to be his lady's adoring slave for all time and the lady going into an ecstatic swoon.

She frowned and applied herself to her task. She and Lord Farthing were strolling in a garden. He had just paid her a very pretty compliment and she looked up modestly to dazzle him with a smile—when she saw—Kenyon's face!

"Since you do not seem to be engaged for this dance, Lady Chattington, may I have the honor?"

He was no dream! He was actually standing before her dressed in evening black and white, the face above the starched shirt points as mocking as his tone.

To Cynthia's horror, she felt herself blushing. This, of course, was caused by her being so rudely interrupted in the middle of a daydream by this odious creature. "I—I do not care to dance, sir."

From the corner of her eye she saw Lady Sedgegood start with amazement. "Of course she cares to!" exclaimed the chaperon. "How can you be so impolite, Cynthia?"

"If we are to satisfy your chaperon, it appears we shall have to stand up together," remarked the earl sardonically. "Not that I would wish you to feel in any way *indebted* to me."

Cynthia gasped. How dare he remind her of Bramford's IOU in such a blatant manner and in front of Cousin Alice so that she could not give him a set-down. For the first time in her life Cynthia was conscious of a strong desire to slap a gentleman's face. She controlled the impulse, saying in a repressive tone, "I seem to have forgotten my manners, my lord, but I am certain you will understand how such a thing might happen. Indeed, I am told that even more highly born personages than I have been known to commit far worse indiscretions."

Lady Sedgegood was fanning herself vigorously, as if she might be about to suffer a spasm. As for the earl, he merely grinned at Cynthia in the most maddeningly unruffled way as she stood and allowed him to escort her to the dance floor. She was immediately the target of envious glances from young ladies who were close enough to see the earl requesting her company in the dance but far enough removed to be unable to hear the oddly unflirtatious remarks exchanged by them.

"I confess myself taken aback at finding you playing the role of wallflower," remarked Kenyon, when it did not appear that his partner intended to exert herself by offering a topic of conversation.

"I told you I did not care to dance. I'd already turned down several offers before you approached me."

"Ah," observed the earl, "so jaded for one so young.

I've been observing you this past quarter hour, and I can only guess that you find these decorous surroundings so boring that you prefer escaping into a trance. Dreaming of the gallant Lord Farthing, no doubt!"

"Pray tell me, Kenyon, what concern that is of yours? And you needn't raise your brows over my familiar form of address, either, for I find it quite impossible to think of you as the Earl of Graybroughton. You will always be Kenyon the moneylender to me, sir!" In spite of her pert remarks, Cynthia was careful to keep her voice low. She was not unmindful of the appearance of refinement, even in her present plight.

As for the earl, since the ladies whom he chose to honor with his attentions did not ordinarily persist in insulting him at every opportunity, even in such extraordinary circumstances as might cause them to suspect him of being less than honorable—as Lady Cynthia did—he discovered that he was momentarily thrown off balance. Even given the ludicrous conditions under which they had met and his failure to set the chit straight in her amazing misjudgment of him, he saw now that he had expected her to weaken *somewhat* in her contempt of him by this time. His ease of manner and handsome demeanor—not to mention his wealth and station—had never before failed to bring the most contentious lady to heel. Recovering, he laughed. "A heavy rake-down! Can it be possible that I have the ill fortune to offend you, Cynthia?"

"Is that so wonderful?" she countered forthrightly. "Since you seem to delight in speaking improperly of a gentleman who I deem to be all that is excellent and—and accomplished."

"Don't be absurd, my girl!"

Further aroused by his maddening refusal to take her

interest in Lord Farthing seriously, she added, "And he is *by far* the best dancer I have ever been honored to stand up with."

Since Kenyon's own grace on the dance floor had never been called into question, he found this latter remark too impudent by half. "Oh, well! That is certainly a preeminent accomplishment for a potential husband. Almost as important as a docile disposition. You must thank the gentleman's mama for molding him so well for you."

She flushed. "It is most unbecoming in you to speak so disrespectfully of Lord Farthing. I cannot credit that he has ever done anything to cause you to mislike him so."

"Indeed, I have not taken the gentleman in the least dislike. In fact, I feel quite sorry for him. In the unlikely event that you carry off this mad scheme of yours, you will probably cause the poor man to go distracted."

For the second time that evening Cynthia was aware of an almost overpowering urge to slap that handsome, mocking face. Somehow she managed to say aloofly, "I might take umbrage at such ungentlemanly slurs on my character, sir, if I were not aware of the scandalous nature of your person. Apparently you have consorted with rascals and rake-shames for so long that you have forgotten how to go on in polite society."

"This is the outside of enough!" growled the earl, the sudden fire in the blue eyes giving Cynthia a start. Fortunately, they were separated at that moment by a movement of the dance. When they came together again, she had collected herself enough to say frostily, "I cannot think why you asked me to dance when we have nearly come to cuffs every time we have met."

"Don't flatter yourself with any fancies as to the desirability of your company, my girl. One of the patronesses was attempting to steer me toward little Anne Bloomhedge. I took a moment to weigh insults against giggles and chose the former. I have noticed a marked tendency in you to be unimpressed by my presence and, therefore, not given to titters and speechlessness. But your outrageous incivilities are beginning to wear thin, so perhaps it is time I corrected the incredible assumption you have made about me. I am not the infamous Higgins's associate."

If he had expected this information to send Lady Chattington into raptures, he must needs have been profoundly disappointed. She stared at him in the most astonished way, and then a frightened cloud fell across her face. "Oh, you cannot mean that he still has Bram's IOU!"

"No, no," Kenyon corrected her quickly. "I have the vowels in my possession. Be assured of that."

She continued to stare at him fixedly for a moment, a look of deep cogitation on her face. At last, comprehension dawned. "So, you have set up on your own, have you? Well, I cannot feel excessively comforted by that! Although I do suppose the devil one knows is preferable to the devil one does not."

"Hell's teeth!" barked the earl.

She disregarded this, but said matter-of-factly, "The dance has ended, sir. You needn't return me to my chaperon. I want to find my brother and remind him tò ask Miss Bloomhedge to dance. Sometimes Bram forgets his manners, too."

She set off with a determined look, leaving Kenyon to gather his reeling senses as best he could.

Lady Sedgegood had had her eye on Cynthia, however, from the moment she had left her chair on Lord Marlbridge's arm. She saw her seek out her brother and, after what appeared to be a somewhat heated exchange, watched him making his bow very creditably in front of Anne Bloomhedge, after which the two of them took up positions in a set of country dances. When Cynthia did not move to return to her, Lady Sedgegood shouted her excuses into the trumpet of her companion and went forth to do her duty.

By the time she had reached her young cousin, Cynthia had found a chair, turned down two invitations to dance, and, from all appearances, had sunk back into the dismals.

Lady Sedgegood tapped the girl's shoulder with her fan. "Taking everything together," she announced, "I feel it is time we made our adieus."

"What?" Cynthia looked up at her with a vacant expression. "Oh, is it time at last? I didn't think we should ever be leaving." She got up with alacrity and followed her cousin from the hall.

Lady Sedgegood contained herself admirably until they were seated in their curricle. Cynthia, totally oblivious to her cousin's disapproving stare, had turned her face in the most disinterested way toward the side window, where an occasional glimpse of the London street was afforded by light from a gas lamp.

Lady Sedgegood bit her lip and regarded her charge searchingly. It flashed across her mind to wonder if mental instability ever came on of a sudden. She thought back over Cynthia's family tree, those individuals on both sides known to her, but could not recall a single instance of real madness. Oh, Lord Dahlmere's elder son, Oliver, was certainly never called clever by those who knew him, but he had been an amiable sort and there had never been any harm in him. Not that Lady Sedgegood didn't think it just as well that he had passed on without marrying and leaving behind what might have turned out to be several replicas of himself.

Lady Sedgegood shook her head, admonishing herself. Why, Cynthia had always been as clear as a bell in her upper works. Her ladyship sighed heavily. Well, she was not getting any younger and she was tired and her feet hurt atrociously and she must surely be excused for thinking that *something* was wrong with the girl. She had first noticed a suggestion of strange behavior at the Bloomhedges' ball. And Cynthia's conduct tonight had been bewildering beyond anything. Vagueness had never been one of the girl's faults before—and turning down all those gentlemen, quite as if she had not always reveled in parties and admirers—and capping it off by saying she thought the evening would never end! Furthermore, although she had always been spirited and even lamentably unbiddable at times, she had never behaved with rudeness before. Tonight she had not bothered to hide her reluctance to dance with Lord Marlbridge, behavior that, in Lady Sedgegood's mind, showed as little decorum as that of an unschooled shop girl.

This latter thought brought Lady Sedgegood up short. On both occasions when Cynthia had behaved in so uncharacteristic a fashion, the Earl of Graybroughton had been involved in it. If her ladyship had been so fanciful as to entertain even the remotest possibility that reincarnation might figure in the scheme of things, she would have been forced to the conclusion that Lord Marlbridge and Cynthia had been sworn enemies in an earlier life. Since she had not a hair of fancy in her nature, however, she was thrown back on illness as an explanation, even though this had its puzzling aspects, too. The girl had not had the sniffles or the fever or any other common manifestation of

114

physical ill-being. Only this odd behavior. Lady Sedgegood sighed yet again. Well, if one could not hit upon the disease, one must attack the symptoms, bizarre though they be.

"I never thought to see you behave in such an ill-bred manner, Cynthia. I must tell you that it is a reflection upon me as your relative and chaperon. With very little encouragement, I would go back to Sussex tomorrow, and then where would you be?" She watched Cynthia's face to see how she would rally to this threat.

"I don't see why you shouldn't go home if that is your wish, Cousin Alice," responded Cynthia with little trace of concern.

"Oh, well, if you don't care for *me*," said Lady Sedgegood crossly, abandoning that unpromising track, "I wonder you don't care for your grandfather whom you confess to hold in such affection!"

Cynthia, who had never felt in such low spirits and who was, in addition, beginning to suspect that her thwarted expectation of seeing Lord Farthing that evening and making a further push to fix his attention could in no small way account for such a fit of the blue devils, said with a fretfulness that was alien to her character, "How can you utter such a preposterous charge when everything I am trying to do is for Grandfather!"

"I wish you will tell me," countered Lady Sedgegood, "how insulting the Earl of Graybroughton will help your grandfather."

"Oh, that does not signify."

"Does not signify!" ejaculated Lady Sedgegood, roused to real dismay. "You have made a figure of yourself, treating the most eligible gentleman in all of London as if he were no better than an undergroom! No, worse than that.

115

You wouldn't treat the lowliest servant in such a way—for you have ever had a kind heart, Cynthia. I confess I cannot *conceive* what has brought on such unforgivable conduct and to one whose consequence is unassailable. I pointed out to you this distressing quirk after the Bloomhedges' ball, and tonight you did not seem to be making the least push to set yourself right with him!"

"I haven't the wraith of a desire to set myself right with him!" her young cousin informed her in trembling accents. "And a great many persons of impeccable taste have told me that my company is *quite* enjoyable!"

"Well, if they had witnessed tonight's imbroglio and could still hold to that opinion, they are all caper-wits!"

Cynthia was strangely silent for a long moment, and Lady Sedgegood very much feared that she was about to dissolve into the weeps. This, too, was unlike Cynthia and the thought wrung Lady Sedgegood's heart. She was preparing herself to offer the comfort of her ample bosom at the first sign of a tear. But Cynthia merely swallowed hard several times and then said mysteriously, "There are things you never dreamed of, Cousin Alice, living your innocent rustic life."

This pronouncement was so unfathomable and so far from anything she had expected to fall from Cynthia's lips that Lady Sedgegood's brain whirled with confusion. Since she could think of no sensible rejoinder, she beat a retreat into silence.

Some distance away in a distinctive barouche, Lady Madeline Witherspoon was having no better luck at discovering what lay at the root of her companion's musing expression.

"Who would have thought," remarked Lady Witherspoon, "to have found so many unexceptionable young ladies at Almack's this early in the season?"

"You would," her brother answered promptly. "That's why you dragged me there tonight, isn't it, Maddy? And pray don't take offense because your ploys are so obvious. After all, I have known you all your life, dear sister."

She lifted her shoulders in the blue velvet pelisse and smiled. "So you *did* think there were some pretty ones?"

"A virtual hothouse full of flowers, old girl. Daisies, roses, pansies, azaleas—but, alas, not a brain among them."

"Dearest Kenyon, you are just as abominable as you ever were!"

"Yes, I daresay I am," agreed the earl amiably. "But you needn't put yourself about. I behaved with a circumspection even you could not fault. Did you proud."

"Well, you did give me a twinge early on when Lady Jersey was hinting that you ask Anne Bloomhedge to dance. You made up for it later, however, by standing up with her twice." She peered into his handsome face, which was partially in shadow. "She seems a sweet little thing. So modestly behaved."

"I should rather say vacuous. You'd best forget about her if you have any ideas in *that* direction. I don't fancy spending the rest of my days with someone whose only topic of conversation, as far as I can discern, is ladies' fashions."

"Gracious!" Lady Witherspoon said dauntingly. "I did not realize you had become a cynic. What has given you such a jaundiced view of females?"

"Most of the females I have known," retorted the earl, "always, of course, excluding you, dear Maddy."

"At least," she said teasingly, "you have not forgotten

117

how to turn a compliment when doing so will get you out of the briars."

"On further thought," drawled the earl tolerantly, "perhaps I must be grateful to you for all your efforts to get me up to London since I returned from the Peninsula. I do not believe that the rustic environs of Northumberland have dulled *all* my town bronze, but it may be that I've ventured back into civilization none too soon. Fact is, someone told me recently that my veneer has become lamentably tarnished."

Lady Witherspoon, hearing the ironic tone underlying this surprising speech, did not quite know what to make of it. "Fustian, Kenyon! You can't take seriously the remark of someone who is undoubtedly envious of your station."

"Oh, you couldn't be farther off the mark, Maddy. She may harbor a number of unladylike emotions where I am concerned, but I think I can tell you that envy is not one of them!"

Lady Witherspoon turned to stare at her brother's rugged profile. "She? Surely you are not speaking of any of the ladies in attendance tonight. None of them would make such an impolite remark except in jest." Kenyon did not reply to this and, in fact, appeared to have fallen once more into the attitude of preoccupation that she had noticed earlier. She was feverishly curious about the cause of such clear ponderment but, alas, knew that a frontal attack would advance her knowledge of the matter not at all.

Rather than set out on an investigation that was predestined to failure, she began to review in her mind all the ladies whom her brother had favored with his company during the evening. It occurred to her that the only time when Kenyon's handsome features had suggested anything other than mild amusement or tolerant boredom had occurred as he danced with the Chattington girl. In fact, had she not been so well acquainted with her brother's sometimes infuriating composure, she might even have interpreted his expression in that brief moment at the end of his dance with Cynthia Chattington as astonishment. Lady Witherspoon had given the notion so little credence at the time that she had immediately dismissed it. Now, however, the memory returned to puzzle her.

"Well, I shan't badger you to escort me frequently to Almack's. I only thought that one or two appearances there would give you the best opportunity to meet the majority of the members of the ton near your own age who are in town."

"Come, Maddy," responded Kenyon mildly, "you hoped to find an acceptable female who might be thrown into my path as often as possible."

Undaunted, Lady Witherspoon said, "It would be futile for me to deny that I hope you will choose a wife before too many more seasons pass."

"Futile, indeed," observed the earl.

"I will confess," continued Lady Witherspoon carelessly, "that my earlier assessment may have been exaggerated. To own the truth, the current crop of eligible misses is not, on the whole, outstanding. There are, naturally, one or two exceptions. Anne Bloomhedge's father plans to settle a sizable fortune on her when she marries, but since you have already expressed your disinterest on that head, I hardly think you will be moved by money. I daresay if your fortune was depleted, as is true of several of the unmarried gentlemen of the ton, you might view Miss Bloomhedge somewhat differently. It does seem, doesn't it, that the wealthiest young ladies are often the least capable of inspiring strong emotions in male hearts, while the most attractive—well, take Cynthia Chattington, for example. The poor child hasn't even the hope of receiving anything upon her marriage. The latest on-dit has it that her grandfather has suffered another financial setback, after several years of dwindling resources. But she is a taking little thing and, from all I have seen, of a pleasant disposition."

Unprepared for the sudden bark of laughter that escaped her brother, she could only stare at him in surprise. Kenyon's shoulders shook for several moments before he could speak. "Oh, Maddy, that is the most hilarious thing I have heard this past age!"

"What have I said?"

But the earl was unable to enlighten her, even had he been so inclined, for every time he tried to speak, he broke into fresh whoops of laughter.

Set down on her own doorstep, Lady Witherspoon could only wonder at her brother's reaction. It was obvious, however, that a mystery—though probably of unremarkable character—lay behind Kenyon's hilarity over her assessment of Cynthia Chattington. Having her fair share of feminine inquisitiveness and propensity toward romantic intrigue, Lady Witherspoon resolved to invite the young lady and her chaperon to tea soon so that she might become better acquainted with the girl. Perhaps then she would discover why Kenyon had found her remarks so amusing.

8

Cynthia, however much Lord Marlbridge might anger
and disconcert her, was well enough pleased with the
results of her strategy as far as Lord Farthing was concerned. That gentleman gratified her by calling on her
several times during the next few weeks, in addition to
sending her flowers and a delicately painted ivory fan.
Cynthia could only suppose that Lady Farthing did not
know of her son's destination when he left their house on
these occasions, for she did not accompany him. Even
Lady Sedgegood grew accustomed to seeing Percy Farthing's pleasant face in the house in Grosvenor Square,
and although she could not be said to approve, at least she
ceased harassing Cynthia about the unsuitability of such
a potential alliance. As for her grandfather, he kept to his
rooms during much of this time, fighting the continuing
discomfort of the gout with prodigious amounts of excellent port.

Encouraged by Lord Farthing's resourcefulness in

finding frequent opportunities to call on her without his imposing mama's knowledge, Cynthia began to believe in her own ability to wrest his allegiance from his mother to herself. The gentleman was clearly developing a *tendre* for her, and she could not but feel flattered by this, considering his unquestioned eligibility.

Lord Farthing's attentions to her, however unknowing his mother might be of their number and seriousness, did not go unnoticed by other members of the ton. Cynthia and Lady Sedgegood found themselves the recipients of several invitations to tea from ladies who previously had not shown any special interest in advancing more intimate acquaintance with them. Therefore, when Lady Madeline Witherspoon's invitation arrived, it created no particular uneasiness in Cynthia, even though she was aware of the relationship existing between Lady Witherspoon and the Earl of Graybroughton.

The earl had shown no further interest in seeking her out in recent weeks, and Cynthia, who had seen him in company with several young ladies of the ton during that same period, had managed to put aside any compassionate, but unwise, impulses to enlighten those young ladies concerning the earl's true character, reminding herself that one should certainly think carefully before besmirching the name of someone who seemed, for whatever reason, charitably inclined toward the collection of a debt long past due. Such thoughts proved soothing enough to her conscience until it came to someone whom she considered a special friend. This new dilemma was presented to her on the afternoon when she and Cousin Alice joined Lady Witherspoon at her house for tea.

They were not, in the event, the only guests. Lady Bloomhedge and Anne had arrived before them and were already ensconced in one of the most elegant saloons Cynthia had ever seen. The room, called appropriately the Ivory Saloon, was furnished in velvet, damask, and satin, all in shades of ivory, which contrasted tastefully with the forest green leaves in the carpet and the gold tassled ropes that held the heavy draperies away from the wide windows, allowing the April sunlight to bathe the room in a cheerful glow.

Lady Witherspoon, an attractive matron in her midtwenties with beautiful deep auburn hair and a complexion that was flawless, except for a light sprinkling of pale freckles across her up-tilted nose, advanced toward the latest arrivals as they were admitted to the saloon by the butler.

"Do come in, Lady Sedgegood and Cynthia," she greeted them. "I'm so glad you could find time to accept my invitation in what I am sure must be a busy social schedule. You know the Bloomhedges, of course—Anne and her mother."

Greetings were exchanged and the newcomers were seated on a velvet settee with the Bloomhedges and Lady Witherspoon facing them, a tray laden with a variety of dainty sandwiches and sweetmeats within convenient reach. A young maid served tea in fragile china cups and then withdrew.

"You can't think how charmed we were to receive your note, Lady Witherspoon," Lady Sedgegood said with becoming frankness. "I was quite disappointed last season that we were not able to become better acquainted. My late brother spoke affectionately of your dear father. They were, I believe, fast friends in their school days." Although this might have been an exaggeration, Lady Witherspoon did not seem to mind at all.

"I was so busy last season bringing out my husband's youngest sister. You may recall that she made an excellent marriage this past summer and so I find I have fewer responsibilities this season."

"I am sure we are all indebted to you," interposed Lady Bloomhedge, "for persuading Lord Marlbridge to leave Northumberland for a spell. Gracious, but he is dedicated to the management of his estates, isn't he? So laudatory when one sees many gentlemen turning those things over to overseers—and often with disastrous results. I am sure your brother is to be admired for such devotion to duty— and after so many years spent in the Peninsula. I declare, he has made such an impression on my little Anne that Lord Bloomhedge and I are almost daily treated to a recital of his excellent qualities."

Anne Bloomhedge's face was rosy with embarrassment, which she attempted to hide by pretending to be intent upon selecting a sandwich from the tea tray. Lady Sedgegood frowned disapprovingly at such an obvious maneuver to enlist the earl's sister in aid of Anne's quite obvious infatuation with the man.

Lady Witherspoon merely laughed and said, "I wish I could claim credit for Kenyon's decision, but I must confess that he has some business in London at this time."

Cynthia wondered wryly if this plainly coddled lady had the faintest idea what sort of business had lured her brother to the metropolis. But, of course, she did not and Cynthia found herself possessed of the oddest conviction that Lady Witherspoon must *never* know the depths of her brother's fall from propriety. It would quite devastate her, Cynthia was certain.

"Now, Cynthia," said Lady Witherspoon, fixing her deep blue eyes on Cynthia's face, "I wish you and Anne will tell me the latest on-dits among the younger set. I confess I am quite content being married, but I do miss those carefree confidences I used to share with my bosom bows."

Cynthia did not know when she had formed such an instant liking for someone, but Lady Witherspoon's totally unaffected manner and infectious smile were fast winning her devotion. Cynthia was quite willing to be obliging, and the next quarter hour was spent in lively discussion of who had offered for whom, what lady had been seen riding in the park with what gentleman, and other such goings-on among the quality.

It was Lady Bloomhedge who put a slight damper on the lightheartedness of this exchange for Cynthia by asking coyly, "And may we expect an announcement from Lord Dahlmere soon, Cynthia? I am told that Lord Farthing is a frequent caller at your house."

"We do not see Lord Farthing any more frequently than Lord Silverstone or others that I could mention," Lady Sedgegood said promptly and, for once, Cynthia was grateful for her cousin's reservations concerning Percy Farthing. Feeling that he was still far from the point of offering for her, Cynthia did not want exaggerated rumors to reach the ears of Lady Farthing, who might be expected to throw obstacles in the path of Percy's intention.

She saw that Lady Witherspoon was eyeing her with interested speculation and smiled brightly. "I noticed your extensive gardens as we approached the house," Cynthia said. "I don't believe I've seen so many varieties of early-blooming roses before." It was clear that she had touched on a subject dear to Lady Witherspoon's heart, but before they could pursue it, the butler appeared to announce the arrival of another guest, and Lord Marlbridge stepped into the saloon.

"My dear Kenyon," exclaimed Lady Witherspoon rising from her chair to cross the carpet and draw her brother into the room. "Such an unexpected pleasure to see you here!"

Kenyon placed an affectionate kiss on his sister's smooth cheek and remarked, "I had no idea you were entertaining, Maddy. I certainly don't mean to intrude upon this pleasant gathering."

"As if you could intrude," reprimanded Lady Witherspoon. "What brings you here at this time of day?"

"I had to make a call in Clarges Street, and since my return took me so near to you, I decided to look in."

Cynthia was not unfamiliar with Kenyon's audacity. Nevertheless, this offhand reference to the house in Clarges Street caused her to have some difficulty in marshaling her unruly thoughts, which seemed to be a confusion of wonder at a brashness far beyond anything she had ever encountered before and dismay at the deception he practiced so easily upon his unsuspecting sister, not to mention the Bloomhedges and Cousin Alice.

"Come and say hello to my guests," Lady Witherspoon said, upon which Kenyon, with practiced politeness, possessed himself of each of the visitors' hands in turn.

If I were as courageous as—as Joan of Arc, Cynthia thought distractedly, who regardless of what else might be said of her was *French*, I would speak up now and bring his abominable farce to an end. It made her feel quite horridly disgusted with herself to sit there as if her tongue were paralyzed and watch Kenyon playing the role of a perfect gentleman with so little effort.

But, after all, he had been born to the part. For the first

time since their meeting in Clarges Street, Cynthia felt the most blazing curiosity to know how he had come to be associated with Higgins in the first place and what had made him decide to continue Higgins's shameful trade alone.

She had composed herself enough to listen with a set face to Lady Witherspoon's eager suggestion that Kenyon take the young ladies on a tour of the gardens since Cynthia had just expressed an interest in them. Cynthia could think of no possible excuse for declining her hostess's suggestion, and since Kenyon did not, she found herself following an ecstatic Anne Bloomhedge from the saloon.

"Oh, Lord Marlbridge," twittered Anne breathlessly as they emerged from the house, "it is ever so generous of you to take the time to show Cynthia and me the gardens. I saw a pink rose just over there that is the same color as my new gauze gown, the one I plan to wear to Lady Witherspoon's ball." She tripped to one of the rose bushes to finger a velvety bud, then added with a worshipful look at the earl, "Here, this is the one."

Cynthia stole a glance at the gentleman beside her in time to see a sardonic smile cross his face. "A veritable glory of a gown, I am sure, Miss Bloomhedge."

"Oh, yes, sir!" exclaimed Anne, blushing furiously. "And Mama always says that pink *is* my color."

"There you are then," replied Kenyon with amusement. "Who should know better than she?"

Thus encouraged, Anne fell into a rapturous description of two other new gowns that were that very afternoon being conveyed to her house from the elegant establishment of one of London's most renowned modistes. Cynthia, who had never even entered that Bruton Street showroom, could not help feeling a twinge of covetousness as Anne continued her rhapsodizing with blushes and giggles punctuating the whole.

It was soon evident to Cynthia that the earl was paying only token heed to this monologue, a fact to which the enraptured Anne remained utterly oblivious. Despite her feeling of envy over the new gowns, Cynthia could not but feel compassion for the girl whose romantic temperament and limited experience with men seemed to be hurtling her headlong into hopeless love for the earl.

She could only be glad when Kenyon, taking advantage of a momentary pause in Anne's soliloquy, announced that he must beg to be excused to return to his house, where some pressing business matters awaited his attention. This was said with a conspiratorial grin in Cynthia's direction. He urged the two young ladies to continue their stroll through the gardens if they wished.

When he was gone, Anne turned to Cynthia with a dreamy look. "He is so handsome! Don't you think him the most handsome man you have ever seen, Cynthia?"

Cynthia, whose more extensive knowledge of Kenyon nevertheless did not blind her to his lean, broad-shouldered figure, well-carved features, and arresting blue eyes, agreed that the earl was a fine-looking specimen but reminded her enchanted friend that physical appearance was certainly one of the least important qualities to be considered in a gentleman.

Anne gave her a momentarily bewildered look and then said, "Oh, well, I know breeding and manners and such things are vastly important. But, of course, the earl is without flaw in all ways. And, besides, he comported himself with *such* bravery in the Peninsula, risking his life to save others, and he is so—so very gallant, too."

"Gallant!" said Cynthia with irritation, remembering the rude manner in which he had ordered her to hold her peace concerning his affairs and the insulting epithets he had attached to her name during their few conversations. "Oh, you poor misguided babe!"

"I am *not* misguided," snapped Anne, with unusual fire. "And I'm almost as old as you are! What makes you think you know him better than I do? I am sure I have spent as much time in his company as *you* have." The sight of the earl's smart tilbury leaving the house just then attracted their attention and sent Anne into another trancelike state. "Did you hear him, Cynthia? He said he thought I would look glorious in my new pink gown."

Biting her tongue to keep from pointing out that those were not *precisely* the earl's words, Cynthia resolved to speak to Kenyon at the earliest opportunity about casting out lures to someone as basically good and innocent as Anne Bloomhedge. Even if Cynthia had not known Kenyon's dark secret, she would have felt indignant for her friend, for she did not think the earl had any serious interest at all in that direction.

She took a moment, however, to consider that possibility. Anne *was* sweet and certainly eligible, with a fortune to be settled on her by her indulgent papa. Why should not the earl find Anne's blushing adoration—to say nothing of her fortune—to his liking?

This was an unsettling thought, though why it should be unsettling, Cynthia could not have said, except that one would have to be a total cork-brain to imagine that Kenyon and Anne Bloomhedge would rub together at all comfortably.

Confident of this, she was determined to have words with Kenyon before Anne became even more besotted with him. Such a conversation, she felt, could be most easily arranged at Lady Witherspoon's ball, which was only six days away.

As that event approached, Lady Witherspoon herself found that she was looking forward to the evening with unusually marked anticipation. Her husband had returned to London and would be by her side to greet their guests. His mere presence in the house would ensure that things would run smoothly, for her dear Charles had about him a certain aura that elicited prime performances from servants and tradespeople. Thus she could rest assured that everything would be "up to scratch," as Charles would say.

Whenever she bemoaned the fact that the household never seemed to run as facilely in his absence, Charles always said fondly, "You are too familiar with the servants, Maddy, dear, for you have an oddly plebeian desire to be loved by everyone. They take advantage of you. Oh, they love you, sweet—indeed, who could help it? But they *respect* me."

Charles's return then was one cause for her feeling of hopeful expectation, and, of course, she did enjoy a party, especially when she and Charles were giving it. But beyond these things, she wanted to see if her feminine intuition would provide her with any romantic hunches concerning her brother.

She had almost felt *something* when Kenyon had put in that unexpected appearance in the Ivory Saloon in the midst of her small tea party. Her invitations to the four ladies present that afternoon had been anything but haphazard or impulsive, although she had certainly not counted on something so fortuitous as her brother's visit. Having mentally scanned the ranks of eligible misses in

London, and taking careful note of them at early-season parties, she had seen that, regardless of Kenyon's curt denial of interest in one of the misses, Anne Bloomhedge and Cynthia Chattington were among the most favored by gentlemen at such gatherings. Lady Bloomhedge had certainly made it clear that she and her husband would not be averse to a match between their only child and Lord Marlbridge, and the girl herself gave every sign of welcoming Kenyon's attentions.

Cynthia Chattington was something of another matter, for on the few occasions when Lady Witherspoon had seen her with Kenyon she did not appear to be making any effort to fix his attention.

But there was *something*. Take the way Kenyon had whooped when she had paid Cynthia a mild-enough compliment. And there had been that rigid expression on the girl's face when Kenyon had walked into the Ivory Saloon. How Lady Witherspoon would have loved knowing what had been passing through Cynthia's mind at that moment! Oh, if only her brother were the confiding sort! Well, she would keep her eye on Kenyon at the ball to see if he showed a preference for either of the young ladies.

A fond smile touched her lips as she recalled Kenyon's amiable acceptance of her command that he present himself at her ball, even though he had planned an evening at his club with some of his sporting friends.

"Only for you, Maddy," he had said with a touch of resignation, "would I forgo a convivial evening of sport for hours of perspiring in evening dress and inane conversations with simpering misses."

"Poor Kenyon, you are *so* long-suffering!" Lady Witherspoon had told him with a twinkle in her blue eyes. "And I shall see that you are repaid in part by having

Cook prepare all of your favorite dishes for the evening's collation."

"At least I shall have that to look forward to," Kenyon had responded.

At the house in Grosvenor Square, Bramford had been pressed into service as escort. His acceptance of the inevitable, however, had been somewhat less graceful than Lord Marlbridge's. In fact, he was still mumbling about the disagreeableness of the situation when Cynthia came downstairs wearing one of the few new gowns Lady Sedgegood had contrived to supply her with for the season—an attractive creation of pale yellow Indian muslin with a low neckline that displayed her creamy shoulders and a hint of her bosom to lovely advantage.

"Don't see why Silverstone wouldn't serve as well as I," Bramford greeted her.

"If I had made such a request," Cynthia told him, "he might have thought I wanted to encourage his attention. Besides, that would have been quite presumptuous of me, since Lord Silverstone is at the Bloomhedge house as often as he is here. And I hope you will not be in this dreary glump all night. Perhaps Cavey will be at the Witherspoons' ball and—"

"Cavey's gone out of town for a few days," Bramford interrupted.

"Oh?" Cynthia was putting on her satin pelisse, which she had carried downstairs over her arm. "At the height of the season? Where has he gone?"

"How should I know?" Bramford inquired petulantly. "He don't confide in *me!*"

"So you are still feuding because he won't tell you the source of his new-found fortune?" Cynthia said. "Well, I still believe he's received something from that merchant cousin of his father's."

"Suggested that to him," Bramford responded. "Just gave me a fish-eyed stare and muttered that nonsense about not wanting it spread about there was a tradesman in the family. As if *I* care a straw for that! Been acting like a dashed loose screw for weeks now."

"Don't put yourself about so," Cynthia advised sympathetically. "You know Cavey can't keep a secret from you forever. He probably wants to allow people to become accustomed to the idea that he has come into a comfortable living before he lets it be known that his inheritance came from trade. It will perhaps seem more acceptable after the fact. And since Cavey's out of town, you've no one to rattle about with, so you may as well enjoy tonight's ball."

"Why didn't you ask Farthing to escort you?" persisted Bramford, though with less petulance. "You still want to encourage his attention, don't you?"

Cynthia sighed. "Yes, but I must move very carefully on that head, for there is his mama to contend with. I believe," she added with a musing expression, "that she may be less opposed to me than in the beginning, for I did receive an invitation to her rout." She glanced toward the stairs. "Oh, here is Cousin Alice. Shall we go?"

When they were settled in the carriage, Cynthia thought it well to inform her chaperon that Lord Farthing had already engaged her for two dances in addition to requesting her company at supper.

"Two dances *and* supper?" said Lady Sedgegood disapprovingly. "I shall have to remind that gentleman that taking up too much of your time when there is no under-

133

standing between you may subject you to disagreeable gossip."

"Bramford will be on hand after each of my dances with Lord Farthing, won't you, Bram?" Cynthia said appealingly. "So there will be no question of impropriety."

"Besides," added Bramford, "Farthing ain't at all forward and his mama's always watching him, so I shouldn't think anyone could find anything to gossip about. Expect him to offer for her any day, anyway."

"Oh, do you think so?" Cynthia inquired, trying to feel encouraged.

"Bound to. Stands to reason. He's head over heels already. Waiting for his mama's approval, I expect."

"*That* may be a long time arriving," remarked Lady Sedgegood stiffly.

"Can't think what you see in old Percy, Cyn," Bramford said. "If it was me, I'd go after someone like Lord Marlbridge. Shows you I'll never understand women, don't it?" Cynthia did not see fit to reply to such a rhetorical question.

The street outside the Witherspoon house was already crowded with vehicles when they arrived, so it was several minutes before their carriage could be brought up to the front door. Cynthia alighted, feeling some of the elation with which she had, until recently, approached a party.

She thought that her dismal mood of late had been caused by a combination of things, all of which seemed to be coming right now. Her shock over learning that the moneylender who held Bramford's IOU was none other than the Earl of Graybroughton had leveled off into mere disapproval. Even the most astounding knowledge became rather mundane upon long familiarity, she supposed. Her grandfather had not raised any strong objections to an alliance with Lord Farthing, which Cynthia was certain was yet more evidence of the grievous state of his finances. The earl seemed willing to wait until her marriage for repayment of the IOU, and her push to fix Percy Farthing's interest was moving forward satisfactorily. Tonight she would concentrate on breaking down more of Lady Farthing's resistance to her as a daughter-in-law. Of course, there was the unpleasant necessity of speaking in private with Kenyon, but she resolved not to let that throw a pall over the whole evening.

On Bramford's arm she ascended the wide blue-carpeted staircase to where Lord and Lady Witherspoon stood to receive their guests. They were welcomed warmly by Lady Witherspoon, and Cynthia was introduced as a "special friend" to the lady's husband, a tall, rather stern-looking gentleman whose features took on a surprising warmth when he met his wife's glance.

They entered the long ballroom where candlelight flickered from crystal chandeliers and several sets of French doors opened onto a large balcony that ran the entire length of the room.

Cynthia was immediately approached by Lord Farthing, who solicited her hand for the set of dances just forming. When they had taken their places, that gentleman said earnestly, "I say, Lady Cynthia, you look—ahem, magnificent!"

This compliment was received prettily with a dazzling smile that further captivated the gentleman. He begged her promise of the first waltz and, upon handing her over to Bramford at the end of the set, left with clear reluctance to see if his mama required a glass of punch or a breath of fresh air on the balcony. During the past several weeks Lord Farthing had managed to spend a surprising amount of time with Lady Cynthia while at the same time remaining on relatively amiable terms with his mother, and he believed that he was becoming rather adroit at the art of subterfuge.

He would have been surprised to know that his mother, far from having the wool pulled over her eyes, was fully aware of his increasing attentions to Cynthia Chattington. She had attempted, after his first call at the house in Grosvenor Square, to put a stop to any attachment on that front by throwing a tantrum. To her utter amazement and complete bewilderment, her son had walked out of the room in the middle of her melodrama and left her without an audience. Further attempts to dissuade him by more subtle means had, likewise, been met with uncharacteristic stubbornness. For once in his life Percy refused to be governed by his mother.

Lady Farthing had, therefore, seen the wisdom of a retreat of sorts. Not that she was any less opposed to Percy's marrying "that silly chit" who was the detested Lord Dahlmere's impoverished granddaughter. She had merely changed her tactics, realizing finally that the only hope of stopping a marriage was for Percy to see the unsuitability of such a match for himself. This, Lady Farthing was certain, would only come about if he could be made to realize that Cynthia Chattington was at heart strong-headed, high-strung, and tempestuous—in short, everything that would make poor Percy's life miserable. It had dawned on Lady Farthing that the more time Percy spent in the chit's company, the more likely it became that she would forget herself and show him her true character.

In keeping with her new battle plan, Lady Farthing greeted Percy upon his leaving the dance floor with a grudging remark concerning the gracefulness with which

136

he and his partner had performed the patterns of the dance. She found it impossible, however, to resist adding that she *did* feel that Cynthia's gown was cut a shade too low for a miss of her age and position. This suggestion of poor taste in the object of his growing regard did nothing to unsettle the expression of foolish enchantment on Percy's face, so she let it pass and sent him after a cup of punch. She would have much preferred retiring to the game room for whist, but she could not do that and keep the enemy under surveillance. The sacrifices one makes for one's children, Lady Farthing told herself, were often out of reason inconvenient.

It was some time later before Cynthia caught sight of Kenyon and was able to arrest his eye with what struck the earl as a strangely earnest grimace and an unfathomable gesture made with her ivory fan. Amused and slightly intrigued, he approached Cynthia as she finished a dance with Lord Silverstone.

"Good evening, Lady Cynthia," he said. Then, indicating the dance program that dangled from her slender wrist he added, "I hope I have not delayed too long in laying claim to you for a dance."

"As it happens, I have the next one free," she replied with remarkable congeniality and, laying a hand on his arm, led him around the edge of the dance floor. "I must speak to you," she told him in an earnest, if impatient, whisper. "Perhaps we could talk more privately on the balcony."

"I shouldn't be at all surprised," he agreed, following her from the room, his curiosity quickening. Much of the balcony lay in shadow and at the moment the major portion of it was unoccupied. Seeing this, Cynthia was much relieved and immediately made for a dim corner farthest from the doors leading into the lighted ballroom.

"Aren't you afraid," Kenyon said, "that leaving the ballroom with me will give rise to speculation in—certain quarters?"

"Oh, I suppose you are referring to Lord Farthing," said Cynthia with a touch of agitation. "Well, I couldn't think of any other way to talk to you. At any rate, I shall think of a good explanation."

Kenyon grinned. "I don't doubt you will conjure up an excellent explanation, but you will forgive me if I find it hard to swallow that you could think of no other way to talk to me. Why not hop on a post chaise and drive to my house? I assure you it rests in a far more respectable neighborhood than Clarges Street."

"As if *that* wouldn't be all over the ton in hours, you abominable man! I am taking a slight risk even coming out here with you, but it cannot be helped."

Kenyon's grin became a soft chuckle. "You *do* understand that consorting with such a low person as myself will very likely brand you as *fast?*"

"Nonsense—you *are* Lady Witherspoon's brother," said Cynthia, unable to suppress a small smile, "and everyone thinks you are all that is proper. So if we are noticed at all, I will be the envy of every female present for having managed to capture your attention. I half believe that most of them would continue to fall into raptures over you even if they knew your disgraceful secret. One lady told me that she thought you were *unutterably dashing* but so far above her touch that she felt quite destroyed. Silly innocent!"

"Just as I expected," said Kenyon. "You have brought me here to administer another rake-down. Lord, Cynthia, are you so free with your disapproval with other gentle-men, or am I the sole recipient of your fits of temperament?"

"You," Cynthia pointed out, "have *earned* my disapproval. I sometimes think you are quite mad! Why, the way you strolled into your sister's saloon the other day and announced that you had just come from Clarges Street! If you must involve yourself in such unsavory practices, you could at least have the good sense to cover your tracks more carefully."

"You needn't concern yourself with my tracks," said Kenyon reassuringly. "I can promise you that nothing is more unlikely than that anyone should give the least credence to a taint on my name."

"Well, I daresay you are right," Cynthia acknowledged, "though how you have managed to bamboozle everyone, I cannot think. Devious undertakings require a devious mind, I suppose, and—"

Kenyon looked down at her, his face partly in shadow, but there was in the way he held his head a certain challenge that made Cynthia's virtuous renunciations come to a sudden halt.

"There is something I want you to understand, Cynthia," he said. "I am not in the habit of being guided in my conversation or actions by anyone other than myself. If you imagine that these shatter-brained reprimands of yours are apt to work a regeneration in my character, you have a far too lofty notion of your talents. You are too wide in the mouth, my girl. It becomes you ill."

"Becomes *me* ill!" Cynthia retorted, much rankled. "And what of you, Kenyon? A peer of the realm engaged in—in usury. If that is not enough to land you in Newgate, it should be!"

"I daresay it should," Kenyon responded calmly, "but I do not think you will be unwise enough to lay such a charge at my door."

Cynthia swallowed an indignant rejoinder. "You know I will not since you hold Bramford's IOU and you have been—considerate enough to give me time to set things right. Only I wish you would not always be reminding me of this *hold* you have on me, for it throws me into an awful temper and makes me speak before I think."

"Yes, I *have* noticed that in you," said Kenyon sardonically, "but I continue to hope that you will be able to master it in time."

Cynthia glared up at him. "I do not consider that it is anything so horrid. Nor have I any wish to be retiring and—gooseish."

"Indeed? Has Farthing discovered this?"

"Lord Farthing thinks I am accommodating, for he told me so himself. Soon I expect I shall be able to be . . . more myself in his company. I never intended to deceive him—but merely to gain his mother's approval. I am determined to do so, too."

"I do not think there is much chance of that," remarked Kenyon feelingly.

"I am sure that is meant to put me in my place, but never mind. I want you to know that I think it is *odious* of you to make yourself so attractive to Anne Bloomhedge that she is falling in love with you—unless you mean to offer for her, of course."

"Falling in love with me! I have done nothing to foster such an emotion in Miss Bloomhedge. Far from it, in fact. As for offering for her—that is the dottiest thing you have said to me yet!"

"Oh." Momentarily daunted, Cynthia gazed into the

shadowy planes of his face. "Well, she is wearing the willow for you, I am sure of that. She says that you are handsome and gallant and so brave to have saved so many lives in the Peninsula. I am very fond of Anne, and it is so distressing to think of her suffering from unrequited love. Do you suppose you could tell her some Banbury tale—that you showed yourself to be a coward while you were with the troops—left under a cloud of dishonor or something of that sort?"

"Paint myself a regular flat, eh?" Kenyon laughed. "Well, I did not think you needed any aid on that front! A cloud of dishonor! Oh, Cynthia, where *do* you come by such crack-skull notions?"

"You think of a better plan then!" said Cynthia, affronted. "And don't imagine that anything *I* might say would make the least impression on Anne. She would merely think I've developed a *tendre* for you myself."

"Yes, that is probably true," commented Kenyon, his tone full of amusement, "for I believe I am considered a reasonably good catch in some quarters."

"Fiddle!" said Cynthia loftily. "It is really quite amazing how easily people are blinded by a title and polished manners."

Kenyon heaved an exaggerated sigh. "I shan't attempt to defend myself, for I am well aware that such words would be wasted on you. You almost tempt me to resort to other means."

There was something different in his tone, all at once, something that sent a small, unsettling shiver up Cynthia's spine. "What other means?" she inquired uncertainly.

"Just this," said Kenyon, and before Cynthia had any notion of what he was about, she was gathered into his arms and pressed firmly against the hard length of his

141

body. The astonished protest she would have made was stifled when his mouth descended and captured hers with what was, Cynthia would think later—when she could think at all—bold assurance that could only have resulted from considerable practice.

Cynthia had been the recipient of two furtive kisses before, one each from the young men who had offered for her the previous season. These had been unexpected, too, pecks stolen when she had by chance found herself briefly alone with the gentlemen at parties. In both instances, the outcome had been embarrassment on both sides and stammered apologies from the gentlemen who confessed themselves to have been quite overcome.

Nothing in either of those experiences had prepared her for this kiss which, for one thing, lasted much longer, although strangely Cynthia lost any conception of time. How long it might have continued, she was never to know, for she was brought to the full realization of where she was and with whom by a startled cough from near at hand.

"Oh, I say—Lady Cynthia—*ahem!*" croaked Lord Farthing.

This was followed by Lady Farthing's shriek, which could surely be heard throughout the ballroom: *"They are embracing!"*

9

For a moment the earth seemed to tilt dangerously. And then Kenyon said, "Oh, it's you, Farthing. I'm glad you've come. Lady Cynthia's fainted, I'm afraid. I only managed to catch her before she collapsed at my feet."

Lady Farthing clutched her son's arm. "Did you see it, Percy? I am sure they were *kissing!* Shocking, eh, what? Simply shocking! Not that I'm at all surprised by such behavior. The gel's—"

"Forgive my rudeness in interrupting, ma'am." Kenyon's firm tone cut into Lady Farthing's relish at having her opinion of Cynthia so blatantly confirmed. "Farthing, will you help me get her to that bench over there? She seems to be coming around now."

"Oh, I say—ahem," sputtered Lord Farthing, breaking free of his mother's clutches to grasp Cynthia's arm tentatively. A gentleman on either side of her, Cynthia was guided to a nearby bench and lowered to a sitting position. It required little pretense to lift a hand weakly and pass it across her brow as she took in several deep gulps of the cool evening air, for indeed she did feel rather weak. Nor, she discovered, could she bring her skittering thoughts into any clear, reasonable arrangement. Fortunately, Kenyon again came to her rescue.

"If you will stay here and see to the lady, Farthing, I'll go and fetch a cold drink for her."

"By all means, old boy." Lord Farthing, after a brief hesitation, seated himself beside Cynthia. He watched concernedly as she pushed falling curls back from her brow with both hands and, taking another deep breath, sat straighter. "Feeling better now?" he inquired.

With Kenyon's departure, Cynthia's clarity of thought was returning. "Yes, I believe I am," she murmured, looking at the man beside her with a grateful expression. "I—I don't know what came over me. I have never fainted before or even suspected that I might—but all of a sudden I just felt so queer, as if I couldn't get my breath."

"Humph!" Lady Farthing advanced to face the couple on the bench. "Shameless gel! Brazen creature! I ain't to be taken in by *that* farradiddle!"

"Mama," said Lord Farthing, squirming on the bench, "can't you see that Lady Cynthia isn't feeling quite the thing?"

"Nonsense!" brayed her ladyship, incensed. "Caught out, that's what she is!"

"Mama," cut in her son, his voice taking on a firmer tone, "we will discuss this later at home. I am sure you will be able to see things a little more . . . clearly then. Please go and ask Lady Sedgegood to come here."

"Eh, what?" Lady Farthing was much disconcerted by this assertive speech. "Don't be such a bird-wit, Percy!"

"And stop making a figure of yourself," Lord Farthing

added, gathering enough courage to look the furious woman in the eye, causing his parent to choke on the remainder of her scathing denouncement of Cynthia, turn, and leave the balcony with a rigid set to her lumbering form that boded little good for anyone.

"I apologize for her," said Lord Farthing ruefully. "I believe I mentioned before that when she gets an idea in her head, it takes a great deal to dislodge it. I hope she has not made you feel even more discomfited."

"I am much better, really I am," Cynthia said, vastly relieved to see the last of Lady Farthing for the moment. "I can't conceive how your mama could have misunderstood so completely what happened."

"Ahem—well, it is dark out here and, coming from the lighted ballroom as we did—"

"Yes, I see," said Cynthia, "and though it makes me sad to say it, your mama does not care excessively for me, which explains her tendency to think the worst."

"Oh, I say . . ." stammered Lord Farthing, clearly embarrassed by this. "You mustn't let her plain speaking throw you into the dismals. You are so amiable and even-tempered that I am sure she will come to like you when she is better acquainted with you."

Much fearing that this was not to be, Cynthia nevertheless decided not to dwell on it. Poor Lord Farthing was uncomfortable enough as it was. "It was so fortunate that you came out here when you did."

"Oh—Mama wished to take a stroll," said Lord Farthing, seemingly relieved to change the subject.

The arrival of the Farthings at that particular moment now became perfectly understandable. Cynthia was certain that Lady Farthing had seen her and Kenyon leave the ballroom and had hoped to catch them in what she could construe as a compromising circumstance. She should have realized that the old harridan would be watching her!

Cynthia suppressed a smile. Even the suspicious Lady Farthing could not have expected to witness anything so compromising as what had met her eyes. Fortunately, it did not appear that Lord Farthing was going to accept his mother's version of what had happened. It was fervently to be hoped that none of the other guests at the ball would accept it either; it was widely known that Lady Farthing disapproved of any young woman in whom her son showed an interest.

"I—I must confess, my lady," Lord Farthing continued after an embarrassed pause, "that I saw you leave the ballroom with the earl and—well, I felt a bit apprehensive since I did not think you were at all well acquainted with the gentleman, and so I was glad to accompany my mother. Not," he added quickly, "that I thought he would behave—ahem—improperly."

"You are most considerate, sir, to be so thoughtful of me." This seemed to please the gentleman, and Cynthia decided to carry her earlier explanation a bit farther in an effort to set it more firmly in Lord Farthing's mind. "Lord Marlbridge had just asked me to dance and suddenly I felt faint. He must have seen my . . . dilemma, and he was kind enough to insist on accompanying me here. I—I thought for a bit that the night air would totally refresh me, and then, just as you came out, I—I felt weak again."

She was saved from the necessity of embroidering any more on the story that Kenyon had supplied, with such instant wit, by the earl himself, who appeared at that moment with a cup of punch.

"Thank you, sir," said Cynthia demurely, taking the

cup but not meeting Kenyon's look. She sipped slowly, wondering uncomfortably what she should say next and wishing Kenyon would remove himself and his silent amusement from the balcony. And then she saw Lady Sedgegood approaching.

"Oh, Cousin Alice," Cynthia greeted her, "don't look so worried. I am quite all right. I only had a spell of weakness, but it is gone now."

Lady Sedgegood peered down into her young cousin's face. "Everyone inside is saying that you swooned dead away and that Lord Marlbridge caught you before you fell and injured yourself."

"That is a tolerable summary of what transpired, Lady Sedgegood," said Kenyon, and Cynthia wondered if anyone other than herself could detect the faint hint of irony in the words. "But as you can see, she has come back to us now."

"It was merely the heat in the ballroom," Cynthia put in. "All those candles and . . . so many people squeezed together. These . . . gentlemen have been very kind to me and I feel quite all right now."

Lady Sedgegood continued to regard Cynthia with a frown. "Are you certain it was nothing more than the heat? You have never fainted before, and you have not been acting quite yourself lately. I am not at all convinced that you are completely well."

"Of course, I am well," Cynthia assured her. "Please don't concern yourself about me anymore. Why, I feel utterly famished for something to eat. Surely that is a sign of good health."

"It is almost time to go in to supper, Lady Cynthia," said Lord Farthing hopefully. "If you are certain you wish to partake, I'll remind you of your promise to allow me to escort you."

"Indeed, sir, I had not forgotten." Cynthia disposed of her punch cup and stood. She could no longer ignore Kenyon, who waited with such maddening ease beside Lady Sedgegood, a droll expression tugging at his mouth. "Thank you, Lord Marlbridge, for coming to my rescue. I am sure your quick thinking saved me from an embarrassing situation."

"Embarrassing?" inquired Kenyon wickedly.

"Why, yes. It would surely be embarrassing to find oneself stretched full-length on a balcony with a party going on nearby. I might even have damaged my gown."

Kenyon bowed with what seemed to Cynthia mock politeness, though neither Lady Sedgegood nor Lord Farthing appeared to find anything unusual in his manner. "I look forward to being of—uh, service to you again at some future time, Lady Cynthia. If you will excuse me now, I believe my sister may have engaged me to escort one of her guests in to supper."

That guest, Cynthia saw a few minutes later, was Anne Bloomhedge, who sat with Kenyon at a table some distance removed from the one Lord Farthing had claimed. There were two other couples at the table, as well, but the way Anne's rapt attention stayed riveted on Kenyon's rugged face, one must suppose she was unaware of the other four. Anne seemed to be doing most of the talking at that far table, also, and Cynthia might have spared a brief moment to wonder what she was saying if it had not taken all of her wits to parry Lady Farthing's pointed barbs.

"Oh, here is Hetta Larchmont—and Pendleton," Lady Farthing announced after Cynthia had explained again, under her ladyship's detailed interrogation, what had happened on the balcony. "I have invited them to share our table." She threw Cynthia a sly look, which Cynthia did not at first understand. "You don't mind, do you, gel?"

"Not at all," Cynthia assured her. Although she and Hetta Larchmont could never have been said to be friends, she rather liked Lord Pendleton and, anyway, she hoped that another couple at the table would take some of Lady Farthing's attention away from her.

When the newcomers were seated, Lady Farthing inquired of Hetta, "Is your aunt, Lady Hallum, planning another of her lovely breakfasts this season?"

"Yes, my lady," Hetta replied, "although not until summer. The weather is too uncertain until then, and she does enjoy having her breakfasts out of doors."

Lady Farthing fingered the gaudy ornament that adorned her crimson turban. "Been trying to think for weeks—who *was* that ridiculous gel who fell into the Hallums' fishpond last season?"

Cynthia's gaze flew to meet Hetta's. They had certainly had their differences, but Cynthia hoped the presence of Lord Pendleton at the table—who, after all, had been the cause of that dust-up—would prevent Hetta's saying much on the subject. "I have been thinking about that myself, Lady Farthing, since you mentioned it earlier," Cynthia announced, inventing rapidly. "It seems to me it was one of the Courtney girls. I believe her father is a Scottish peer." The look she was giving Hetta was unabashedly pleading now.

"Courtney?" boomed Lady Farthing. "Never heard of any Courtneys!"

"To own the truth, I had forgotten all about that incident," Hetta said, casting covetous eyes upon Lord Pendleton, who was looking from her to Cynthia with curiosity.

"Seems to me," said Lord Pendleton, his interest engaged, "I heard there were *two* young ladies involved in that. One pushed the other, or so I heard, although I can't imagine any well-born girl behaving in so farouche a manner."

Seeing where wisdom lay, Hetta said, "I remember now. It was the *two* Courtney girls, isn't that right, Cynthia?"

Cynthia released a long breath. "Exactly so, Hetta. And I haven't heard of them since. Gracious, Hetta, that blue gown is becoming with your blond hair. Don't you think so, Lord Pendleton?"

"Reminds me of a June sky in Kent," agreed that gentleman. "The same color as Hetta's eyes. Don't know any other girl with eyes quite so blue."

Hetta flushed prettily. "Thank you, but I am afraid that blondes are not at all in vogue this season."

"Like blondes myself," said Lord Pendleton gallantly before returning his attention to his plate, and Hetta blushed even pinker than before.

"Still can't recall ever hearing of any Courtneys," announced Lady Farthing darkly. "Eh, what? Percy, ever hear of them?"

"Ahem—no, Mama, I can't say that I have. But if their father is a *Scottish* peer, well . . ." Lord Farthing's voice trailed off, but his tone left no doubt how little importance he placed on such a personage.

"Well, they can't be of much consequence, that's true." Her ladyship stared at Cynthia for a moment, then attacked a large piece of walnut cake with some relish.

"I am looking forward to your afternoon rout, Lady

Farthing. Lord Pendleton has done me the honor of offering to escort me," announced Hetta coyly, darting a complacent glance at Cynthia, who was perfectly willing to allow Hetta her triumph. "Mother says you have redecorated some of your house in the striking new Egyptian style. I am simply pining to see it."

"Eh, what?" Lady Farthing had demolished her cake and started on the plum pudding. "Oh, yes. Had everything brought from Cairo. Like bright colors, you know. Percy adores everything Egyptian, don't you, dearest?"

"Yes, Mama," Lord Farthing agreed. "Striking. That's the very word for it, Miss Larchmont." He turned abruptly to Cynthia. "Want to show you the new rooms—whole house, in fact. At the rout."

"Why, that will be very interesting, I'm sure," said Cynthia, not quite certain what hidden meaning, if any, was contained in this sudden announcement.

"The gel wears puce and shades of green, Percy," observed Lady Farthing. Her glance fell momentarily on Cynthia's muslin gown. "Insipid yellow. Dull colors. Probably hates red and such hues."

"Oh, no," Cynthia said. "I—I happen to like red very well."

Lady Farthing scowled over her pudding while her son beamed at Cynthia, then took a sliver of sole into his mouth, which he chewed with seeming concentration. Cynthia realized suddenly that she found Lord Farthing's habit of chewing with his mouth slightly ajar irritating. She brushed this revelation aside quickly and glanced away. Lord Pendleton was engrossed in his food and Hetta was engrossed in Lord Pendleton.

Cynthia sighed inwardly, wishing that the meal would end. She suddenly felt an outsider at the table, as if she were an invisible observer, watching and feeling unutterably bored by it all. Her glance drifted briefly across the room to Kenyon. There was an expression on his face, as Anne Bloomhedge spoke to him, that was—what? Tolerance? No, more nearly boredom, the same thing Cynthia was experiencing. She looked back at her plate, picking up her fork to toy with the cake crumbs. She somehow did not like the feeling that she and Kenyon were reacting to their surroundings in a similar fashion.

Try as she might, she could not keep her mind, in such idle moments, from going back over that kiss on the balcony, like a persistent tongue probing at a sore tooth. She tried to recall the exact order of words and events that had led up to it, but she could not. The thing that did come back whenever she thought of it was a confusion of feelings—shock, indignation, but also a rush of enervation, a melting sensation quite unlike anything she had ever experienced before.

The man was clearly without shame. He did not exhibit the slightest remorse for the way he was adding to his already considerable fortune. And that bold kiss had been a way of showing his contempt for her disapproval. Fully aware of this, Cynthia could not deny a sense of consolation, knowing that he did not plan to marry Anne Bloomhedge. This was because Anne was her friend, she told herself, and had nothing to do with that bewildering kiss. He had meant nothing by it, she was obliged to remind herself. He had merely intended to shock her and prove his disregard for the rules of decorum by which other well-born people lived. It was indeed fortuitous that he did not mean to offer for Anne. The girl would probably never know how truly fortunate she was to be out of it.

Had she but realized it, Lord Marlbridge, pretending to

be listening to Miss Bloomhedge's detailed description of her new riding habit—he could only assume the chit hoped by such unique means to elicit an invitation to go riding with him in the park—was not feeling at all bold or arrogant or shameless or any of the other things that Cynthia was silently accusing him of being.

Rather, he was berating himself for his inexplicable action on the balcony. What the devil had induced him to behave as if the chit were anything other than an impertinent child who had conceived the most outrageous opinion of him and seemed determined to persist in that opinion, regardless of what he said. Oh, he supposed he could *make* her understand that she was mistaken in her judgment of him, if he tried. But then mightn't he be called upon to explain why he had purchased Bramford Chattington's IOU from Higgins? Since he was not absolutely clear about that himself, he preferred not being asked the question. Furthermore, for some unfathomable reason, he wanted Cynthia to come to a more appropriate conclusion about him herself, rather than be forced to it by him.

Pride, he thought with wry amusement. He had to admit that the girl had made a small dent in his pride. The mere idea that anyone could believe him capable of being such a rogue rankled. No doubt that explained the kiss, which had surprised the earl almost as as much as it had surprised Cynthia. Certainly he could not have been moved to such action by the fact that she had looked so absurdly young and vulnerable, standing there on the balcony in her yellow muslin, that it had suddenly seemed an inhuman thing to allow her to go on with her fantastic scheme, which would put her under Lady Farthing's thumb for the rest of her life. He had had an impulse to turn her over his knee and paddle some sense into her, but knowing that was totally inadvisable, he had kissed her instead.

All right, Kenyon, he reasoned with himself, if your only motive was to save the chit from herself, why didn't you allow that turbaned monster to spread her vicious tale? Such an indiscretion probably would have ended Percy Farthing's interest in Cynthia—the fellow was such a deuced rigid stickler! But, no, a gentleman must offer a lady protection, particularly when he is solely responsible for her defenseless position.

"Don't you think so, my lord?" Kenyon became aware suddenly that Anne Bloomhedge had asked him a question.

"Oh, yes, indeed," he muttered. What was the little fool talking about now? Undoubtedly another item of her extensive wardrobe. Wouldn't the chit ever run out of gowns to describe? Lord, one could be expected to perform only so many absurd indulgences, even for a much-loved sister.

The opportunity to advise Lady Witherspoon of this arrived the next afternoon when she called on Kenyon. She found him in his study perusing an account book.

"Can't you leave that sort of thing to your overseer?" she inquired as she swept through the door, bringing fragrance and color to an otherwise uninspiredly masculine retreat.

Kenyon looked up with a smile, closed the account book, and came from behind the desk to greet his sister. "You know Papa taught me better than that. I had no other choice while I was in the Peninsula, but upon my return I discovered that—just as Papa warned me—things had been somewhat neglected. It has taken three years to get everything up to the mark again."

"Oh, I know." Lady Witherspoon offered her cheek for

his kiss, then settled into a leather chair near the window. "And that is why you refused to come to London until now. At least, that is the excuse you have always given me."

"You *know* I hadn't the time for languishing in town." Kenyon sprawled comfortably on the well-worn brown couch facing his sister's chair. "Maddy, I am sure Charles has explained to you the necessity of my remaining in Northumberland until now."

"Indeed, yes!" Lady Witherspoon agreed with a laugh. "My husband is quite as boringly devoted to duty as you are."

Kenyon summoned Drabney, who appeared with the tea tray. "My wife has prepared the spice cake again, my lord," said the valet, "and the date muffins especially for Lady Witherspoon."

When Drabney was gone, Lady Witherspoon poured tea into china cups, handing one to her brother. "I have always thought you are extremely fortunate to have such devoted servants as the Drabneys."

"Quite," said Kenyon with a twinkle in his eye. "The fact that the old boy idolizes you is certainly no mark against him, either. 'Sainted,' I believe, is his most recent appellation for you. Of course, I gave him my considered opinion that he was doing it a *trifle* too brown with that one."

Lady Witherspoon chuckled good-naturedly and helped herself to a muffin. Cradling his teacup in one hand, Kenyon stretched his long legs, clad in tan inexpressibles, in front of him. "Tell me, Sister, what brings you here? I was sure you would be exhausted after your ball and would lie abed until much later in the day."

"I am not at all exhausted," Lady Witherspoon informed him. "Besides, I couldn't wait any longer to hear how you enjoyed the festivities."

"I will own I suspected that the moment I saw you. Well, I am glad you are here, for I must speak to you about the want-witted creature whose company you seem to have decided is eminently suited to my tastes. I confess I thought you knew me better, Maddy. I must tell you that I shall very likely run mad if I have to listen to much more of Anne Bloomhedge's monotonous conversation."

Lady Witherspoon shrugged helplessly. "I know that you told me the girl's talk runs rather too much to fashions."

"It does not merely run to fashions," Kenyon corrected her. "That is the sole topic upon which Miss Bloomhedge discourses—at any rate, when she is in my company."

"I daresay," mused Lady Witherspoon, "she is a bit overawed by you. If you could put her more at ease, Kenyon, I am sure you would find she is capable of discussing other things."

"Fact is, Maddy, I have no interest in discussing *anything* with Miss Bloomhedge. I am very much afraid the girl is developing an—ah, attachment for me."

Lady Witherspoon giggled appreciatively. "Mercy, Kenyon! The child is madly in love with you! And her parents approve heartily. Actually, that is the reason I asked you to escort Anne in to supper last night. Lady Bloomhedge hinted so broadly that I could not think how to decline."

"Hereafter," growled Kenyon, "refer Lady Bloomhedge to me, since I am the one being imposed upon. I don't think she has enough cheek to make such a suggestion to *me*, but if she does, *I* have enough cheek to refuse. Your assessment of Miss Bloomhedge's feelings confirm what someone else told me last night. It was suggested that I might try to make myself less attractive in her eyes by spreading it about that I left the Peninsula under less-than-honorable circumstances."

Lady Witherspoon's eyes widened. "Oh, that would not be the thing at all! What a cork-brained notion!"

"So I said," Kenyon told her. "I daresay the chit will be head over ears for someone else soon enough, anyway. I intend to encourage that by avoiding her in future so, pray, do not offer my services again. I feel I should tell you, Maddy, that I am quite capable of making my own assignations."

"That certainly would *seem* to be the case," commented Lady Witherspoon, a small smile quirking her lips.

Kenyon eyed her narrowly for a moment. "I perceive there is some hidden meaning in that remark."

"I was only thinking," said his sister with studied casualness, "that you managed a meeting with Cynthia Chattington on the balcony last night without the least push from me, and all the time I have been under the impression that you had taken little notice of the girl."

Kenyon chuckled. "I wondered how long it would take you to arrive at what, I am convinced, was the real motive for this visit. Well, I am sorry to disappoint you, Maddy dear, but I am sure you have already heard the whole story. You will find me unable to add any delicious tidbits to the tale, I'm afraid. I rescued the girl in a moment of need. That is all that transpired."

"But how," prodded his sister, "did you come to be on the balcony with Cynthia in the first place? It was said you asked her to stand up with you and she became overheated, so you took her outside for a breath of air, but—"

"You will learn nothing different from me," stated the earl.

His sister's expression was touched with a lingering dissatisfaction. "Of course, no one would have given the incident more than passing notice, had not that *odious* Lady Farthing carried on so, insisting to anyone who would listen that you were *kissing* the girl."

Kenyon gave her a brief, measuring glance. "The old termagant *is* rather desperate to detach her son's interest from Lady Chattington. But I am certain everyone in attendance was aware that Lady Farthing had her own reasons for wishing to discredit the girl."

"Undoubtedly," agreed his sister. "Lady Farthing is quite the most ridiculous woman. Why, Percy Farthing is thirty-five if he's a day and surely is capable of knowing his own mind. Still, I cannot think that Cynthia and Lord Farthing would suit well at all. Of course, one can never be sure what another will find to his liking. Perhaps the match would be a good one, after all."

"Hell's teeth!" ejaculated the earl. "I cannot conceive of a *worse* alliance. She would be bored out of her mind before the honeymoon was over!"

Lady Witherspoon watched her brother with acute interest, somewhat astonished at the sharp reaction her observation had brought forth. She cleared her throat and ventured a mild comment to the effect that Mrs. Drabney had certainly done herself proud with the date muffins.

"Furthermore," said Kenyon, disregarding the muffins altogether, "Percy Farthing does not possess enough strength of character to curtail that young woman's hoydenish impulses."

"Indeed?" said Lady Witherspoon with interest. "How acute of you, Kenyon, to see the flaws in such an arrangement, and on such brief acquaintance with Cynthia Chattington, too."

"Not at all!" Kenyon demurred. "My acquaintance with the lady may be brief, but it has been—er—informative. But, hold, Maddy. I must confess that I believe we are needlessly pursuing a moot point, for I do not think she will ever bring Percy Farthing to offer for her. It's an insane notion, anyway! Totally daft!"

"Well, I can see *you* are convinced of that, at any rate," said Lady Witherspoon. "What I do *not* understand is why it should make the slightest difference to you whether or not Lord Farthing offers for her."

"You mistake me, Maddy," said the earl tersely, "if you imagine it *does* matter to me."

"I stand corrected then," said Lady Witherspoon obligingly. "By the by, you *didn't* kiss the girl, did you?"

"Maddy," retorted the earl evenly, "I must tell you that you do me an injustice if you can suppose I would take advantage of a well-born and obviously innocent girl when there is no question of marriage."

Lady Witherspoon smiled. "I meant no discredit to you, dear. Of course," she added after a moment, "you could not be said to have taken advantage of Cynthia if she welcomed your advances. But then that is not at all likely, for it does seem to me that Cynthia does not find you as captivating by half as Anne Bloomhedge or, indeed, a number of other young women. Oh, I see I am trying your patience with this silly chatter, so I will cease tormenting you. I will own, Kenyon, that you *do* appear to have lost some of your well-known sense of humor. Ah, I expect advancing age accounts for that, and your increasing interest in more serious pursuits, such as the running of your estates."

Fully conscious that his sister was still twitting him, despite her protestation to the contrary, Kenyon laughed outright. "I can only be grateful, Sister, that you had the uncommon good sense to marry Charles Witherspoon, for I cannot think of any other gentleman who would tolerate your barbed tongue."

"Well, I shan't pass along that observation to Charles, for he is quite well enough satisfied with himself already!"

The remainder of Lady Witherspoon's visit was passed in casual chitchat. As far as Kenyon could discern, his sister had dismissed the faint suspicion that he had, on the balcony the previous evening, done anything more intriguing than catch a girl as she swooned.

In point of fact, Lady Witherspoon was more suspicious than ever that her brother had been involved in something of a romantic interlude on the balcony. It seemed clear to her, however, that Kenyon did not want it known. His reluctance might result from a desire to protect the young lady's reputation, in which case it seemed he had spoken the truth when he said there was no question of marriage. What Lady Witherspoon could not guess was how her brother really felt about the girl—or, indeed, how Cynthia felt about him. It was obvious that she was not to be enlightened on that head by her brother. She therefore made no attempt to prolong their conversation, but excused herself, saying that she must return to her house and submit to the ministrations of her dresser, since Charles was escorting her to the theater that evening.

When she was in her carriage, however, she instructed her driver to take her to Lord Dahlmere's house in Grosvenor Square. Although it was not expected, her appearance there was greeted with evident pleasure by Lady Sedgegood.

160

In the green saloon that lady made her guest comfortable and ordered refreshments, in spite of Lady Witherspoon's demurral, which she explained by saying she had already taken refreshment.

"One can always drink another nice cup of tea," observed Lady Sedgegood as a maid entered with a tray that was placed on a low table before the hostess.

"Now," said Lady Sedgegood, waving the maid from the room, "do you take both sugar and cream?"

The tea was served and Lady Witherspoon accepted the unwanted offering with grace. "I hope you will forgive me for dropping in unannounced, but I was passing and, remembering Cynthia's unfortunate indisposition last night, I wanted to know how she is feeling."

"Perfectly fine," Lady Sedgegood told her, "or at least that is what she says. And she did *look* fine before she left for a ride in the park with Lord Farthing."

"I *am* relieved to hear that. I shouldn't like to think it was anything she ate at my party that caused her to feel . . . unwell."

"Oh, it couldn't have been that," Lady Sedgegood pointed out, "for it happened before she went in to supper."

"Is she subject to frequent spells of that nature?"

"To my knowledge," said Lady Sedgegood, "last night was the only time Cynthia has fainted in her life. She has always been robustly healthy, much more so than her brother, Bramford."

"I see," said Lady Witherspoon meditatively.

Lady Sedgegood was frowning. "I *have* noticed some rather strange behavior in the girl lately. I was convinced at one point that she was coming down with a malady—

perhaps one of those exotic Eastern ailments—but, fortunately, I seem to have been mistaken."

"What sort of strange behavior?" inquired Lady Witherspoon in the most offhand manner imaginable.

"Well, I know it will not make the slightest sense to you—nor, indeed, does it to me—but Cynthia has seemed vague, or deeply preoccupied, on occasion. I have also had to give her several set-downs for impolite behavior. I am excessively sorry to say that your brother seems to be the most frequent recipient of these freakish fits."

"Indeed?" Lady Witherspoon's arching brows rose. "Kenyon has not mentioned it to me, so I daresay he has not taken it amiss."

"Such an outstanding gentleman," remarked Lady Sedgegood. "Of course, he would be too gallant to criticize the girl's conduct."

Lady Witherspoon suppressed a smile. It was clear that her hostess had a rather romanticized view of Kenyon. Apparently, Cynthia did not share that view, however, if one were to judge by what her chaperon called the girl's "impolite behavior."

"I am very sorry," Lady Witherspoon said, "that one of my guests made such a spectacle of herself over last night's incident."

"Lady Farthing, you mean?" inquired Lady Sedgegood. "Well, if you should ask for my opinion, I would have to say that Cynthia will find herself hard pressed to please *that* woman, no matter what she does. Not," she added hastily, "that I believe that . . . embrace was anything other than an effort to keep the girl from falling, except in Lady Farthing's overheated imagination."

Lady Witherspoon perceived that her hostess's words were meant to reassure herself as much as her guest. The lady seemed to share Lady Witherspoon's suspicion that the alleged kiss was, at least, within the realm of possibility. She finished her tea and excused herself as soon as she could, certain that there was, indeed, something of a mystery surrounding her brother and Cynthia Chattington. Its nature, regrettably, she could not begin to fathom.

10

Cynthia had spent a good portion of the morning, before giving up all effort to sleep and arising from her bed, sunk in recollection of that "romantic interlude" on the Witherspoons' balcony. Far from seeing what had happened as romantic, however, she had grown more and more indignant, telling herself that Kenyon's behavior was too familiar by half and that she had never been more insulted in the whole of her life. She then berated herself for being so naive as to have expected anything better from a *moneylender*.

By the time Lord Farthing arrived to take her, with Mary's chaperonage, for a carriage ride in Hyde Park, she had convinced herself that nothing could be so desirable as to be able to pay Bramford's debt, thus rescuing her brother from disgrace while at the same time ridding herself of any further necessity of ever seeing the odious Lord Marlbridge again. Further convinced that Lord Farthing was the only solution on the horizon to her pressing problems, she met that gentleman wearing a pale pink walking dress adorned with dainty rosebuds and narrow ribbons, determined to lose no more time in casting a net of enchantment over her unsuspecting escort.

Had she but realized it, Lord Farthing was half enchanted already. Until the previous evening, although he found Cynthia charming and quite breathtakingly beautiful, he had, to own the truth, been a bit in awe of her. Lord Farthing did not need his mother's constant reminders to know that he was not the cleverest gentleman in England, but he was not simpleminded, either. And something told him there was more to Lady Cynthia Chattington than met the eye—*his* eye, at any rate. His mother, with her usual dogged insistence upon upholding her own opinion, had pried until she had discovered that her dressmaker held a shockingly overdue bill for the latest additions to Cynthia's wardrobe. Upon further interrogation the dressmaker confessed she had reason to believe that Lord Dahlmere also owed bills at the tailor's and the blacksmith's, adding that she would not care to say how many other establishments. Lady Farthing had not delayed in passing along this on-dit to her son.

To her chagrin Lord Farthing was not at all put off by this information, for it seemed to him that any lady as lovely as Lady Cynthia had every right to select a husband with a fortune, particularly if she was without a living of her own, that, indeed, she would be quite foolish not to do so. Something in Lady Cynthia's manner on one or two occasions, however, had caused Lord Farthing to wonder if she might not be as willful, in her own way, as his mother. It was this, rather than the knowledge that her family was impoverished, that had made him somewhat cautious in his attentions to her.

But the incident on the balcony on the previous evening had banished the lingering suspicion that Lord Farthing now believed had been wholly unjust. All of that gentleman's protective instincts had been aroused by seeing her helplessly aswoon in the arms of another. His mother's unreasonable attack on the girl had merely fixed more firmly in his mind the image of Cynthia as a frail wraith tossed about on the cruel winds of fate and in need of the sanctuary that could be provided by a peaceful home in the country—namely, Farthingate—and a well-heeled husband—namely, Lord Percy Farthing.

Consequently, it took even less effort than Cynthia was prepared to expend to bring out a theretofore unsuspected trace of resolution in the gentleman. When they had reached the park and departed the carriage, leaving the abigail to engage in conversation with the groom, Lord Farthing steered Cynthia along a little-used path and behind a screen of tall shrubbery.

"Why, sir! I didn't even know such a cozy hideaway was to be found in the park," Cynthia teased, amused by the beet-red color of the gentleman's face. "La, I am half convinced you have had occasion to use it before, for you guided me here so unerringly."

"Oh, I say—" stammered Lord Farthing as he ran his finger around beneath his collar in an effort to loosen its suddenly tight grip on his Adam's apple. "You are quite wrong, Lady Cynthia. Ahem—that is, I knew of it because I noticed another couple coming here once and came later to investigate. Actually—Mama would allow me no peace until I did. The young lady was the daughter of Mama's cousin, you see."

"Ah," said Cynthia, "and your mama felt it her *duty* to

keep an eye on the girl and, of course, report all of her actions to her cousin?"

"Er—ahem—yes. I believe there was some sort of dust-up over it. Mama and her cousin created a great miff-maff. Totally unnecessary, for I am convinced the incident was innocent. Should have said so, if anyone had asked my opinion. But then," he added ruefully, "nobody did. All forgotten now, anyway, since the girl is married."

Lady Cynthia, stifling a giggle, strolled over to the shrubbery and traced the veins of a leaf with her slender fingers. Lord Farthing followed hesitantly. "It—it only goes to show you, Lady Cynthia, that a respectable marriage seems to wipe out any—ahem—unpleasantness in which a lady might have been embroiled in the past."

Lady Cynthia turned to look up at him with wide gray eyes. "Are you still speaking of the daughter of your mama's cousin, my lord?"

"Well, ahem—yes, but I am sure there are many examples of similar situations."

"I expect you are right," Cynthia agreed. "I believe there was a girl last season who ran off with a coachman. But her father sent a gentleman after her—I have heard that a great deal of money changed hands, although I do not know how much truth there is in it. At any rate, she married a baron and in less than a month they were being invited to all the best houses."

"Oh, I say, that *was* a close shave, but I was not thinking of anything so indecent as that. Little fool was dashed lucky the gentleman needed money so badly."

"Lord Farthing," Cynthia said, blinking her sooty lashes at him, "do you think it is quite proper of us to stay here any longer?"

"Mean to make it proper," announced that gentleman,

squaring his shoulders and thrusting his finger beneath his collar once more. "That's what I've been trying to say. Be honored if we could become betrothed, Lady Cynthia."

Although she had been steering the gentleman toward such a declaration, Cynthia found that she was oddly unprepared for this sudden display of dash. "Oh, sir! Betrothed—you have quite taken my breath away."

"Didn't mean to do that! You ain't going to faint again, are you?"

"No," Cynthia assured him. She did not understand the reluctance she was experiencing—wasn't this what she had hoped for? Nevertheless, she felt compelled to add, "It is just that—well, are you quite sure you wish us to be betrothed, Lord Farthing?"

"Might as well be frank," said the gentleman earnestly. "If we're to be betrothed, I should think it's the best way in the long run. Might as well tell you that I know of your grandfather's debts—know you ain't got sixpence. Don't care a reed about that, for I've enough money to see Lord Dahlmere well set up and provide comfortably for you, too."

"Sir, you are everything that is generous," said Cynthia, flushing slightly at this bald assessment of her situation. "But I am not at all certain your mother will approve."

"Mean to see that she does," stated Lord Farthing, but then his uncharacteristic burst of courage wavered slightly. "May need a little time to bring her up to scratch. Needn't send the announcement to the papers yet. I am prepared, however, to return to your house with you and solicit your grandfather's blessing. If he agrees, we can discuss a financial settlement."

Knowing what a settlement would mean to her grandfather, Cynthia was able to brush aside her feeling that things were moving ahead too fast. Lord Dahlmere had been so despondent in recent weeks that she had begun to fear a serious physical decline. Being relieved of his debts would do much to return him to his normal spirits. "I am honored, Lord Farthing," she said impulsively. "If you are absolutely certain—"

"Course I'm certain. Wouldn't have spoken otherwise." Lord Farthing's flushed face broke into a smile of relief. "Does this mean you want to be betrothed?"

"Provided Grandfather approves," Cynthia told him.

Emboldened by this, he gripped her hand with surprising strength and bent to plant a moist kiss on her knuckles. Straightening, he stammered, "Well, I say—ahem—no reason to waste any more time here. I'll go and speak to Lord Dahlmere."

"Very well . . . Percy."

"Like you to use my Christian name," announced Lord Farthing. "Shall like being betrothed to you, too . . . Cynthia."

Lord Farthing was bound to admit to himself that a bit of the surge of well-being that had emboldened him in the park had left him by the time he was admitted to Lord Dahlmere's study. Nevertheless, having set his course, he struggled bravely on. "Good of you to see me, sir. Know you haven't been feeling well."

"Gout," uttered Lord Dahlmere by way of explanation. He was sitting at his desk, but got up now to peer from beneath beetling brows at the clearly uncomfortable gentleman before him. "Sit, Farthing," he directed imperiously. "We'll have a touch of brandy." He poured the drinks himself and thrust one into Lord Farthing's hand.

"Thank you, sir. Kind of you." Lord Farthing, who had never particularly liked brandy, threw back the contents of the snifter with one deft movement. He immediately felt even warmer, but somewhat less anxious.

Lord Dahlmere strolled with a slight limp to the window, where he gazed out for some moments, causing Lord Farthing to wonder disconcertedly if the old gentleman had forgotten him. But just as he was summoning his courage to speak, Lord Dahlmere turned around.

"I've been confined to my chamber for several weeks, Farthing, but I'm told you've been running tame in my house and escorting my granddaughter about town. Don't take much cleverness to know what you're doing here now. Want to marry her, don't you?"

"Why, yes, sir—that is—yes." Lord Farthing was taken aback by the elderly gentleman's blunt approach, but he was nevertheless relieved that his mission had been so quickly perceived.

Lord Dahlmere took several moments to finish his brandy before he spoke again. "What about Cynthia? Does she want to marry you?"

Lord Farthing moved nervously in his chair. "She has done me the honor, sir, of agreeing to a betrothal, provided your approval is forthcoming."

"Are you aware, Farthing, that she has no dowry? She would come to you with nothing."

"Oh, I say, sir—I don't care for that. I am prepared to pay over to you a goodly sum in return for your granddaughter's hand." Lord Farthing cleared his throat, then added impetuously, "I'd be content with the bargain, Lord Dahlmere."

The baron frowned at him. "My granddaughter is a damme fine bargain, sir, without a groat to carry with her!"

"Just so," agreed Lord Farthing hastily. "That's what I meant."

"Don't care for your mother above half," observed the baron candidly. "She don't care for me, either. But I daresay that's little to the purpose. However, I own I am curious as to what Lady Farthing had to say upon this subject."

"Nothing, sir. What I mean is—I haven't told her yet. Thought there would be time enough for that after we reach our agreement."

"Oh?" The baron's shaggy white brows rose. "Daresay you preferred to stay out of the briars as long as possible. She'll kick up the devil of a dust, you know."

Lord Farthing attempted a denial, but he was basically an honest man. He stammered for a bit, gave up, and finally said truthfully, "She'll enact me a Cheltenham tragedy, sir, but she'll have to accept Cynthia when she sees I mean to marry her."

"Do you really think so?" inquired the baron with a trace of irony. "I would be most interested in knowing, Farthing, *when* you intend telling your mother."

"When the—ahem—right moment presents itself, sir."

"Eh," said the baron. "I see." He shrugged and, feeling a sudden twinge in his toe, lowered himself with a grunt into the chair behind the desk. "Now about the marriage settlement, Farthing," he said, going without further ado to the crux of the matter.

Some minutes later Cynthia, who had been pacing restlessly about the green saloon under Lady Sedgegood's reflective eye, was summoned to the study. She was relieved to find Lord Farthing and her grandfather in a reasonably congenial mood.

"Cynthia," said the baron, "Lord Farthing has asked

171

for your hand in marriage and we have reached a—ah, mutually satisfactory agreement. He says that you are ready to accept his proposal. Is this true?"

All at once the reality of the situation was brought home to Cynthia, and she realized that, deep inside her, she had not expected her grandfather to agree so readily. Disconcerted, she nodded hesitantly and then, seeing how very much her grandfather wanted to believe her, she said, "Yes, Grandfather."

Lord Dahlmere gazed into her gray eyes for a moment, scowling. "Are you sure, Cynthia?"

"Yes, Grandfather," she repeated.

"Well, then—" His voice rose, as if it had suddenly been released from some confinement. "Congratulations, Farthing. What date have you decided on?"

"Oh, we haven't even discussed dates," Cynthia interposed.

"I would like to speak to my mother before the betrothal is announced, sir. We will send the notice to the newspaper after she has—ahem—gotten accustomed to the idea."

"Still like to know when," said the baron with interest, "that might be."

"Never mind, Lord—er, Percy," said Cynthia. "Gracious, there is certainly no *rush* to have the announcement published—or to fix a date. There will be plenty of time for all of that later. In fact, I think it is just as well that we don't spread it about at all—for the time being."

"My feelings exactly," said Lord Farthing with obvious relief. "Never knew such an accommodating girl, Lord Dahlmere, if I may say so."

"Indeed?" said the baron dryly.

"Well," said Cynthia briskly, "I must go and speak to

172

Cousin Alice about . . . something. I expect I shall be seeing you soon, Percy."

Lord Farthing readily confirmed this assumption, and after making her curtsy, Cynthia left the study and returned to the green saloon. A moment later Lord Farthing was shown out of the house by Hobson who, having stationed himself near enough to the study, had heard most of what was said and was, therefore, well aware of what had just transpired there. Later the butler would observe to the housekeeper in grave accents that if he was any judge of the matter, the old lord had made a serious mistake in agreeing to the union, for Hobson owned that should he be pressed to name anyone *less* capable of keeping Lady Cynthia in hand than Lord Farthing, he would find it an excessively difficult—if not impossible—task.

This was dealt with by Mrs. Hench's remarking reprovingly that she was sure it was no part of *her* duties to pass judgment on Lord Dahlmere's decisions. To which Hobson replied calmly that this was undoubtedly true, but then *she* had not been with the old lord for more than thirty years, either.

In the green saloon, Lady Sedgegood was speaking: "I must say you don't seem completely comfortable with this . . . arrangement, Cynthia."

"I can't think *where* you came by that opinion," said Cynthia testily. "Why shouldn't I be comfortable? I set out to find a rich husband, and I have found one."

"He isn't your husband yet," observed Lady Sedgegood reasonably.

"Well, he *shall* be. You would not be twitting me like this if you had seen how the tension had gone from Grandfather's face just now. Percy and Grandfather must have agreed on an *excessively* generous marriage settlement."

173

She paused to run a hand across her brow, a slightly distracted gesture that did not escape Lady Sedgegood's notice. "I am sure," Cynthia added, "you will understand, Cousin Alice, if I go to my chamber now. It has been a rather tiring afternoon, and I believe I shall retire early."

During the next few days Lady Cynthia's betrothed was less in evidence in the house in Grosvenor Square than had been the case before the betrothal. Cynthia might have been hurt by this evidence of her future husband's neglect had she not been so occupied with rehearsing the disdainful phrases with which she would inform Kenyon of her coming marriage and the impending payment of Bramford's IOU. Besides, Percy explained to her that he would be spending more time with his mama, a mollifying tactic that would, the gentleman hoped, put Lady Farthing in the proper frame of mind to receive the news of her son's engagement. The day of the Farthings' afternoon rout arrived early in May, however, without Lord Farthing's having found "the right moment" to confess all to his mama.

Unfortunately, both Cynthia and Lord Farthing had not taken into account servants' gossip, and as it fell out, Lady Farthing was in possession of the detested information a full week before the rout. She had her own reasons for continuing in pretended ignorance while at the same time treating her son, during their hours together, with uncommon consideration.

Had Lord Farthing been a more questioning sort, he might have suspected that his efforts to keep his mother in the dark until the moment of his choosing had failed. Being rather naive, however, he believed that his renewed attentions to his mother were the cause of her unusually mellow mood, which was eagerly reported to his intended.

Perhaps, Cynthia thought—unaccountably not with all the satisfaction this reflection should have caused her—Lady Farthing will not be such a troublesome mother-in-law after all. This speculation could not have been farther from the fact. She was made aware of that the instant she stepped inside the Farthings' spacious Egyptian saloon on the afternoon of Lady Farthing's rout, for the first person her eyes fell upon was her hostess, and the look she received in return was pure rancor. If looks could kill, Cynthia would undoubtedly have found herself supine upon the carpet and drawing her final breath.

Cynthia had chosen to wear a modest white muslin gown for the occasion, thinking to give her ladyship no possible cause for criticism, but that look of Lady Farthing's pricked her temper momentarily, and she experienced a brief impulsive wish that she had instead worn something more daring as a gesture of defiance. The mild pleasure she received from this provocative thought was quickly dissipated when she spied the Earl of Graybroughton lounging on a quite horribly garish red and black settee, the gilt arms of which were fashioned into sphinxes. He was engaged in conversation with Hetta Larchmont and Lord Pendleton, and his brief glance in Cynthia's direction seemed to contain a hint of scorn, which, of course, made her angrier with him than before.

Lord Farthing came to greet her and escort her to a black and white zebra-striped settee, this one resting on the back of what Cynthia thought to be a bronze likeness of a hippopotamus.

"Mama has arranged some entertainment," Lord Farthing told her, "after which we will partake of the collation that is being spread in the Egyptian dining saloon." He seated himself beside her, an expectant expression on his face. "What do you think of it?" A gesture indicated the newly decorated saloon in which they found themselves.

"It's . . . interesting," observed Cynthia tactfully. "But what is that in the corner? It looks like one of those things they buried people in."

"Sarcophagus," Lord Farthing informed her, his glance resting proudly on the gilt atrocity that occupied the near corner of the saloon.

"Wh-what's inside it?" Cynthia inquired. "Not a mummy, surely."

"Oh, I say!" Lord Farthing laughed at such a silly notion, unaware that his intended had been speaking facetiously. "Inside there's a coat rack. Clever, don't you think?"

"Hmm—yes," Cynthia agreed.

"Want you to see the dining saloon," Lord Farthing told her. "Got columns running the full length with pictures all over them—like something out of those pyramid tombs. Never saw anything like it."

"I daresay I haven't," Cynthia observed. She was rescued from the strain of phrasing any more carefully noncommittal comments on the decor by the string quartet occupying a small patio beyond the saloon's open French doors, which began to play at that moment.

Cynthia might have found the entertainment enjoyable had not her hostess assailed her with malevolent looks throughout the performance. Can it be possible, Cynthia wondered, that she already knows of the betrothal?

But responding to a whispered inquiry, Lord Farthing confessed that he had not as yet found a propitious moment to break the news. Apparently, Cynthia told herself, Lady Farthing is either suffering from acute indigestion or

176

she is merely being her usual abominable self, and she contrived to ignore the malicious looks.

Nevertheless, it was a decided relief when, after the collation, Lord Farthing expressed a wish to show her the rest of the enormous house. Desiring nothing so much as to escape from Lady Farthing's relentless regard, Cynthia eagerly agreed.

The house was a depressing maze of chambers, decorated either in the new Egyptian style or in more subdued, but often clashing hues. "Our apartments will be on the second floor," Lord Farthing told her as they ascended one of several staircases in the house. "Mama might even agree to your decorating them to your own tastes. We can ask her—after we're married."

"I had supposed—" Cynthia said hesitantly. "That is, I had hoped we might have our own house."

Lord Farthing looked astonished. "Two town houses for three people? Dashed extravagant, it seems to me. Besides, I daresay Mama would be lonely in this place, even with so many servants. One can't converse with servants overmuch. Makes them uppity."

"Well—I hadn't thought of that," Cynthia murmured. "And, anyway, there will be plenty of time to discuss things of that nature . . . later."

They had reached a wide landing, and Lord Farthing gazed at her meditatively for a moment, then said, "Thought we might have a winter wedding—January or February. See what Mama thinks of it, after I've told her of the betrothal." He paused, then added optimistically, "Expect to do that any day now."

"I had a feeling earlier than she might already know."

"Couldn't," stated Lord Farthing. "Ain't told her yet. *You* ain't mentioned it outside your family, have you?"

"No," Cynthia assured him.

"There you are then," concluded Lord Farthing with childlike logic.

Suddenly another voice intruded into the quiet of the wide hall. "Git *up*, ye bloody urchin! Sick of ye're snivelin', I be!" This was followed by an earsplitting howl that suggested someone was in the throes of excruciating pain.

"What the deuce—?" Lord Farthing said.

"It's coming from this room." Cynthia moved to one of the closed doors along the hall, opened it, and stepped inside. Lord Farthing followed. A dirty, unkempt stick of a man was standing in front of the room's wide fireplace. He glanced over his shoulder as Cynthia and Lord Farthing entered, and Cynthia felt a jolt of revulsion at the evil she saw in that grime-creased face. Inside the fireplace, two small legs, clad in sooty rags, dangled from the chimney opening.

"Oh, I say," said Lord Farthing, "it's only the chimney sweeps. I believe today was the only day they could come —dashed inconvenient, but otherwise we'd have had to wait indefinitely."

"Be out of ye're way in a trig, guvner," said the evil-faced man as he crouched to look up at the tiny being whose limbs dangled from the chimney. His hand gripped a long ghastly-looking needle. Before Cynthia's horrified eyes the man thrust the needle viciously into the small bottom attached to the dangling legs. "Up ye git, ye whinin' riffraff!"

"*Yeee—owee—*" The sound that issued from the chimney curdled the blood in Cynthia's veins.

In an overwhelming rush of fury she ran to the fireplace. "Here, what do you think you're doing, you despicable creature!"

The man straightened to peer at her in amazement. "Needs a bit o' encouragement, he do, miss. Ye'd best stand back e'er ye git that fine frock dirty."

The small being had slipped from the chimney opening and now huddled in a corner of the fireplace, hiccuping sobs issuing from his throat. Even covered with soot from head to toe as he was, Cynthia could see that it was a small boy, a child of no more than seven or eight years.

The pitiful sobbing created a devastating effect on her. She turned a wrathful eye upon the child's persecutor. "Get away from him, you wretched beast!" And ignoring the sullen look she received in return, she bent and pulled the child from the fireplace. Trembling with fear, the boy huddled against Cynthia, further wringing her heart. She threw her arms about him, her compassion stronger than her concern over the streaks of black soot that were being deposited all along the front of her white gown.

"Ahem—Cynthia," stammered Lord Farthing. "Shouldn't interfere in things that are none of your business. Oh, I say—you're ruining your gown."

Rounding on him, Cynthia demanded in a voice that could be heard over most of the house, "How can you stand there and babble about a—a *gown* when this child is being *tortured!*"

The boy buried his face in white muslin and pleaded in the most pitiful accents, "Please, lady—don't let 'im 'urt me no more. Don't make me go with 'im. 'E'll beat me when 'e gits me outta 'ere."

"There, there," Cynthia soothed, pressing the child's head against her side. "I can't *conceive* of a father treating a child with such cruelty!"

The boy lifted a sooty tear-streaked face to say, " 'E ain't me da', lady. 'E bought me from th' gent what stole me away from me 'ome."

Cynthia regarded the filthy personage before her with the utmost loathing. "Fiend!"

At that moment Lady Farthing and Lord Marlbridge burst into the room, followed by several other guests.

"What is the meaning of all this commotion?" demanded Lady Farthing, coming to a sudden halt as she took in the scene before her.

Her son stood in the center of the room, a look of total bafflement on his face. His hands worked agitatedly, an action that in a female would have been described as wringing. Near the fireplace stood the grimiest low-born personage Lady Farthing had ever had the misfortune to look upon, since she always left dealings with members of the lower classes to her butler. And facing *that* individual was the despised Lady Cynthia, black streaks covering her face, arms, and gown and a bundle of filth that seemed to be alive clutched against her side.

"*Eeeeek!*" squawked Lady Farthing, pressing an agitated hand against her ample bosom. "Percy, this is *unforgivable!* The gel has gone distracted!"

"Oh—I say—" stammered Lord Farthing, simply perishing with embarrassment and having no earthly idea how to cope with the scene that his betrothed had created. "The boy was crying, Mama. We—we came to see who it was—"

Cynthia pointed with her free hand at the man near the fireplace. "*He* was torturing this helpless babe!"

The little knot of onlooking guests had begun to titter and murmur to each other. Lady Farthing was breathing quite heavily—gasping indignantly, in fact. "They were cleaning the chimney, idiotic gel! How dare you interfere with my hirelings!"

"Oh—I say—Mama," said Lord Farthing weakly. "I am sure Cynthia did not mean—she don't understand—"

"Oh, be quiet, Percy!" ejaculated Cynthia. "I understand *perfectly*. A heinous crime has been committed against this innocent child, and I *shall not allow* that creature to compound his sin by taking the boy out of here with him." In her soot-streaked face her gray eyes glinted with dangerous fire. "I warn you all, if this child leaves here with him, it will be over my dead body!"

It was then that her gaze fell upon Lord Marlbridge, who was standing just behind Lady Farthing, a hand clamped over his mouth, his broad shoulders shaking. "And *you*, sir!" Cynthia uttered in awful accents. "You are—are—" But before she could think of a word that would come close to doing justice to the earl, Lord Farthing found his voice.

"Cynthia—you are—distraught. I daresay you don't realize what you are saying."

"You certainly ain't going to keep that wretched ragamuffin here!" Lady Farthing informed her wrathfully.

"No, I am not," announced Cynthia. "I am going home, and I am taking the child with me." She started for the door, pulling the astonished boy along with her.

"I—ahem—" Lord Farthing took a hesitant step to follow her. "I'll have the groom bring my curricle around—"

"Percy!" Lady Farthing stopped him in his tracks. "You can't be thinking of leaving our guests!"

Lord Farthing stammered helplessly while the man beside the fireplace muttered imprecations under his breath, which drew gasps from the female guests. Into this confusion came Lord Marlbridge's voice.

"No need to cause Lady Cynthia any more embarrassment than she has already suffered," he said calmly, at which Cynthia cast him a vengeful look. "No need, either," went on the earl, "for you to desert your guests, Farthing. I'll see Lady Cynthia home."

Cynthia, her small hand—the one that was not hanging on to the boy—clenching into a fist at her side, informed him tersely that he was the *last* person in London with whom she wished to share a carriage.

"Oh, I didn't ask for your wishes in the matter," Kenyon said with an odd glint in his blue eyes. "Nor do I intend to pay them the slightest heed. I think you have created quite enough turmoil for one day, and if you are a sensible girl you will come along with me without indulging in any further dramatic orations."

Cynthia, her very considerable wrath now centered wholly on the earl, said with as much dignity as was possible under the circumstances that she begged to be excused from the remaining festivities, adding that they would all doubtless enjoy themselves far better without her, anyway. With her head held high she then followed Kenyon from the room, the grimy child grasping the now equally grimy material of her skirt and running to keep up with her.

In his carriage Kenyon, in the most matter-of-fact way, spread a carriage robe over the padded seat to protect it from the soot clinging to his two passengers. He then settled into the seat facing them and ordered his driver to take them to Grosvenor Square.

"Well, Cynthia," remarked Kenyon when they were

under way, "you certainly managed to wreak havoc on your first visit to the Farthing house."

"How do *you* know it was my first visit?" inquired Cynthia, attempting to wipe the soot from her hand on her gown, which was ruined, anyway.

"I have my ways," said Kenyon uninformatively. He glanced at the boy who, clearly awed by his elegant companions and transport, was gazing out the side window, watching mansions pass with an expression of disbelief. "What is your name, lad?"

The boy's startled regard returned to the earl. "Jem, sir."

"Jem what?" asked the earl.

"Jest Jem, sir."

"Well, Jem," said Kenyon tolerantly, "you will make less work for my groom if you will refrain from putting your hands on the side curtains."

The boy jerked his hands back, returning them to his lap where they clutched each other in a convulsive grip.

"Don't take fright, Jem," said Kenyon kindly. "No one here wishes you any harm."

The boy nodded. "Thank 'e, sir."

Kenyon continued to regard his passengers with a wry expression, and then a deep chuckle escaped him. "Lord, I wouldn't have missed that tangle for anything! To think I came near to excusing myself, too."

Cynthia made an effort to possess her soul in patience, but her indignation over Kenyon's amusement at her expense was too much to control. "I am *ever* so happy that you enjoyed it," she said with heavy sarcasm.

Kenyon grinned. "I am sure it will long be remembered as the one bright spot in an otherwise extremely dull occasion. You may have made a cake of yourself, but in addition to rescuing Jem here, the thing surely served another purpose. Lord and Lady Farthing's desertion of you in your moment of need must convince you that you had best cry off from this preposterous betrothal without delay."

"Lud!" gasped Cynthia. "How came you to know of the betrothal? We have told no one except Grandfather and Cousin Alice and Bram."

"Don't be such a gudgeon, my girl. The story is all over the ton. Surely you didn't think to keep it from your servants—and servants love nothing so well as to gossip with servants from other houses."

"Oh, that explains Lady Farthing's aggressive looks all afternoon. She *knows*, doesn't she?"

"I'd lay a considerable wager on it," observed the earl. "How you ever imagined you could tolerate that woman I cannot conceive. You've far too much of the hoyden in you for that."

"I am not the *least* interested in hearing your assessment of me," Cynthia told him stiffly. "And you needn't feel so top-lofty where Lady Farthing is concerned, for she told me that she came extremely close to marrying your father and would have done so had she not fallen in love with Percy's father."

A bark of laughter met this information. "Hell's teeth! I cannot decide whether the woman is an out-and-out fibster or merely self-deceived. My father wouldn't even discuss the alliance, even though the lady's father was quite keen to make the match and she had a considerable fortune. My grandfather was not opposed, but he was never able to force my father to do anything against his will. Even after he married my mother the poor man

184

would fall into a twitter at the mere mention of that woman's name."

"I suppose," Cynthia conceded, "it was after your father turned down the match that she settled on Grandfather's son, Oliver. He wouldn't have her, either, and I've no doubt *he* could have put her fortune to good use. That must be why she has taken me in such dislike."

"That," said the earl with amusement, "and the fact that you are too unbiddable by half."

"Well, she will *have* to accept me, for I've no intention of crying off," said Cynthia, adding virtuously, "I am not so unkind as to do a thing like that to Percy. I am . . . quite fond of him."

"Fiddlesticks! Are you forgetting that a mere two months past you informed me you were on the catch for a rich husband? I daresay it assuages your conscience to tell yourself you're fond of the gentleman. But the fact is you fancy yourself one of those boringly unselfish heroines one finds in romances and have made up your mind to sacrifice yourself on the altar of your family's good name. And if you have any crackbrain notion that your crying off from your agreement will break Farthing's heart, you are even a worse pea-goose than I imagined. The gentleman would count himself fortunate—after today's drama —to escape a lifetime of your mingle-mangles. You saw the way he refused to come to your aid just now."

"He did not refuse!" Cynthia retorted, extremely affronted by this cold appraisal of her intended's behavior. "He—he was merely surprised and didn't, for the moment, know how to help."

"He was mortified, my pippin, utterly mortified. The sight of you standing there covered with soot and vowing so melodramatically to give your life for a sweep was the

185

worst embarrassment the silly chap has ever suffered. And *that* is saying a great deal, when one considers his mama's inclination to insult him in public. Have a little compassion, Cynthia. If you go through with this marriage, you will lead Farthing a dog's life. Isn't his mama enough for him to deal with? Not that he does."

"Oh—you are—*odious!* You know nothing about my feelings for Percy, or his for me, and I will thank you to spare me your ridiculous observations on the way I choose to lead my life."

"So you have told me, repeatedly," Kenyon said cheerfully. "I only hope, for everyone's sake, that somewhere in that fanciful brain of yours there is enough sense to move you to change your mind before it is too late."

"Well, if I do, you can be certain it will be nothing you have said that has caused it!" said Cynthia crushingly. She turned to the boy, Jem, who had been following this exchange with wide, bewildered eyes. "Thank heavens we are home. Come, Jem, I'll turn you over to Hobson. You'll have to be cleaned up before you can be allowed the run of even the servants' quarters."

Kenyon hopped from the carriage and helped her and the boy to alight with elaborate formality. Cynthia raked him with an aloof stare, said curtly, "Good day, sir," and ascended the steps to the front door with the child close on her heels.

When she reached the door, Hobson had already opened it and was standing there with his mouth agape. "My lady! What has befallen you? You have been in a carriage accident!"

"I have not been in a carriage accident, Hobson," Cynthia said, sweeping past him, followed by Jem, who took one look at Hobson's face and knew where sympathy lay. He cringed against Cynthia, his teeth chattering in fright.

Hobson looked down his long nose at the boy. "May I inquire, my lady, what *that* is?"

"This is Jem, Hobson, a horribly abused child whom I have rescued from a life of unutterable horror. Will you ask Mrs. Hench to find some clothes for him and see that he has a good scrub? Where is Mary? I'll need her help immediately to set myself to rights."

"Mary is, I believe, in the kitchen having a cup with Mrs. Hench. If you wish to go directly to your chamber, I'll send her to you." Hobson walked carefully around the blackened child, sniffed disdainfully, and said, "It is not my intention to question you, Lady Cynthia, but if the waif has been taught anything other than to steal, I'll admit to an error in judgment. Follow me, boy, and see you don't touch anything or you'll answer to me for it."

"Go with Hobson, Jem," Cynthia instructed, as the child looked up at her with pleading eyes. "Don't be frightened. You'll find Hobson's bark is far worse than his bite."

This was amended a few moments later by Hobson after Cynthia had ascended the stairs. "You'll discover much more than you want to know about my bite if I catch you putting a hand on anything in this house that don't belong to you, chappy. Now come with me and be quick about it."

Jem's past life had made it incumbent upon him, if he were to survive, to develop a shrewdness uncommon in one so young, and only a few days were required for the boy to discover that Lady Cynthia's assessment of the butler was nearer to the truth than Hobson's own. In fact, Jem, who lost no time in making himself useful in the stables and about the house, quickly won the sympathy of all the servants. Mrs. Hench took it upon herself to see that more flesh was added to Jem's skeletal frame, and the boy was permitted to eat in the kitchen with Mrs. Hench and Hobson, rather than at the long table in the servants' hall behind the kitchen. It was during these shared meals that Mrs. Hench learned all that Jem could tell her of his background.

Every scrap of the information thus elicited was passed along to Cynthia. "I tell you it just tears my heart to hear the boy talk, my lady," Mrs. Hench said to Cynthia about a week after Jem's arrival at the house.

Cynthia had sent for the housekeeper in the hope that some new bit of knowledge had been added to the little Mrs. Hench had learned already. Cynthia had been sitting at the small escritoire in the green saloon when the housekeeper appeared. She had immediately left the letter she was writing, impatient to know what clues the housekeeper might have turned up since their last conversation.

"He don't remember his parents at all," Mrs. Hench continued with a mournful shake of her head, "or any names other than that he was called Jem. He remembers playing in a garden, but has no idea in what part of the country it might have been. He recollects a cow and a big dog, so it's my opinion he lived on a farm or in a small village. His father might have been a farmer."

"Poor child," Cynthia murmured. "He must have been taken from home very young."

"Yes, miss," agreed Mrs. Hench. "He recalls that he was playing in the garden when a man came up to him and began to talk, as Jem says, 'ever so friendly like.' I believe the man lured Jem away from the garden for then—he don't recall the details—he found himself being carried in the man's arms and when he started to cry the man clapped a hand over his mouth. Jem says it was night— although I believe several hours must have passed, for what would a small child be doing playing in a garden after dark? Anyway, he must have fallen asleep—"

"Or was given something to make him unconscious," Cynthia put in.

"That would not surprise me, either, Lady Cynthia," stated Mrs. Hench, "for he woke next day in a house in London."

"He told me," said Cynthia, "that he was sold to the master of the chimney sweeps."

"Yes, my lady, and it seems the house where he found himself is the one where many sweeps live all crowded together. From what Jem has said, their master is cruel to them and they aren't given enough to eat—of course, abody could see *that* from looking at Jem—and they are forced to go up into those dark, narrow, filthy chimneys where there's not enough air to breathe, and if they object they get a beating."

"Or a needle buried in their flesh," said Cynthia with a shudder. "Well, the more we hear, the more horrible the tale grows. From all Jem has been able to tell us, most of the sweeps are kidnapped as very young children and never see their families again. With the treatment they receive, I don't see how many of them could live to be grown men." She broke off with a sigh of frustration.

"Aye, Miss," said the housekeeper grimly, "they would be of little use to their masters once they grew too big to climb up chimneys."

"Jem belongs with his parents, Mrs. Hench, but finding them seems an impossible task. I've thought of one thing I might do, however—place an advertisement in the *Gazette* describing Jem. Perhaps his family or someone who knows them might see it."

"Oh, my lady," said Mrs. Hench earnestly, "that is a fine idea. You are very clever to have thought of it."

Cynthia brushed this aside dispiritedly. "It's only a small thing. The chances of Jem's parents seeing the advertisement are probably not good. And what of all those other children who have been taken from their parents and are even now suffering as Jem has suffered for so long? I wish it were possible to do something for them."

"You have saved Jem's life, Lady Cynthia," the housekeeper told her, "for I am convinced he could not have lived much longer if he had stayed with the sweeps. Even if we never find his family, he'll make a good groom, maybe even a driver. He's that bright, he is."

When the housekeeper had returned to her duties, Cynthia paced restlessly about the saloon, seeing in her mind the cruel picture that Jem's fragmentary memories were painting, and becoming more indignant and determined to do something about this rotten sore festering in the great city of London. By the time Lord Farthing called the next day, she had formulated the outlines of a plan. Unfortunately, not even the first step could be taken without money, and it was for this reason that she was compelled to discuss her plan with Lord Farthing.

It was the third time she had seen him since the afternoon of his mother's rout. According to Lord Farthing, his mother had demanded, after the rout, to know if the rumors of a betrothal were true. He had admitted that they were, and she had not unexpectedly "kicked up the devil of a dust," as the baron had predicted, dwelling at some length on the unforgivably ill-bred scene Cynthia had created and the girl's insane insistence upon taking the boy from his rightful master and installing him in her own house. The afternoon's chaos, pointed out Lady Farthing, was merely a small sample of the imbroglios Percy could expect to characterize his life should he marry the girl.

However, Lord Farthing had told Cynthia, optimistically if unrealistically, that he believed his mother would accept his choice in time. "What else can she do?" he had asked Cynthia naively, but his betrothed had not given voice to any of the possible alternatives that had crossed her mind. Cynthia was, in fact, finding it much more comfortable to put the betrothal out of her thoughts altogether for the time being. Besides, she was caught up in Jem's plight, and it was this that she was determined to discuss with Lord Farthing when he put in an appearance at the house.

After they had been served tea and cakes in the green saloon, Lady Sedgegood excused herself, since Cynthia had told her cousin before Lord Farthing's arrival that it was imperative she talk to him alone. Cynthia had no notion of, nor could she have been said to be to blame for, the hopeful suspicion that was born in Lady Sedgegood's breast by this request. Surely, that lady told herself, she is going to do the only sensible thing and break off the engagement.

The engagement, however, was very far from Cynthia's mind as she faced Lord Farthing over the cakes remaining on the tea tray and came immediately to the point. "I know you must be wondering how Jem is faring."

Lord Farthing blinked at her, his face taking on a blank expression, causing Cynthia to suspect that, far from wondering how Jem was faring, the gentleman had not given the boy any thought at all since the afternoon of his mother's rout.

"Er—ahem—Jem?" inquired Lord Farthing perplexedly.

"The boy I rescued from your chimney," Cynthia reminded him pungently. "He has been working in our stables, and Mrs. Hench is feeding him well. The poor mite was nothing but a bag of bones when I brought him here. Oh, Percy, you would be so saddened to hear that child tell of his past."

"Oh, I say—don't imagine there is any need to concern

yourself with that, for I can't conceive why *I* should engage him in conversation. No, no—don't fret yourself about it."

"I did not mean to imply that I am worried about *you,* Percy," Cynthia informed him, reining her irritation with difficulty. "Did you know that small children are kidnapped and sold for a few guineas to men who force them to go up chimneys?"

"Ahem—" said Lord Farthing. "Everybody knows about climbing boys, Cynthia. Must say I never wondered where they came from, no more than I wonder why other children become pickpockets. Something in the blood, I expect. Poor breeding always comes out, you know. Fortunately we are not required to come into contact with that sort—"

"Yes, we do live such a . . . protected life, don't we, Percy?" responded Cynthia musingly.

"Er—I didn't mean—"

"But," Cynthia continued, "perhaps it is time we *did* think about such things. Jem was *stolen* from his home when he was very young. From what he has told Mrs. Hench, I am convinced that hundreds of children all over England, perhaps even on the Continent, are taken in similar manner, plucked away from their families and sold into slavery."

"Shouldn't addle your brain with thoughts of such unfortunate goings-on," advised Lord Farthing. "Not at all the thing for a lady to be concerned about. Why, if one dwelt on all the evil done in the world, I daresay one would soon run quite mad."

Cynthia leaned forward in her chair to say impatiently, "I'm not dwelling on *all* the world's evil, merely this unspeakable wrong being done to innocent children in a Christian nation. Something *must* be done, Percy."

"Done?" asked Lord Farthing, bewildered. "Oh, I say, you aren't suggesting that you and I—that we—?"

"You won't even have to become directly involved in the undertaking. All I am asking of you, Percy, is financial backing."

Dismay etched unattractive lines in Lord Farthing's normally pleasant face. "Financial backing?" he repeated as if he were parroting foreign words, their meaning incomprehensible.

Taking advantage of his seeming vacillation, Cynthia said, "I want to establish a house where these children can be cared for. We'll have to hire a couple to see after them, and of course we must place advertisements and pursue other ways of finding their families. Once the children learn that a sanctuary exists where they will be protected from their cruel masters, they will come. Jem will know how to spread the word about and—"

She halted abruptly, having become aware that Lord Farthing's face had gone very pale and that he was attempting to speak. Finally, he said in one explosive breath, "Out of the question!"

Cynthia frowned. "But why? Oh, Percy, you aren't going to sit there and tell me your heart is not *touched* by the plight of these children!"

"My heart's nothing to the purpose," Lord Farthing told her. "Must confess to a bit of a twinge when I learned they draw *geese* up the chimneys in Ireland." He grimaced with distaste before going on. "Thing is, Mama controls the purse strings. Shouldn't care to be the one to mention such a scheme to *her*. Must tell you not to consider anything so ill-advised as speaking to her yourself, either.

194

She's already convinced you're a bit—willful. Might give her a spasm."

"*I'm* a bit willful—" sputtered Cynthia. "Oh, never mind that now. We are speaking of children, not geese! And I thought—I mean, I was under the impression you had your own fortune."

"I do," confirmed Lord Farthing, "but Mama's always managed my money, just as she did Papa's. She's quite good at it, you know, and I must own I find thinking about butchers' bills and decorators' fees and the like too boring by half. Told you already I prefer living in the country, hunting, and ambling about the pastures and animal pens. Thought you preferred that kind of life, too."

"Tell me, Percy," said Cynthia reflectively, "do you intend ever to take over the management of your fortune? Surely after we are married—"

"No reason to rearrange things just because I'm married," stated Lord Farthing complacently. "Besides, Mama *likes* taking charge, you know."

"I daresay," murmured Cynthia with an edge of irony that was lost on the gentleman.

Lord Farthing watched her for a moment. "Best thing for all concerned if you will abandon this notion. Didn't want to upset you further but—the day of the rout—when I summoned the butler to show the sweep's master out of the house, the scoundrel threatened to speak to some personage he called 'the gent' who might be expected to do you some harm. Stood outside and argued with my man for a full quarter hour. Finally, I went out to see what was transpiring. Fortunately, Lord Marlbridge returned from seeing you home just then and paid the man eight guineas, which is what the low fellow claimed to have paid for the boy. Said it had not been at all a good investment, though, for the boy was a troublemaker from the start."

Cynthia was staring at him. "Lord Marlbridge did *what?*" She shot to her feet and now stood, glaring down at Lord Farthing in amazement. "You mean he actually bought Jem—paid for him like a piece of merchandise?"

"Said it was the only way of assuring the man wouldn't try to find you and take the boy back—or harm you," said Lord Farthing with unarguable logic. "Must say I agreed with him. Would have done it myself if I'd thought of it," he added righteously. "Can't have a person of such low character and breeding coming around *here.*"

"I do wish that *man* would stay out of my affairs," fumed Cynthia.

Lord Farthing's sandy brows rose in consternation. "Shouldn't think *that* one would care about your wishes, Cynthia."

"I mean the earl," Cynthia uttered exasperatedly.

"Lord Marlbridge? Oh, I say, I thought it was very decent of him. Have to learn to think before you act, Cynthia, and then people won't have to follow you about setting things right. The earl said that, and he was right."

"Indeed!" flared Cynthia.

"Oh, I daresay you will behave with more propriety after we are married. Bound to. Taking up causes is quite unladylike, you know. Even if I could lay my hands on the money, I couldn't put it down for such an unacceptable scheme as the one you've lodged in your head. When you have thought about it, I am sure you will realize it's not at all the thing for a lady of quality to become involved in. Plenty of other things for you to do."

"I know," said Cynthia with heavy sarcasm. "Walking

in the park, going to parties and the theater, keeping up with the latest on-dits—"

A smile of approval wreathed Lord Farthing's pale face. "Exactly so, Cynthia. Sensible gel. Well, I expect I had better take my leave now. May I call again on Friday?"

"Umm—yes," murmured Cynthia, only half hearing the question. "Good afternoon, Percy."

When he was gone, she stood for several moments in the center of the saloon, turning over in her mind other possible means of financing the house for chimney sweeps. It did not take long to discard every idea but one. With purposeful steps, she crossed to the escritoire, sat down, and took out notepaper, ink, and pen. After thinking deeply for a moment, she put pen to paper and wrote hurriedly.

Then she folded the note, sealed it, and carried it from the saloon. A few minutes later she found one of the grooms in the servants' hall and instructed him to carry the note to Lord Marlbridge's house in Bedford Square immediately.

Returning to the front of the house, she heard voices in the entry hall. "But, Cavey, I thought your father had sworn to have nothing to do with his cousin—or the fellow's money."

Cynthia reached the entry hall in time to see Bramford and Lord Caverset putting away their coats and beavers in the ebony wardrobe.

"So he did," Lord Caverset was saying, "but my father's pride, I believe, has given way to what one might call necessity. I need not scruple to tell you, Bram, for I fear it is common knowledge, that my father's fortune is now totally depleted. Circumstances have been straitened for some time. You know how he's forever summoning me to the family seat, giving me a set-down for being such a scattergood. Well, I will own that I looked forward to the trip this time. When I told him his cousin had settled a fortune on me, he began to rant that he hoped he should never stoop so low as to touch a farthing made in trade and claimed he was excessively disappointed in me for doing so. I pointed out to him that for someone whose situation was desperate, he was a great deal too nice in his requirements. He rattled on for some time, but he saw my point nevertheless."

"Well, I still don't know why you couldn't have told me at the beginning, instead of letting me think you'd hit a run of luck at the races."

"Just bamming you a bit, Bram," said Lord Caverset good-naturedly. He had turned from the wardrobe and was smoothing the perfectly aligned folds of his cravat. He settled his shoulders comfortably in a deep blue coat of the finest kerseymere, glanced up, and saw Cynthia. "Oh, hallo, Lady Cynthia. You're looking in fine fettle."

Bramford turned from the wardrobe. "Dash it, Cyn, where is Hobson? Seems I've had to fetch and carry for myself this past week. Deuced inconvenient!"

"I daresay he is in the kitchen with Mrs. Hench and Jem," Cynthia told him.

Bramford's blue eyes rolled heavenward. "Should've known. Seems the man has forgotten where his duties lie."

"Don't be cross," Cynthia said cajolingly. "Surely it is not excessively inconvenient to put away your coat now and then. Why don't you and Cavey come into the green saloon. Tea is still laid."

The gentlemen followed her into the saloon and made themselves comfortable while she poured tea and set the tray within their reach.

"Well, my lady," said Lord Caverset, "I hear congratulations are in order."

Bramford shot Cynthia an apologetic look. "Didn't tell him, Cyn. Swear it."

"It's all right," Cynthia assured him. "It seems the whole ton has been aware of it for days."

"First on-dit whispered in my ear upon my return from Kent yesterday," Lord Caverset confirmed. "There was also some mention of a Cheltenham tragedy supposedly enacted by you, Lady Cynthia, at the Farthings' rout. Something about dragging a filthy chimney sweep away from his master and daring anyone to stop you. I perceive the Jem you mentioned is the sweep who figured in the dust-up."

"I am resigned," said Cynthia with a sigh, "to being the talk of the ton for the time being, at least until something else comes along to catch their attention."

Bramford grinned at his friend. "The old dragon, Lady Farthing, didn't like it above half." His blue eyes danced with amusement. "Tried to get Farthing to cry off."

"Indeed?" said Lord Caverset. "Well, I collect Farthing's too rigid a stickler to pull anything so dastardly as that."

"I say," Bram interposed, "he was supposed to call today, wasn't he, Cyn? Did you set the wedding date?"

Cynthia shook her head, a rather distracted look on her face. "No, we didn't talk of that. I—I solicited Percy's help with my plan to rescue more climbing boys, but he refused. Said it wasn't ladylike to take up causes."

Bramford laughed. "Told you he'd never agree. Should have taken my advice and kept quiet. Must say, Cyn, the scheme's too fantastical for even you to push. Ladies of quality have no business running around setting up houses for chimney sweeps and raking the back alleys for the little ragamuffins. It wouldn't do at all, and you know that Grandfather would not approve of it, even if Farthing had agreed."

"I don't mean to go into the alleys *myself*," Cynthia said impatiently. "And I would hire a couple to stay in the house with the boys. Honestly, Bram, you're as unfeeling as Percy."

Lord Caverset, who had been following this exchange with a deeply interested expression, set his teacup down and said, "No, no, Cynthia. Bram is quite right. You can't seriously be considering anything so—unseemly. Leave such things to Parliament—or those who are equipped to deal with them."

Cynthia, who had been behaving in an uncharacteristically nervous fashion ever since they had entered the saloon, started abruptly for the door. "I am sure you will both excuse me. I believe I will go to my chamber now."

As the door closed behind her, Bramford got to his feet and went to a small cabinet near one of the room's large windows. "Rather have brandy than tea, Cavey. Will you join me?"

Lord Caverset said that, indeed, he would. As he watched his friend pour the drinks and carry them across the room, he added, "Bram, you have to stop her, you know. Can't let her go dashing about town like—like Lady Caroline Lamb."

Bramford chuckled appreciatively and selected a cake from the tea tray. He sat down, ate the cake, then sipped his brandy slowly. "Shouldn't think the comparison is quite apt, old boy. Wee Jem's hardly in the same league with Byron when it comes to capturing ladies' hearts. Although—" He paused momentarily before continuing.

"Cyn has certainly got up on her high ropes over the climbing boys. Convinced they've all been kidnapped and sold into slavery."

"Expect that tyke Jem's an accomplished fibster," mused Lord Caverset, staring into his brandy. "I mean, he'd have to be to have lived in the London streets. He's probably filled her ears with the most shocking Canterbury tales—to gain her sympathy, you know."

Bramford shrugged, losing interest in the chimney sweeps. "Possibly. Anyway, there is little Cyn can do about the sweeps now since Farthing turned down her request for money. She's no one else to turn to."

"Good thing," observed Lord Caverset. "It's my opinion you ought to push for a hasty marriage. Your sister needs a husband to haul her up short when she gets these sap-skull notions."

Bramford looked at his friend, then gave a crack of laughter. "Lord, Cavey, if you think Farthing's man enough to do that, you're short of a sheet. Old Percy's got no backbone and my sister, while she may look fragile, is as tough as whit leather."

The next afternoon Mary appeared in Cynthia's chamber with a reverential look on her freckled face. "Lady Cynthia, you have a caller waiting in the green saloon. The Earl of Graybroughton." This last was uttered with the air of one announcing the arrival of royalty.

Cynthia dropped the embroidery on which she had been trying to concentrate and stood abruptly. "Well, he has certainly taken his time about it!"

Mary seemed taken aback by her mistress's antagonistic reaction. "You were expecting him, my lady?"

"Certainly I was expecting him, Mary," Cynthia responded as she moved toward the chamber door. "I asked him to come."

The abigail's mouth pursed in a moue of consternation, at which Cynthia said, "Oh, you needn't look so disapproving, Mary. I want to see the earl on a matter of business." She walked from the chamber, leaving Mary to stare after her in bewilderment.

In the green saloon Kenyon was lounging with one long arm resting on the mantelpiece. He straightened as Cynthia entered, his blue eyes regarding her with a watchful expression.

"Good afternoon, Kenyon," she said in cool tones.

He made his bow. "Your servant, ma'am."

She scanned his face closely. "I expected you yesterday."

"Your impatience is well known to me, my girl, and I confess I was intrigued by your note inviting me to call upon you at my earliest convenience. Unfortunately, I was otherwise engaged until now."

Cynthia had not expected to find it so difficult to voice her request, but under Kenyon's steady and much-too-insightful regard, she discovered that she was casting about for the proper words.

As she hesitated, Kenyon strolled to one of the saloon's armchairs, inquired "May I?" and, upon receiving her nod, sat and leaned back in the chair, watching her. "If you have brought me here to deliver another set-down on behalf of your friend, Miss Bloomhedge, I believe I can save you the effort. The young lady cannot have failed to notice my aversion to her conversation of late, and she has, so my sister tells me, been paying marked attention to Lord Silverstone. I would not be at all surprised to hear an announcement from that quarter before the season is out. Obviously, if she felt anything at all for me, it was mere infatuation, certainly not love." He smiled teasingly. "Bit of a blow to my pride."

"That's nice," murmured Cynthia absentmindedly. She moved to a settee facing Kenyon's chair and sat down almost gingerly. His eyes watched her with curious interest. "I—I didn't ask you here to talk about Anne Bloomhedge," she said after a moment.

"May I hope," inquired Kenyon with wry amusement, "to hear the true reason for this summons, or must I guess until I hit upon it?"

"Oh, don't be so condescending," Cynthia said crossly. "I am trying to decide how to give voice to what I have to say."

"Indeed?" The thick auburn brows rose sardonically. "Well, this *is* a new development, for I have never seen you at a loss for words before. Has your—ah, approaching marriage brought about this surprising transformation?"

Cynthia rose abruptly from the settee and began to pace back and forth in front of him. "Oh, you *are* the most irritating man! Well, that does not signify. I dislike this excessively, but I could think of no other way—"

Kenyon's eyes followed her as a chuckle escaped him. "I perceive you are in the suds again and don't know how to extricate yourself."

Cynthia stopped pacing and stood in front of his chair. Kenyon stirred. "I do wish you would sit, however, for you are making me feel most ungentlemanly, taking my ease while you walk back and forth in the manner of a caged jungle beast. I do have a bit more regard for the niceties than you credit me with."

She returned to the settee and gave him a puzzled look. "You do amaze me sometimes, Kenyon. Imagine worrying about sitting while a lady stands when all the time you're—Oh, I didn't bring you here to speak of your indiscretions."

"Well! I am certainly grateful for the reprieve!"

"I need your help," Cynthia said abruptly. "I thought I could depend upon Lord Farthing for assistance, but it seems I cannot."

"Ah, the bloom is fading from the romance already, and the announcement hasn't even been published yet."

"My betrothal is . . . neither here nor there," said Cynthia stiffly. "I wish to consult you in your capacity as . . . moneylender." She paused as he sat forward in his chair, an expression of rapt attention settling over the rugged planes of his face.

"Yes?" he said expectantly.

She spoke in a sudden rush of words. "Oh, Kenyon, I have uncovered the most horrid hell right here in London, and I am convinced that even you must be shocked by it."

His sudden bark of laughter unsettled her for the moment. "Horrid hell! I am constantly amazed at the expressions that fall from those lovely lips. Well, tell me, am I to understand that you have come to believe that even a *usurer* is capable of tender feelings? I must say I am surprised, Cynthia—and *excessively* flattered. Pray, what is this 'horrid hell' to which you refer?"

Deciding, in the interest of gaining her ends, to ignore the heavy edge of mockery in his tone, Cynthia said, "The most unspeakable crimes are being committed even as we speak. Children—mere babes—are being stolen from their parents and forced into service as chimney sweeps. Jem was kidnapped from his family, and he says that most of the climbing boys are acquired in this way."

Kenyon's expression became suddenly grave. "I will

204

own that I have heard rumors of this activity. In fact, I have endeavored for some time to bring a bill before the House of Lords to abolish the employment of climbing boys altogether. I am hopeful that an official enquiry will be launched this year, but unfortunately the Earl of Lauderdale leads a very vocal contingent in opposing any such legislation."

"Oh," said Cynthia with a deep-drawn breath of relief. Yet, somehow, she had known that the earl would react with compassion, just as she had known, deep down, that Lord Farthing would feel nothing but disapproval at having such an unseemly topic of conversation thrust upon him. Nor did the knowledge strike her as incongruous as it perhaps should have done. "I am so glad that you are already concerned about this. It—it makes it easier for me to make my request. I do not know how such things are arranged, but I would like to borrow money to rent a house and employ a couple to care for these boys until their parents can be found or, failing that, suitable homes for them. I never thought when I gave Bram such a rake-down that *I* would find myself approaching a moneylender. But sometimes one *must* do things which one finds distasteful."

Kenyon had listened to this speech with a dawning astonishment. "Let me see if I understand you correctly. You are suggesting that the sweeps be stolen back from their masters?"

"I am sure that would not be necessary," Cynthia told him quickly. "When they learn there is a house where they can go, they will come to us of their own accord. We can place advertisements in the *Gazette,* and although I cannot say precisely when I could repay the loan, I know that after my marriage I will be able to find the money—somehow."

The earl was shaking his head. "God's beard! I had thought you could no longer astonish me, but I see I was wrong. Do you not realize that what you are suggesting could put you in dire danger? Men who make their living by kidnapping children would not scruple to dispose of anyone who tried to stop their ignominious trade."

"I cannot wait for Parliament to act," Cynthia said stubbornly, "for that might take years. Something must be done *now*, Kenyon, and if you are worried about repayment—"

"Be quiet and listen to me!" instructed the earl with a note of command that momentarily brought Cynthia up short. "There is something I must tell you. Indeed, I have tried to tell you before, but you would not listen."

"But—"

The look he gave her made the protest die on her lips. "You will sit quietly, for once, and listen to what I have to say." The steely tone brooked no argument. "I am not now, nor have I ever been, a moneylender. The day you met me in Clarges Street I had gone there to call on an old soldier with whom I served in the Peninsula." He raised a hand in warning when she opened her mouth. "No, his name is not Higgins. That house is a lodging place for several gentlemen. I saw you walking up and down in front of the place, trying to get up the courage to come in. Suspecting that you were in some kind of trouble, I intercepted you."

Cynthia would not be silenced any longer. "But this is unbelievable! You let me think you were Higgins's associate!"

"You chose to think that, my girl. You jumped to the

206

conclusion and refused to be budged from it. After meeting you, I realized you had no idea what sort of person you were bent on involving yourself with. When you left, I made myself known to Higgins and relieved him of your brother's IOU."

Cynthia was on her feet once more, pacing agitatedly. "I do not understand this at all! You bought Bram's IOU? And Percy tells me you paid that vile sweep master for Jem, too. I cannot conceive why you seem moved to these —these rescue missions, for I must say you do not strike me as being excessively chivalrous. I suppose I must be grateful, but I cannot fathom why you have done it."

"Oh, I have given that some considerable thought myself," Kenyon said with an odd narrowing of the blue eyes, "and I believe I have come upon an explanation, which I'll reveal to you at the proper time and in the proper place. At present, though, I am more concerned with disabusing you of this insane penchant you seem to have to sacrifice yourself for others."

"I certainly do not wish to get into a brangle with you over that again," she exclaimed. "Truly, Kenyon, how *could* you have allowed me to think—Oh, this is the outside of enough! Well, it seems I shall have to look elsewhere for aid. But you needn't concern yourself with that. This is *my* problem, not yours, Kenyon."

"By confiding in me, you have made it mine," the earl pointed out. "Besides, I have a strong notion that you will not rest until you have created the worst tangle of your life if I do not intervene."

"I haven't time to worry about your notions," Cynthia told him. "And if you are thinking of speaking to Grandfather—"

Kenyon shrugged. "I shall not hesitate to do that, if you

207

persist in defying me. You foolish child! This is not a game. If the rumors are true, the depraved creatures involved in this network of child-stealing are wicked beyond anything you have ever imagined. You would not have the least idea how to cope with them."

"Are you suggesting that I *ignore* what Jem has told me?" asked Cynthia loftily.

"I am asking you—no, I am *telling* you, Cynthia—to wait." She tried to respond once more with hot disapproval, but he forestalled her. "No, I've had quite enough of your indignation for one afternoon! I am willing to concede that your idea of establishing a house for sweeps has some merit. There are, however, ways of going about such an undertaking without exposing yourself to criminals. Do I have your promise that you will do nothing until you hear from me?"

After a moment's hesitation she nodded reluctantly. "I—I have just realized," she said with dismay, "that regardless of how you acquired it, you do hold Bram's IOU and I am still under obligation to repay you."

"By all means," Kenyon agreed, his face grave, but his eyes alight once more with amusement. "And I assure you, I have every intention of demanding payment at the proper time. There are, however, other means of restitution besides money."

"I am sure I do not know what you mean," put in Cynthia.

"Never mind," advised Kenyon complacently. "We shall leave that for another day at which time, I promise you, you will understand completely."

She stared at him in perplexity, then said, "Oh, I am afraid I have quite forgotten my manners. I should have offered you some refreshment."

"Don't fret yourself," recommended Kenyon, coming slowly to his feet. "I haven't time for that. If you will excuse me, I must be on my way."

"Of course." Cynthia saw him from the saloon, unable to understand the sense of disappointment she was feeling. It was almost as if she *wanted* him to stay for refreshment. She shook her head. No, it was more than that. Kenyon's startling revelation that he was not guilty of the shameful activities of which she had repeatedly accused him had quite thrown her. She had a strong suspicion, too, that he had been amusing himself at her expense, allowing her to go on for such an unforgivably long time in her mistaken assumption. What a wretched, infuriating man he was!

12

A few days later, having received an invitation to tea from
Lady Madeline Witherspoon, Cynthia was not excessively
surprised to find Kenyon present as well. The earl's mo-
tives might continue to bewilder her, but after his call at
the house in Grosvenor Square she felt she could no longer
be amazed by him. On the other hand, Lady Sedgegood,
who accompanied Cynthia, was not only surprised to see
the earl but clearly pleased. That lady exchanged a knowing glance with Lady Witherspoon, which suggested that
she was aware of certain undercurrents here, even if her
hostess were not.

To say the truth, Lady Witherspoon was more befud-
dled than anyone present. Her brother had come to her
and asked that she invite Cynthia to tea. Lady Witherspoon had pressed to know the reason for such a startling
request, but had been told merely that he wanted to discuss some sort of charitable society with both Cynthia and
herself. Lady Witherspoon had had to be content with

that, but she, like Lady Sedgegood, suspected there was more going on than the formation of some vague society. She had, of course, heard the rumors of a betrothal between Cynthia and Lord Farthing. She had mentioned the rumors to Kenyon, who had shrugged and further confused her by saying enigmatically, "A betrothal and a marriage are two very different kettles of fish, Maddy."

As soon as greetings had been exchanged, however, Lady Witherspoon began to experience a feeling of disappointment, for Kenyon immediately dispensed with chit-chat and said in a brisk manner, "Cynthia and I have spoken previously about the plight of young boys employed as chimney sweeps." He went on to explain, much to the dismay of his sister and Lady Sedgegood, whose hopes for a romantic intrigue were being quickly dashed, how such children were stolen from their homes and forced into servitude to hard masters. "I have decided," continued the earl after this explanation, "to establish and fund a society for the protection of climbing boys. I have rented a house near—but, no, I think it wise to keep the location of the place a secret. I have employed a couple to live there and arranged to place advertisements in the *Gazette* to inform the general public of the society's purpose and to solicit further contributions. I am hopeful that you ladies will help me in that aspect by putting in a good word for the endeavor with your friends."

Cynthia had listened to the earl's discourse with growing excitement. Finally she interrupted to say, "It's the perfect solution, Kenyon! I cannot imagine why I didn't think of establishing a society myself. No one will know who is behind it."

"At least, no one who might wish harm to the society's founders," Kenyon amended.

Lady Witherspoon listened to this exchange with some confusion but a resurgence of hope. How, she wondered, had her brother and Cynthia Chattington become so well acquainted that their address had been shortened to the familiar Christian names? It was evident that they were so accustomed to addressing each other in this way that they had not even noticed the breach of etiquette. But they hadn't, as far as she knew, been in each other's company above five times. Occasionally, as she was well aware from personal experience, an unexplainedly intimate rapport can be established between a man and a woman after what others might consider only a few casual encounters. Yet, she told herself in mystification, if *this* is a courtship, it is a strange courtship indeed.

When Lady Sedgegood and Cynthia had gone, Lady Witherspoon attempted by a roundabout means to gain some indication of her brother's feelings for the young lady. She poured him a glass of Madeira and said, as she looked closely into his handsome face, "So, now you've become a founder of charitable societies! I hardly know what to expect next."

He laughed and said good-naturedly, "Is this the preamble to reading me one of your scolds, Maddy? For if it is, I must tell you that I can well afford the sum I mean to invest."

"No, dearest Kenyon," she said gravely, but with a smile lurking in her blue eyes. "In fact, I think it is a laudable thing you are doing. And Cynthia certainly seems to approve of it."

"Of course she does, for it was she who suggested some of the details of the plan in the first place."

"I suppose I should have realized that," said Lady Witherspoon, "for I recall hearing something about a

212

chimney sweep at work while Lady Farthing's recent rout was in progress—although I must say I think that an odd time to have hirelings about, but when one considers that this is the busiest time of the year for cleaning chimneys, I expect Lady Farthing had to use them on that particular day or wait weeks for another appointment." Realizing that she was straying from the thrust of her inquiry, she continued quickly, "At any rate, there was some exaggerated tale about Cynthia's coming to the sweep's aid."

"I am inclined to think," said the earl, "that the tale was not exaggerated at all. I was there, you see, and Cynthia did create a rare bumble-bath."

"And then *you* took her home, I am told," observed Lady Witherspoon in careless accents.

"I confess I did, Maddy," said Kenyon, "for it was obvious that poor Farthing hadn't the *least* notion of how to cry halt to the Cheltenham tragedy that Cynthia was enacting for the Farthings' guests."

Lady Witherspoon's look was meditative. "I have become fairly well acquainted with Cynthia these last few weeks, and I must own I feel, more than ever, that she is not the proper wife for Lord Farthing."

"In that," remarked the earl blandly, "the gentleman's mother would agree."

"Yes, the on-dits have it that Lady Farthing is making the most impolite comments about Cynthia to her friends. Do you know, I am rather surprised that Lord Farthing defied his mother to the extent of offering for the girl."

"Maddy," Kenyon told her, "it is clear that you are not aware of the lengths to which Cynthia will go once an intention takes hold of that capricious brain of hers. In the present instance, however, I fear she, as well as Farthing, is coming to regret her precipitousness."

"Indeed?" inquired Lady Witherspoon with interest. "Has she told you that?"

"Oh, no," admitted her brother. "*She* swears they are well pleased with the bargain."

Lady Witherspoon frowned perplexedly. "Then I don't see—"

"Dear Maddy," interrupted the earl, smiling at her, "I would be willing to sit here for some time discussing with you Cynthia Chattington's eccentricities, but I want to be at the newspaper office to place an advertisement before closing time."

"Fustian!" exclaimed Lady Witherspoon, concealing under indignation her fondness for her brother. "Don't think you can flummery *me!* You know I am intrigued by this odd acquaintanceship that has evidently developed between you and Cynthia Chattington. And you don't mean to satisfy my curiosity, do you? Well, I had a comfortable coze with Lady Sedgegood one afternoon not long ago, and she told me that Cynthia has been behaving in a positively Gothic manner—particularly where you are concerned."

Kenyon prepared to make his departure. "Sister, I must tell you that Cynthia's behavior is frequently Gothic, and without the least nudge from me. I do feel that there will be no marriage with Farthing, not if Lady Farthing is up to her usual mark."

"Am I to understand," inquired Lady Witherspoon meaningfully, "that you are prepared to throw some obstacle in the path of this alliance yourself if Lady Farthing fails?"

"Why, Maddy, you have a strangely indelicate opinion of me," said the earl reproachfully. "Besides, I am sure the need for anything so inelegant will not arise, for I have the utmost confidence in Lady Farthing."

She burst out laughing. "Scoundrel!"

He smiled. "Ah, you have caught me out, Maddy."

"I should rather think I have!" she responded with another gurgle of laughter.

Nevertheless, even the earl could not have expected Lady Farthing to bring Cynthia to the end of her rope so quickly. Cynthia should have suspected what her ladyship was about when she began to receive almost daily invitations to take tea at the Farthing town house, and undoubtedly she would have, had not her mind been almost wholly occupied with her efforts at fund raising for the Society for the Protection of Climbing Boys. These efforts consisted of penning notes to friends among the quality requesting the opportunity to introduce them and their acquaintances to the society, and then speaking to small groups of women brought together in their homes by these friends.

An initial advertisement had appeared in the newspaper announcing the formation of the society and its avowed purpose to rescue young sweeps from a life of drudgery and, undoubtedly, an early death. There was also a detailed description of Jem and his few memories of the time before he was taken from his home. Anyone having information concerning the boy's family was urged to write a letter to that effect, addressed to the society, and leave it with a well-known firm of London solicitors.

Because of these speaking engagements, Cynthia was unable to accept all of Lady Farthing's invitations, but she appeared as often as she could in the dreadful Egyptian saloon, where Percy's mama seemed to pass a great deal of her time. She told herself that the invitations were by way of a peace offering. Before the end of the second afternoon thus spent, however, she realized that nothing could be farther from the truth. In fact, Lady Farthing's conversation seemed to center upon certain conditions under which Percy's wife must expect to live her life, conditions that Cynthia might not find completely to her liking.

Cynthia was left in no doubt that she and Percy would make their home with Lady Farthing for the greater part of the year at Farthingate, that Lady Farthing would continue to manage Percy's fortune, and that Cynthia would be expected to fit herself, as best she could, into the routine that Lady Farthing had worked out for herself and her son years ago and found so very much to her taste.

As usual, Lady Farthing did most of the talking. But Percy, who was present also, did not contradict her, from which state of affairs Cynthia could only suppose that he was in agreement with everything her ladyship said.

Still, Cynthia might have managed to keep her own counsel against the time when she would be Percy's wife and in a much better position to assert herself, if Lady Farthing had not chosen, upon the occasion of Cynthia's fourth visit to the Egyptian saloon in late May, to take her to task for her role in the activities of the charitable society.

"Lady Hallum told me something yesterday," said the clearly disapproving matron, "and I must tell you, Cynthia, I can hardly credit it."

Cynthia sipped her tea and said cautiously, "Oh? What is that, my lady?"

"If Lady Hallum has the straight of it, the Earl of Graybroughton is behind those gauche advertisements that have been appearing in the *Gazette,* the ones appealing for contributions to some organization meant to wrest climbing boys from their rightful masters and put the urchins in the homes of complete strangers."

"I believe," murmured Cynthia, "that the main goal of the society is to find the boys' own families from which they were stolen. Apparently you have been misinformed about another matter as well, Lady Farthing. The masters cannot, by anyone's definition, be said to be the 'rightful' ones, for they are involved in a criminal network in which the children are kidnapped and placed under their dictate."

"You," observed Lady Farthing, stiffening, "seem to be remarkably well advised on this matter. I collect Lady Hallum's information was not all false. Can it be true, gel, that you are lecturing on behalf of this society?"

Cynthia, seeing the trap laid before her, glanced at Lord Farthing and found him unwilling to meet her eye. "I—I have spoken to small groups of women a few times."

Lady Farthing's eyes appeared to be about to pop from her head. "Eh, what? Didn't like to believe it, seeing that you are betrothed to Percy. Well! It is fortunate I heard of it this early. Since you have no mother, I can only assume you have not been instructed in the finer points of ladylike behavior. You will have to stop this sort of thing at once, of course! I'll not have anyone in *my* family taking up causes like a—a common member of the working class!"

Lord Farthing's face had gone quite pale, but Cynthia could only guess at what he was thinking, for he did not speak. She set her teacup down on a side table and lifted her chin. "I am not, Lady Farthing, a member of your family yet. Nor do I see anything common or unladylike in what I am doing. Since the earl, who I am sure you will agree is a person of some consequence, is involved, I cannot think you will persist in this unreasonable attitude."

"Unreasonable!" ejaculated her ladyship, casting a darkling glance in her son's direction. "Did you hear that, Percy? Eh, what? Said all along she wasn't up to the Farthings' weight. Didn't I say that, Percy?"

Lord Farthing, now blushing furiously, was bound to admit that she had done so, but added, "I say, Mama—don't see any reason to discuss this at the present."

Further aroused by this hint of insubordination, Lady Farthing said in tones of awful determination, "Should have been discussed *before* this! Always knew any granddaughter of that old rumstick couldn't be everything that she should be. Thank my lucky stars I didn't accept his son's proposal!"

By this time Cynthia's tautly confined temper had begun to seep past its bounds. "It is my understanding," she said with portentous calm, "that it was my Uncle Oliver who turned down your father's proposal."

Seeing the confrontation gathering force quickly, Lord Farthing at last attempted to sound a note of conciliation. "Mama—Cynthia, I wish you will not say things you will later regret."

"Be quiet, Percy!" ordered her ladyship. "I would expect that old mawworm to twist the actual happening to suit himself!"

"Are you suggesting that my grandfather is a fibster?" asked Cynthia, a flame leaping in her gray eyes.

"Ain't suggesting!" thundered Lady Farthing, lumbering to her feet to stand glaring down at the seditionist in their midst. "Saying it outright! What do you say to that, gel?"

"I suppose Lord Marlbridge is another, for putting out

218

that his father, too, refused your hand and your fortune."
By this time, Cynthia's temper had lost all restraint. She got to her feet, trembling, and stood watching the furious woman facing her.

"Viper!" shrieked Lady Farthing. "This, Percy, is the shameless creature you propose to install in my house!"

Cynthia, who had never been in quite such a heated imbroglio before, discovered that she felt faint. Somehow she managed to hold up her head and say, "If you think for one moment that I would live in the same house with a—a *sarcophagus,* you are very much mistaken!" She swept one disdainful glance about the Egyptian saloon, shuddered, turned on her heel, and strode from the room, her skirts swishing about her.

Descending the stairs hastily, she went to the door, ignoring the questioning butler, and seeing her grand-father's carriage with the waiting groom outside, she departed. To her vast relief, no one tried to stop her.

Safely on her way to Grosvenor Square, she sank back against the squabs, tears of mingled rage and horror at what she had done trickling down her ivory cheeks.

There were no more invitations to take tea with Lady Farthing, even though Lord Farthing continued to escort Cynthia to social gatherings. It was too much to be expected that the story of that angry verbal exchange—at least Lady Farthing's version of it—would not reach other ears and soon be commented upon in all the houses of the quality. Adding fuel to the rumors, her ladyship lost no opportunity to enlarge upon Cynthia's shortcomings.

Members of the haut ton were of two minds about Lady Cynthia Chattington's involvement in the Society for the Protection of Climbing Boys. The vacillation was caused by the knowledge that the Earl of Graybroughton was the prime mover of the organization and, it was further rumored, intended to introduce a bill in the House of Lords to have the employment of child chimney sweeps outlawed.

To further obscure the issue, it was said that the earl's sister, Lady Madeline Witherspoon, whose husband's family was as highly regarded as her own, had, at elegant breakfasts in her town house, invited her closest friends to contribute to the cause.

As for Lord Farthing, he was extremely careful to avoid any mention of the society or the harsh words exchanged by his mama and his betrothed, although at home he was frequently subjected to long harangues on the subject from his still-irate parent. In truth, Lord Farthing found himself in an almost constant state of misgiving, for he was beginning to have a premonition of the sort of life he might expect to have in the future. It would be fraught with continual upheavals instigated by either his mother or his wife. Unhappily, Lord Farthing loved peace above all things.

Sensing his dilemma over the situation, Cynthia did not speak of unpleasant topics to him, either. But as June progressed, she felt more and more depressed whenever she thought of marrying Percy and subjecting him to the permanent state of being caught between two strong-willed females.

When she was being totally honest with herself, she had to admit that her reluctance to press for a formal announcement of the betrothal was not caused solely by her concern for Percy's peace of mind. To own the truth, she found herself, at various entertainments and gatherings of the ton, more and more aware of the earl. His disclosure that he was not engaged in dishonorable activities made her wonder what other things he was hiding behind that aloof exterior.

The kiss she had shared with him on the Witherspoons' balcony, instead of fading from memory as one might have expected, continued to return with utter clarity, and Cynthia found herself at such times comparing the earl's resolute manner with Lord Farthing's timorous equivocation. It was a comparison in which her betrothed came off very poorly.

It was Lady Sedgegood who finally brought the situation to a head. It was an unusually fine June day, and Lord Dahlmere had recovered sufficiently from the gout to have paid an early visit to his club. He found Bond Street filled with shoppers and his club pulsing with the convivial spirits of his peers. By the time he returned to his house, he was feeling better than he had in months.

He found Lady Sedgegood awaiting him in the entry hall. "I beg your pardon, my lord," said the lady with that look of determination the baron had come to distrust, "but I must speak to you at once."

Lord Dahlmere handed his hat and cane to Hobson and, favoring Lady Sedgegood with a stare of vexation, proceeded to his study, where he installed himself behind his desk. Not to be put off by these tactics, Lady Sedgegood followed him. "It's Cynthia," she announced. "The girl is desperately unhappy and it is up to you to do something about it."

"Confound it!" snapped the baron. "Can't a man have peace in his own house? What is it now? She is betrothed to a man of her own choosing and, against my better judgment, I've permitted her to engage in these fundraising activities."

"But that is just it," stated Lady Sedgegood, moving to

a chair near the desk and slumping into it. "Percy Farthing is not of Cynthia's choosing."

"Nonsense!" he began in a high state of indignation. "She stood in this room and told me herself that she wanted to marry the man!"

"Of course she did!" said her ladyship. "She knew it would please you—at least, that the marriage settlement would. If you will recall, sir, I warned you months ago that Cynthia's wish to see you comfortably set up would result in the most dreadful snarl, and so it has fallen out."

"What *are* you talking about, madam?" exclaimed the baron, unable to restrain his impatience and suffer quietly under these insinuations that he was to be faulted in some matter concerning his granddaughter. "The girl made her own choice. I will own Percy Farthing is not the gentleman *I* would have picked for her, but there's no *harm* in him."

"And does it not seem odd to you, sir, that the announcement has not yet been published? It has been near two months since Lord Farthing offered for her. I know he said he wanted to inform his mother of the betrothal before an official announcement was made, but Lady Farthing has known for weeks now. She has gone all over the ton proclaiming her disapproval to anyone who will listen."

The baron surveyed her with an extremely jaundiced expression. "The draggle-tailed hussy! Cynthia will have to stand up to that shocking fright if she expects to find any contentment in this marriage."

"Oh, she has already done so, sir," said Lady Sedgegood. "The on-dit has it that Cynthia set the woman straight on the supposed offers for Lady Farthing's hand by Oliver and Lord Marlbridge's father. She also made a

222

rather disparaging remark about the woman's taste in home decor. I don't expect I need tell you that Lady Farthing very nearly had apoplexy."

"Indeed not! Oh, famous!" exclaimed Lord Dahlmere, looking much gratified.

"Of course, that will not be the end of it," said Lady Sedgegood portentously. "I cannot think you want Cynthia to be subjected to that woman's interference for the rest of her life. Nor does your granddaughter relish the thought, I assure you. Have you not noticed that she has been walking around in a dreary glump for weeks? But she's given her word, you see, and does not know how to cry off."

"Are you trying to tell me Cynthia means to go to the end of a road that is not exactly to her liking without setting up a screech? Poppycock! Ain't like her at all!"

"Under other circumstances, I would agree with you," said Lady Sedgegood forthrightly. "But you know that Cynthia is kindhearted, indeed so much so that she has sometimes plunged into quite a bumble-bath merely to avoid hurting someone's feelings. Cynthia does not want to disappoint *you,* sir—or hurt Lord Farthing, who is already so put upon by his mother. She fears she will break the gentleman's heart by retracting her promise."

"Fine girl, my granddaughter," said the baron with great fondness. "But Percy Farthing's heart is none of *my* concern. If Cynthia does not wish to go on with this— Deuced queer start, but there must be some honorable way of calling off the wedding."

"I believe there is, sir," said Lady Sedgegood with evident eagerness. "You see, it's my opinion that Percy Farthing is as dissatisfied with his bargain as Cynthia is. I daresay he has some ridiculous notion about being chivalrous and is determined to go to the stake before behaving ungallantly."

The baron scowled. "If you know whereof you speak and Cynthia and Farthing are neither one satisfied with the match," he said, still unconvinced, "yet both refuse to admit it, I do not see what can be done to remedy the situation."

"I do," Lady Sedgegood told him. "This needs an objective intelligence to sort it out. You must step in, sir."

"Oh, I say!" Lord Dahlmere interrupted, but it was plain he felt flattered by the unusual happenstance of Lady Sedgegood paying him a compliment. "What are you suggesting?"

Lady Sedgegood was on her feet, moving toward the door. "Lord Farthing is with Cynthia in the green saloon now. Talk to them, sir. Please. Show them the course of reason."

The baron sighed heavily. "Send them in then, madam. Might as well see what they have to say for themselves."

A few minutes later Cynthia and Lord Farthing came into the study with Lady Sedgegood, their faces revealing that, as the baron had feared, it would be left to him to explain the reason for the summons.

"Sit down, Cynthia—Farthing," he said abruptly. He did not have to tell Lady Sedgegood to do so, for she had perched on the edge of a chair in the corner, watching the others with the same resolute expression she had worn earlier. It was clear that she meant to hold Lord Dahlmere to his reluctant intention.

The baron leaned back in his chair. "It has come to my attention, Farthing," he said gruffly, "that your mother continues to withhold her approval of this match with my granddaughter."

"That is—ahem—regrettably true, sir," admitted Lord Farthing, moving his head about in an effort to loosen the constriction of his collar.

"What do you intend doing about it?" demanded the baron.

"I—I can only hope that in time—"

"The devil take it, man! My granddaughter is being maligned by *your* mother and you expect time to make all right? I am coming to think that you are not as keen on this alliance as I was led to believe."

"Sir!" said Lord Farthing. "I should like to know how you came by such false information. I have offered for your granddaughter and we are betrothed. There is an end to the matter."

"A betrothal that has not, after many weeks, been officially announced." The baron noticed that Cynthia was strangely quiet as she stared at the hands folded in her lap. He sat forward in his chair and attempted to inject a sympathetic note into his tone. "Look here, Farthing, we all make mistakes. But they are not, in most cases, irrevocable. There is no reason why we must live with a bad bargain for the rest of our lives if it is possible to extricate ourselves in an honorable fashion."

"I do not, my lord," said Lord Farthing stiffly, "consider it would be an—ahem—honorable thing to leave Cynthia at the altar."

Cynthia lifted her gaze to her grandfather's strained countenance. "I—I have no wish to be the one to cry off, either, Grandfather. The marriage settlement has been agreed upon and—"

"Forget the deuced marriage settlement!" exclaimed the baron. "I have managed this far without Farthing money, and I daresay I can continue to do so. As for anyone's being dishonored by a—a rupture, that is all a hum. A quiet announcement to your friends to the effect that the engagement has been terminated by mutual consent will take care of things satisfactorily—if that is what you both wish."

Lord Farthing was finding his collar so uncomfortable that he, probably without being aware of what he was doing, was fumbling with the closing. "I—I cannot be responsible for my mother's poor conduct, Lord Dahlmere, but I—I am a man of my word, I assure you."

Lady Sedgegood spoke into the silence that followed this assertion. "No one is calling that into question, Lord Farthing. I have kept silent all these weeks, hoping that you or Cynthia would realize the unsuitability of this alliance. I ask you, frankly, Lord Farthing, have you ever seen two people so badly matched as you and Cynthia? Only consider the uproar over that chimney sweep. Your mother is still livid over the tangle which, I must own, did place her in such a dreadful fix with so many guests in the house. Surely you must have realized by now that this is probably quite tame compared to what Cynthia might do after you are married."

Cynthia was staring at her cousin in speechless wonder. She might have managed to give voice to her indignation at being so maligned by her own chaperon, had not Lady Sedgegood forestalled her. "You may rake me down later, Cynthia. Believe me, I am thinking of your happiness, even more than Lord Farthing's."

An involuntary shudder had shaken Lord Farthing. "Rare dust-up, that sweep business. Mama was thrown quite out of her stride, you know. Said she'd never dreamt such a coil would be played out in her own house."

226

Cynthia gave him a speaking look and sniffed indignantly.

He glanced briefly at Cynthia, then away. "I will own, I never knew anyone *quite* so inclined to fall into the briars as Cynthia. But she doesn't mean any harm, I am sure, and if she is satisfied with the match—"

"But is she?" put in the baron, fixing his granddaughter with a penetrating stare. "Speak up, Cynthia. *Are* you satisfied with Farthing?"

"Yes!" said Cynthia, but with such a scathing look at her betrothed that a bark of laughter escaped the baron.

"Must say that's a good bit short of a protestation of undying love! But never mind. Farthing, do you want to go on with this marriage? And I warn you, if you say yes, you had better be prepared to deal with your mother's detractions, publish the announcement, and set the date. I'll have no more of this dillydallying."

Lord Farthing, unable to look his intended in the eye, said stiffly that *he* had already expressed his feelings on the matter.

"There you are," said Lady Sedgegood, jumping into the breach. "That is nothing but a refusal to answer. I daresay Lord Farthing is not an accomplished fibster, which is why he is unwilling to reply."

"You—you mistake me, madam," said Lord Farthing hotly. "I—I do wish to marry Cynthia."

"I ask you, sir," said Lady Sedgegood, addressing the baron, "did you hear a trace of conviction in that?"

The baron glanced from Cynthia to the squirming Lord Farthing, his brows rising. "Perhaps a trace," he replied, "but hardly more than that. I tell you what, Farthing. I gave my consent to this marriage because Cynthia vowed she wanted you. Needed the marriage settlement, I'll not deny that. I confess, for the moment, I forgot that your role in such a proposed marriage was likely to be—Well, you shall probably be browbeaten by your wife, as well as your mother."

"I am nothing like Lady Farthing!" Cynthia interjected in furious denial.

"Not yet, my girl," agreed the baron, "but who's to say you wouldn't turn out to be—almost as bad, anyway. Don't think Farthing has enough rumgumption to stop you."

"I am beginning to perceive the purpose in this . . . meeting," said Lord Farthing indignantly. "It is you, sir, who is having second thoughts. You wish to withdraw your permission for the marriage."

"You're wrong there," the baron told him. "If you both want to go on with it, I'll not put barriers in your way. But I say now, if either of you wishes to stand aside, this is the only chance you are ever likely to have—and hang all this talk about honor!"

Lord Farthing sighed miserably. "Oh, I say, sir—never thought to find myself in such a ticklish situation."

"Then you *do* want out of it!" Cynthia said accusingly.

"Didn't say that," stammered Lord Farthing. He tried to smile, then gave it up. "Unless you do, of course."

"So typical of you, Percy!" said Cynthia with trembling forbearance. "Putting everything on my dish. Well, I shan't scruple to tell you that I shall be extremely happy to call the whole thing off!"

"Oh, I say—ahem—" sputtered Lord Farthing. "Want to make you happy, above all things. We'll say it was a mutual agreement, naturally."

"That settles it then," said the baron, sinking back in his chair once more, obviously glad to have the session finished. He bestirred himself, however, to speak bracingly to his granddaughter. "Don't fret yourself, Cynthia. I have no doubt at all that you will find a husband more suited to you."

"That is highly unlikely, Grandfather," Cynthia told him with a rigid countenance, "for I do not believe I shall ever marry. My experiences with men thus far have been excessively disappointing."

"Oh?" inquired the baron. "Pray, how do you mean to fill the remainder of your life?"

Cynthia got to her feet, squaring her shoulders. "I shall devote myself hereafter to charitable causes. If you will all please excuse me now, my work with the Society awaits." With a slight inclination of her head in Lord Farthing's direction, she walked out of the study, three pairs of eyes watching her with bemused interest.

"She *is* a lovely girl, sir," said Lord Farthing when no one else moved to break the heavy silence. "But I don't think I could have made her happy. To tell the truth, sir, I'd just as lief lead a bachelor existence. Women can be so . . . unsettling."

"A useful bit of knowledge to have acquired, Farthing," uttered the baron. "Well, I am sure you wish to hasten to your mama with your news."

"Yes, sir," agreed Lord Farthing. "Don't mind saying she has made my life near unbearable lately. In fact, I believe I shall return to Farthingate early, even if Mama disapproves."

"That's the ticket, Farthing," approved the baron. "Time you started to make a few decisions on your own."

Lord Farthing left with a noticeable spring in his step. Lady Sedgegood said over her shoulder as she departed the study, "You have done a wonderful thing for Cynthia, sir."

"Talked myself out of a goodly sum of blunt, too," grumbled the baron to himself as he got up to pour himself some port.

13

Cynthia acknowledged, but only to herself, that her pride had been wounded a bit by Lord Farthing's hasty acceptance of a way out of the engagement. Still, she managed to go on very well, since wounded pride was balanced by her feeling of relief at being free of the Farthings for good.

True to her word, she spent more and more of her time "lecturing" and engaging in a letter-writing campaign on behalf of the Society. Her efforts were spurred by the organization's first success. Jem had been moved to the "chimney sweeps' house" some days previously so that his knowledge of where and how the sweeps could be contacted and informed of the haven awaiting them could be utilized.

One day Kenyon arrived at Lord Dahlmere's house to inform Cynthia that, the afternoon before, a woolen merchant and his wife, in London on business from their home, a small village in the north, had seen the advertisement in the *Gazette,* presented themselves at the solicitors' offices, been directed to the sweeps' house, and identified Jem as their son, who had disappeared more than three years earlier. It was, said Kenyon, an extremely tearful and joyous reunion, and Jem was leaving with his parents that very day.

There was other gratifying news as well. Word of the safe house had spread among the climbing boys and nearly a dozen had already presented themselves there and had been taken in by the couple in charge.

It required some debate, but Cynthia finally persuaded Kenyon to take her to the sweeps' house so that she could say good-bye to Jem and see for herself how the others were being cared for. He warned her sternly that she was never to consider coming there without his escort, but seeing her desire to become more involved in the organization, he charged her with the task of shopping for needed items of clothing for the sweeps in residence.

Returning to the house in Grosvenor Square, Cynthia collected Mary to accompany her and set out for Bond Street in her grandfather's carriage. Determined to spend the Society's money thriftily, she spent more than an hour wandering from shop to shop, comparing prices. So engrossed was she in her shopping that she did not for some time notice her abigail's extreme weariness.

"Oh, Mary, I am sorry for dragging you about like this," Cynthia apologized when her eye fell on the white-faced woman slumped against a counter. "How inconsiderate of me to have forgotten that you have only recently arisen from a sickbed. You haven't got your strength back yet. Why didn't you speak?"

"I'll be all right, miss," Mary said, passing a hand across her perspiring brow. "If I may only have a minute to collect myself."

"Nonsense!" exclaimed Cynthia. "You will return immediately to the carriage and wait for me there. Come, I'll accompany you."

"But I don't like to leave you alone," protested Mary.

"Gracious, I won't be alone. Look at all the shoppers about. And besides the carriage is just around the corner. I'll make my purchases and return to you shortly."

Berating herself for failing to notice sooner her abigail's weakness, Cynthia realized it was a measure of Mary's indisposition that she ceased arguing and submitted to being led to the carriage by Cynthia, who instructed the groom to keep an eye on the woman and hurried back to the shop where she had determined to buy a bolt of fabric for shirts and several pairs of shoes.

Upon leaving the shop, after having made her purchases, she almost ran headlong into two men waiting just outside the door, both of whom wore the rough clothing of the working class.

"Lady Cynthia Chattington?" the taller of the two inquired. He had black hair and a long, pinched face, and he bobbed his head and avoided her eyes with great deference.

"Why, yes." Cynthia glanced from the tall man to his companion, a shorter, burlier fellow who was twisting some sort of workman's cap in both hands.

"I—we are Lord Marlbridge's men," said the shorter man. "We take care of 'is 'orses."

"Oh?" Cynthia said, frowning. "But how did you know my name?" A little flare of suspicion disappeared as she saw an expression of the gravest anxiety upon the face of the taller man. "Has—has something happened to the earl?"

" 'E was comin' 'ere, m'lady, to see ye back to yer 'ouse. There was an accident—"

Cynthia's hand went to her mouth, half stifling the exclamation that broke from her. "Oh, dear heaven! What sort of accident? Is the earl badly hurt?" Her eyes flew to the tall man. "He isn't dead, is he?"

"No, no." The shorter man had taken her arm lightly. "It 'appened in th' street a short distance away. We—carried 'im to the nearest 'ouse. The doctor's been sent for. Please, m'lady, won't you come with us? 'E keeps calling your name."

Clutching the bag containing her purchases tightly in front of her, Cynthia began to tremble. The taller man had taken her other arm, and together the two began to urge her along the street.

Apparently making an effort to reassure her, the shorter man's anxious expression was broken briefly by a slight smile. "Don't think the worst, Lady Chattington. I don't think 'e'll die."

Cynthia stared into his face for a moment. "What happened?"

"One of the 'orses—Caesar, m'lady," said the taller man. " 'E be stubborn. When Caesar's stubborn, only the earl can 'andle 'im. 'E got out of the carriage to calm the beast, and Caesar rared. The earl was struck in the side of the 'ead."

Cynthia pressed one hand despairingly against her forehead. "If he had not been concerned about me, this would not have happened. I must go to him at once!"

"Yes, m'lady," said the shorter man in a soothing tone. " 'E asks for ye."

She nodded and, guided by the two men, mounted into a waiting carriage. The tall man seated himself facing

Cynthia and closed the door securely. "Forgive me bold-ness in forcing me rude company upon ye, m'lady, but ye look lak ye might faint, and the earl would not forgive me should ye 'urt yerself."

"Yes—" Cynthia said distractedly. "Do not concern yourself with the proprieties now. Can you tell me—was Lord Marlbridge conscious when you left him?"

"Yes, miss, and the doctor should be there by now. Please, try to be calm."

Cynthia nodded, biting her lip. She was remembering all the times she had spoken unkindly to Kenyon, accusing him of despicable things, all of them untrue. She censured herself bitterly for jumping to such false conclusions about him and, further, for insisting on taking a more active part in the Society. Kenyon had been reluctant even to send her on this shopping excursion, but she had pleaded with him until he relented. Yet he had continued to worry about her and had been coming to get her. She would never forgive herself for her willfulness if he was seriously injured. But she would not imagine dire possibilities until she had seen Kenyon for herself.

With an effort she forced her mind away from visions of the earl lying in the street beneath the hooves of his horse. Glancing out the side window, she saw that they were on an unfamiliar street. This puzzled her for a mo-ment, for they were obviously proceeding in a direction opposite the one she had assumed they would take, toward Bedford Square.

She looked at the man sitting across from her. He wore a frowningly watchful expression that she put down to his anxiety over the earl. Turning her attention back to the street, she realized the late June dusk had fallen since she'd set out for Bond Street. Her thoughts strayed back to what the man across from her had said. Kenyon had asked for her. Why had he done that unless—But, no, it was not the time to indulge in such speculation.

She became aware of the curricle's increased jolting and realized they were on a rougher road now on the outskirts of the shopping district. She looked back at the man across from her.

"I thought you said it was not far. Have we taken the wrong turning?" Trees were becoming more numerous in the landscape now, and the darkness was thickening. They seemed to be leaving London behind altogether. "We must stop and ask the way! Surely we have come in the opposite direction from the one we should have taken!"

"No, no," said her companion soothingly. "I see I mistook the distance in me worry over the earl. But George knows where we be going, ye can be sure."

In the darkening carriage she peered at the man, for the first time wondering why neither of the earl's drivers was wearing livery. It seemed to her suddenly that something was very much awry.

Perhaps seeing the puzzlement on her face, the man spoke. "I fear I misled you a wee bit, m'lady. We be goin' farther than I led ye to believe. The earl awaits ye in Kent."

"Kent!" Cynthia stared at him, her dark brows drawn together. "But what is he doing in Kent? I have never heard him speak of property there."

"Only a small one, m'lady," said the man. "Nothing like his other estates. 'E spends little time in Kent, and that makes the location good for . . . certain meetings."

Cynthia's feeling of uneasiness grew. Something very odd was going on. Her companion's manner seemed all at once to be one of suppressed excitement. As the carriage traveled farther and farther from London, she began to wonder if these men worked for the earl after all. But if they did not, then why had they lured her into the carriage? How had they known her name? She tried to calm her fears and speak reasonably. "My abigail was waiting for me around the corner from the shop. She will be beside herself by now. I think that perhaps we should go back. I—I will ask my brother to accompany me and we will go to the earl." Almost without being aware of it, she had placed one hand on the door handle as she spoke.

Her companion, whose long face was almost totally lost in darkness now, said with a hard note of warning in his voice, "Do not try to leave the carriage before we stop, Lady Chattington. If ye do anything so foolish, I'll be forced to stop ye."

For a moment Cynthia could only stare into the darkness where he sat. Then she demanded on a note of dismay, "Who are you?" She broke off, forcing herself to think coherently. She had been abducted, and she was very sure Kenyon was not involved in it. But who then?

"I'm known as Will, miss." The tone was calm and deferential on the surface, but Cynthia thought she detected an edge of contempt.

"Where are you taking me?" she whispered hoarsely.

"To Kent, Lady Chattington, just as I said. I'd advise ye to try to rest. We've some way to go yet."

Rest, of course, was out of the question. Cynthia's thoughts raced down one unpromising track after another, seeking a means of escape. There was none. The man called Will did not speak again, but she sensed that he watched her, alert for any unexpected action on her part. So she kept her fears under control as best she could and waited for the journey to end.

She did not know how much later it was when the carriage rattled off the main road and entered a neglected overgrown lane illuminated briefly by the carriage lamps. Ahead she could barely discern the outlines of a small, ramshackle dwelling.

" 'Ere we be," said Will, his voice breaking into the dark silence abruptly, causing Cynthia to start fiercely.

Will flung open the door of the carriage as the driver came around to let down the steps. Will climbed down and instructed Cynthia curtly to follow him. As soon as she had done so, the driver remounted to his seat and the carriage rumbled off down the lane, taking Cynthia's purchases with it. But that no longer seemed important.

A light burned in the window of the house. Cynthia shivered, not certain whether the chill night air or her fear made her feel cold. Will's hand gripped her elbow, making her jump.

"Come with me, Lady Chattington," he said. "My employer is waiting for ye."

"Lord Marlbridge?" she asked shakily, but she was dreadfully sure that she would not meet Kenyon in this tumbledown house. She attempted to pull back. "I—I do not wish to go in," she objected breathlessly. "Are you quite certain we have come to the right place?"

Will laughed low in his throat, a sound that was strangely menacing. "Aye," he told her. "I'm sorry to insist on yer entering such a 'umble dwelling, m'lady, but maybe ye won't feel so scared when ye meet my employer."

"I know it is not the earl," she said in a hoarse voice.

The man beside her laughed again. "No, but someone who is well known to ye."

She had no choice but to allow herself to be led up to

the door. As they approached, it swung open to reveal a tall, lean figure clad in a finely tailored green coat and tan pantaloons, holding a candle aloft. As the light was lifted to illuminate the man's face, Cynthia felt a rush of near-staggering relief.

"Cavey! Oh, thank heavens it is you! What are you doing here?"

"Come in, Lady Cynthia," he said in a voice that seemed to be held tautly under some restraint. He stepped aside to allow Will and Cynthia to enter. "I will explain everything to you shortly."

Will said, "George is 'iding the carriage and—"

"Be still, you fool!" Lord Caverset interrupted shortly. He turned to Cynthia, who had halted just inside the room and was staring up into the close-set eyes. They regarded her with something very close to hatred.

She drew back a little as Lord Caverset gripped her arm and pulled her forward. "What's wrong?" she asked, her voice breaking in fright. "Why have you brought me here?"

"All will be clear to you in good time," said Lord Caverset tersely, his strong fingers irresistibly compelling her forward. The room where she found herself was furnished with nothing but a rude table and benches, and dust covered everything. Clearly the shack had been unoccupied for some time. Lord Caverset continued to press her toward an open door leading into an adjoining room, which contained a narrow cot spread with a ragged coverlet.

In the second room she whirled to face Lord Caverset. "I demand to know what this means!" she cried. "Why are you acting in this odd, secretive manner?" She caught her breath in a sudden gasp. "It's not Bram, is it? He isn't in some serious trouble?"

Lord Caverset stood in the doorway, the candle flickering in one hand, and smiled. It was not a pleasant smile and Cynthia felt again that chill of fear that had passed through her outside. "Bramford is safely tucked up in your grandfather's house, as far as I know."

"But why then—?" She broke off, trying to make some sense of her racing thoughts. Was it possible, she wondered frantically, that Lord Caverset was infatuated with her? Could he hope to force her, by such means, into a marriage? But he had never shown more than the casual interest in her that one might expect of her brother's closest friend.

Lord Caverset seemed to suspect what was going through her mind, for he said mockingly, "Don't flatter yourself that I've brought you here for a romantic tête-à-tête. Your virtue is quite safe. I'm afraid it will take more than a foolish little hoyden to capture my attention!"

"Then—why?" Cynthia's gray eyes were wide as they stared into his face. She wondered why she had never before noticed that streak of cruelty that now was so obvious in the close-set eyes. She shook her head in bewilderment. "It has nothing to do with Lord Marlbridge, has it?"

"Very astute," remarked Lord Caverset, his thin lips curling scornfully. "It is unfortunate that you are not always so clever. You have a most stupid habit of acting precipitously and not at all astutely, but you have thrust your nose into the wrong person's business this time, my dear."

"What *business*, Cavey?" she cried. "I don't understand."

"*Mine*, Lady Cynthia," he said, a sudden snarl in the words. "You should have been content with parties and admirers like other respectable women." He held the candle higher as if he wished to see her face more clearly. "Such a pretty face," he mused. "A pity it shan't be around much longer for the gentlemen of the ton to admire."

She peered at him, utterly confused. But before she could gather her wildly skittering thoughts to ask him for a further explanation, Lord Caverset stepped back out of the room, closing the door behind him. A key scraped loudly as it was turned in the lock.

In the house in Grosvenor Square Kenyon had called to relieve Cynthia of her purchases and transfer them to the sweeps' house. The butler turned him over to Bramford, who took him to the green saloon where Lord Dahlmere and Lady Sedgegood were sharing a rare amicable conversation. Lady Sedgegood was praising the baron for his unselfishness in providing the opportunity for Cynthia's engagement to be broken. The baron, having that very day been notified by his estate manager that the estate's sale of wool had been higher than expected, was enjoying Lady Sedgegood's approval as he poured himself a brandy. Then Bramford appeared with the Earl of Graybroughton in tow.

The earl was introduced to Lord Dahlmere, who had not had the pleasure of meeting the gentleman, and given a brandy.

"Cynthia should be back at any moment," Lady Sedgegood said to the earl, wondering thoughtfully if obtaining the sweeps' clothing was the only motive behind the call.

"Imagine you've heard," said Bramford, "about the engagement being called off."

"Yes," admitted the earl, a smile touching his lips at the young gentleman's obvious eagerness to impart the information. "I must say I believe Cynthia to be well out of it."

Lady Sedgegood gave a shrewd glance to the baron, who wondered blankly what she meant by it. He might, in fact, have blurted out the question had not the sound of excited voices from the entry hall reached them just then.

After some moments Hobson appeared in the saloon doorway, a look of dark foreboding on his face. "Pardon my intrusion, Lord Dahlmere, but Lady Cynthia's abigail has come back and—" He faltered, then thrust Mary, her face white and tear-stained, forward into the saloon. "Tell them what you told me, Mary."

The abigail had begun to wring her hands. "I looked and looked for her, sir. I went back to all the shops where she might have been, but she's *gone!*" Mary's frightened eyes scanned the quartet of astonished faces and she burst into tears.

"Stop sniveling, Mary," commanded Hobson sternly. "You can't help Lady Cynthia that way." He turned to the baron. "Mary has just recovered from an illness, sir. She felt faint while she and Lady Cynthia were in one of the shops, and Lady Cynthia insisted that she go back to the carriage and wait for her."

Mary choked back her sobs to wail, "I waited for a half hour or more! Then I began to wonder why my lady hadn't come back to the carriage. I—I returned to the shop where she meant to go when she left me. She wasn't there, sir. Oh—it's my fault—I should not have left her alone." The abigail broke into another bout of weeping.

The earl had been listening to her recitation with a growing feeling of unease. Now he approached the girl and demanded, "When you didn't find her in the shop, what did you do?"

Mary peered up at him through her tears and gulped wretchedly, "The groom and I went to other shops, sir. On both sides of the street. No one had seen her in the past hour."

"But she must be in one of the shops!" Bramford put in. "Where else could she be?"

"I—I am sure I don't know, sir," returned Mary in a hoarse whisper.

"Get the carriage, Hobson!" ordered the baron agitatedly. "I'll go and look for her myself."

The earl turned to him abruptly. "May I suggest, sir, that your grandson and I go. You and Lady Sedgegood will serve Cynthia better by awaiting us here. My carriage is at the door and I believe Chattington and I can move more quickly if we go alone."

"Ain't one to mince words, are you, sir?" snapped the baron. "Don't want a female and an old man to hamper your progress. Ah, but I know you're right. Well, be off! Hurry!"

After learning the name of the last shop Cynthia and her abigail had entered, Kenyon and Bramford hurried from the house. In the curricle Bramford said excitedly, "Must be some mistake. Silly abigail probably went to the wrong shop."

Kenyon's look was so fraught with anxiety that Bramford stopped talking to stare at his companion. "You don't think so, do you?"

"No," confirmed the earl heavily. "I blame myself com-

243

pletely for what has happened, Chattington. If someone has harmed your sister—"

"But what could have happened?" queried Bramford incredulously.

"I have allowed her to be too active in the Society," said the earl harshly. "She pleaded and cajoled and I confess I gave in against my better judgment."

"Do you mean, sir, that Cynthia's . . . disappearance is in some way connected to that climbing boy society?"

"I very much fear that is the case, but it is a waste of time to speculate. We can only see if the shop owner can tell us anything more. I suspect the abigail was too distraught to question him carefully."

This, in fact, proved to be the case, for when Kenyon described Cynthia to the shopkeeper and urged him to try to remember her presence in his shop, the man thought deeply for a moment, then said, "Yes, sir. I do recall a young lady such as you describe. She purchased some items of boys' apparel and left. I saw her talking to two men outside, and then she walked away between them."

"Can you describe the men?" asked the earl grimly.

"One was tall with black hair, the other short. They wore rough clothing. Whatever they told the young lady, it unsettled her. She looked worried and seemed to be questioning the men. It made me wonder—well, she was alone, sir—and so I went to the door of my shop. I saw her get into a carriage with one of the men, and the other took the reins and drove away."

"Can you remember anything about the carriage?" Kenyon asked. "Anything distinctive? Think, man!"

"It was smart, to be sure," responded the shopkeeper, who was clearly eager to help. "Black—and there was something on the door—a coat of arms. I only had a brief glimpse of it, but I think there were two crossed swords—or sabers—and something above them."

"A crescent?" ejaculated Bramford. "Like a quarter moon with the curved side up?"

The shopkeeper nodded. "It could well have been, sir. I only had a glimpse, as I said."

"Cavey!" Bramford's voice rose shrilly on the word.

"You know the carriage?" asked the earl.

"It sounds like the one belonging to Lord Caverset. But neither of the men who were with Cynthia sounds like Cavey. Besides, dash it, what would Cavey want with Cynthia?"

Having ascertained the direction the carriage took from the shopkeeper, Kenyon and Bramford hastened back to the earl's vehicle.

"What a fool I've been!" Kenyon exclaimed as they climbed inside. "I protected Cynthia from low-born persons. It never occurred to me that a member of the ton—Well, he probably sent two of his associates. I must say I never liked that fellow above half."

"Cavey's house is not in the direction the carriage took," Bramford said, frowning.

"I doubt that he's taken her there," said the earl, "but we'd better make certain."

A visit to Lord Caverset's town house confirmed the earl's statement. Lord Caverset had gone out of town for a few days, the butler informed them. Extremely agitated by this time, Bramford insisted, over the butler's haughty disapproval, on searching the house, but he did not find Lord Caverset or his sister.

Returning to the carriage, Kenyon said, "Does he have property in the country?"

"His father lives in Kent on the family estate. It will come to Cavey upon his father's death."

The earl was thoughtful. "The shopkeeper said they went south—toward Kent. Can you direct my driver to the Caverset estate?"

"I should think I can!" Bramford assured him. "Been there dozens of times." He watched the earl as he ordered his driver to head for Kent with the most possible haste. "I say, Lord Marlbridge, I don't have the least notion why Cavey would take Cynthia to Kent. Must be some misunderstanding. He ain't got a *tendre* for her, if that's what you're thinking."

"Tell me, Chattington," said the earl urgently, "is your friend, Lord Caverset, a wealthy man?"

"No . . ." Bramford began. "Not until recently, that is. Hardly had a farthing to bless himself with until two or three months ago. His father's cousin made a fortune in trade, and he decided to make a large settlement on Cavey. Fantastical piece of luck!"

"Is that what he told you?"

"Yes—I say, are you suggesting the cousin didn't make a settlement on him after all? Must say I wondered about it myself. The fellow never had any use for Cavey or his father, you see—nor they for him. But if he didn't get the money from the cousin, where did it come from?"

"From kidnapping children and selling them as climbing boys. That's my considered opinion. Tell me, Chattington, could Lord Caverset's father be involved in the scheme with him?"

"Cavey's father!" Bramford almost choked on his astonishment. "I'd bet any amount of blunt he's not. The man's a rigid stickler! Impoverished, you know, but proud as a Turk!"

The earl was silent for several moments. "Describe to me the structures on the estate—other than the main house."

"There are the sheds and barns for the animals—and in the southeast corner there are two or three old dwellings. Been falling in for years. Used to house estate workers, but they've all moved to the village now. Nobody has lived in them for ages."

"That's where we'll go first," announced the earl.

Baffled, Bramford fell into a pondering silence. Full darkness descended as the carriage jolted through the countryside, and the vehicle's two occupants brooded on their own thoughts. Bramford was castigating himself severely. He'd *thought* there was something smoky about Cavey's sudden inheritance, but he'd let himself be bamboozled because he'd trusted his old friend. Imagine Cavey being involved in criminal activity! It was unforgivable—and if the man had harmed a hair on Cynthia's head, Bramford vowed to make him pay dearly.

In the shack on the Caverset estate Cynthia had sunk to her knees behind the locked door. She huddled there for some time, hardly moving, her brain trying to comprehend what had happened. Eventually, she became aware that Lord Caverset and the man called Will were talking in the adjoining room. She pressed her ear against the rough wood of the door and strained to hear what they were saying over the loud beating of her heart.

"If ye ask me, guvner," said Will heatedly, "we should get her outa 'ere tonight."

"Panic leads to unwise actions," stated Lord Caverset smugly. "I'm in charge of the operation now, and you'll do well to remember it."

247

Will grunted a reluctant assent, then said, "What did ye say in the note ye gave George to take back to London?"

"Let me see . . ." mused Lord Caverset with obvious relish. "I can phrase it almost exactly. After all, I spent some time composing it. 'Dear Lord Marlbridge, if you wish to see Lady Cynthia Chattington alive again, you should be on the wharf at Dover tomorrow night, Thursday, at nine o'clock. Come alone. You will be contacted there and told where the lady is being held. A concerned friend.' "

"How can ye be sure the earl will come?"

"How?" There was enjoyment in Lord Caverset's tone. "Why, because the earl is in love with the silly chit. I've watched them at parties. I've seen it in his eyes when he looks at her. He'll be at Dover, never fear."

Listening, Cynthia pressed her small fist against her mouth to stifle a protest. She could not imagine how Cavey had made such a false assumption about Kenyon's feelings—but it had been a serious error in judgment. Nothing, in fact, would have made Cynthia happier than to believe that Kenyon cared for her, for she could admit —now that she was never likely to see him again—that she loved Kenyon desperately. But he had never shown indications of returning her feelings—except for that kiss on the balcony, but that had been done in irritation. No, Cavey was wrong about Kenyon. But, Cynthia told herself with a small ray of hope, the earl would probably feel responsible for her. Regardless of his personal feelings, he would surely keep the appointment. But the men's further conversation turned this small hope into a fervent wish that Kenyon could be somehow prevented from going to Dover.

"We ain't taking her all the way to Dover, are we?" Will asked.

"Only part of the way," said Lord Caverset. "But I want her well away from here so no suspicion can possibly fall upon me. You'll . . . dispose of her in a secluded spot I know not far off the road. As for the earl, he'll drown in the Channel. With the two of them out of the way, their cursed society will come to a quick dissolution."

In the small dark room behind the door Cynthia got quietly to her feet. Trembling, she moved along the wall, searching for another way out. Cavey was involved in stealing children away from their homes! This, more than anything else, convinced her he would stop at nothing to disrupt the Society—even murder. At last her hand fell upon the room's single window, but her slight feeling of encouragement was quickly doused. Boards had been nailed across the opening, and though she tugged with all her might, they could not be budged.

Eventually, she moved to the cot numbly and lay down, staring into the darkness. She was to be—murdered. And tomorrow night Kenyon would walk into the trap that had been laid for him. Then Lord Caverset would remain free to pursue his wretched crimes.

14

Oddly, Cynthia's acceptance of her dreadful fate caused her brain to stop its futile circular reasoning, and she fell into a fitful sleep that was disturbed some time later by a shout and the sound of scuffling in the other room. Cynthia came awake dazedly, and for a few moments she remained as she was, lying on the cot, her heart slamming against her ribs in strokes of fear. She became aware that there were more than two voices coming from the other room, and then she heard a masculine shout: "Watch out, Chattington! He's got a pistol!"

It was Kenyon's voice, and Bramford was evidently with him. Cynthia's heart stopped—as the full meaning of Kenyon's warning penetrated her foggy mind—and then began to thud again in heavy strokes of dread. She scrambled from the cot and ran to the door to pull helplessly at the handle. Then she sank to her knees, her eyes filling with tears of frustration.

In the other room Lord Caverset's voice cut into the

silence that had followed Kenyon's warning. "I wouldn't come any closer if I were you, gentlemen. I shan't hesitate to put a bullet through either of your heads."

"I'll make you regret this, Cavey!" Bramford snarled. "Where is Cynthia?"

"Your sister is quite safe, old boy," said Lord Caverset in deliberate tones. "*You* are the one who has put her life in jeopardy by coming here."

Cynthia dragged herself to her feet. She must do something, anything to aid Kenyon and her brother. But what? She was imprisoned in the room with no way of escape. If only she could distract Lord Caverset's attention for a moment, Kenyon or Bramford might be able to take advantage of it.

Clenching her hands into fists, she raised them to the locked door and banged them against the wood fiercely as she let out a bloodcurdling scream.

A shot rang out and there was renewed scuffling in the other room. "Kenyon! Bramford!" Cynthia cried, almost beside herself. "What has happened? Are you all right?"

The next voice she heard was Kenyon's. "Get his gun, Chattington."

The sound of running feet reached Cynthia. "I've got it!" shouted Bramford. "You shot him in the leg. I say, if I'd known *you* had a pistol, too, I'd have felt much more encouraged!" There was a shove against the locked door and then Bramford cursed. "He's got her locked in!"

"Keep that gun pointed at the other fellow," said Kenyon in a remarkably ordinary tone of voice. "Caverset probably has the key on his person."

After several more moments, there was the sound of the key scraping in the lock. The door swung open and Cynthia fell into Kenyon's arms. "Oh, thank goodness, you found me! They—they meant to kill me—and you, too, Kenyon! They sent an accomplice to London with a note instructing you to go to Dover."

"We must have passed the fellow on the road!" exclaimed Bramford.

Cynthia turned her head against Kenyon's chest so that her eyes took in her brother with a pistol trained on the cowering Will. Near her feet Lord Caverset lay unconscious, blood soaking through the fine material of his pantaloons above the left knee.

She sighed shakily and Kenyon's hand moved across her trembling back in the most comforting way. "You don't seem much the worse for your ordeal, pippin," he remarked. "I think I should have killed him if you had been." He looked over her dark head at Bramford. "Take that one to the carriage and set my driver to guard him, then come back and help me carry this other foul piece of humanity."

As Bramford herded Will out of the shack, Kenyon deposited his pistol in his coat pocket and gripped Cynthia's arms, setting her slightly away from him so that he could look into her face.

"I expect we'll have little trouble finding the other fellow. But there may be others involved in this. You will retire from active involvement in the Society. Do you understand me?"

"Yes," murmured Cynthia meekly, "although I fear I shall find balls and routs rather boring after . . . all that has happened."

Kenyon cocked his head to one side. "If you had not broken your engagement, you would be busy with wedding preparations."

"I shouldn't have gone through with it, you know. I—I

only thought that I could for a time." She sighed. "But I know now I couldn't have married Percy, even for Grandfather."

He had gone quite still, but his blue eyes probed her expression. "Because of his abominable mama, you mean?"

"Well, of course, there was that," Cynthia agreed, "but, more importantly, I didn't love him."

"Ah . . ." said the earl. "So you mean to marry only for love?"

Her eyes taking in the beloved contours of his face, she nodded dumbly.

"I have a confession to make," Kenyon continued. "I promised myself that if I ever had you back safe and sound, I would demand payment of your brother's IOU."

Cynthia continued to stare at him, a look of bewilderment in her eyes. "But I can't pay you now. The marriage settlement was canceled along with the wedding."

"Oh," said Kenyon lightly, "I didn't mean to ask for payment in money."

"What then?"

"I meant to ask for you."

"I—I don't understand," stammered Cynthia.

His hands tightened their grip on her arms. "I intended to ask you to marry me in exchange for cancellation of the debt." A wry smile gleamed in his eyes. "But now you have told me you mean to marry only for love."

Cynthia smiled up at him in tender incredulity. "Oh, Kenyon! I should be greatly honored to marry you. I love you. Of course, I do! I have for a very long time."

She saw his eyes deepen with fierce emotion, and she was gathered into his arms once more, the embrace so close that she could hardly breathe. "Oh, God, Cynthia,

I've wanted you from almost the first moment I saw you—but you were so bent on your own course. I—I thought you might actually have come to care for Farthing."

"Foolish Kenyon," she murmured happily.

He was silent for a long moment, his embrace threatening to cut off her breathing altogether. Finally, he said, his voice very thick and passionate, "My darling! I adore you!" And then he kissed her—her brow, her nose, her cheeks—and, at last, her lips, with such deep yearning that Cynthia's heart turned over and she responded with her own sweet longing.

Undoubtedly he would have gone on kissing her if Bramford had not returned. "Oh, I say! This is really the outside of enough! Making love when we have two criminals on our hands!"

With evident reluctance Kenyon released her. He smiled down at her with such tenderness in his rugged face that Cynthia felt momentarily weak. "I expect, little love, that we had better turn these fellows over to the authorities and then go and beg your grandfather's blessing before we continue our very delightful occupation."

"Well! Relieved to hear you plan to marry her," observed Bramford. "I mean, if you intend to continue behaving in *that* fashion . . ."

"Of course we do, Bram," Cynthia told him, her gray eyes sparkling with joy in her lovely face.

At this Kenyon chuckled deep in his throat, and, his eyes leaving her face unwillingly, he bent over Lord Caverset, who had begun to moan softly. The injured man was lifted by Kenyon and Bramford and carried outside.

Cynthia followed them, stepping into the velvety gray dawn of a new day, a day that seemed to pulse with wonderful promise of her new life with Kenyon.

Bestsellers